ON HONEYMOON WITH DEATH

ON HONEYMOON WITH DEATH

Quintin Jardine

HEADLINE

First published in 2001
by HEADLINE BOOK PUBLISHING

10 9 8 7 6 5 4 3 2 1

British Library Cataloguing in Publication Data

Jardine, Quintin
  On honeymoon with death
  1. Blackstone, Oz (Fictitious character) – Fiction 2. Private
investigators – Fiction 3. Detective and mystery stories
I. Title
823.9'14[F]

ISBN 0 7472 7176 3

Typeset by Avon Dataset Ltd, Bidford-on-Avon, Warks

Printed and bound in Great Britain by
Clays Ltd, St Ives plc

HEADLINE BOOK PUBLISHING
A division of Hodder Headline
338 Euston Road
London NW1 3BH

www.headline.co.uk
www.hodderheadline.com

This book is for my uncle, Duncan Bell,
the voice of Vancouver

Acknowledgements

The author's thanks go to the incomparable Joanne Ritchie-Giles and, as always, to the equally unique Sue Scarr. (Terry, it's not you!)

1

Ever fancy a quiet life? I did. I was stupid enough, at one time, to reckon that I could just coast it, that I could find a nice lifestyle business and work for as long as I had to, until I'd stuffed my pension full enough to retire to the golf course.

I grew up in the East Neuk of Fife, you see, and while I was switched on enough to realise that I had to broaden my horizons a bit, I never wanted to venture too far from home.

So where did it all go wrong? How the hell did I wind up being chased by seriously nasty people? How the hell did I get involved with a wrestling circus, of all things, and become a (minor) television star in the process? How the hell did I wind up in movies, with my name on posters outside cinemas and multiplexes all over the world? How the hell did I come up with those six lucky numbers that Saturday night, the ones that piled all that extra dough into an already fat bank account?

And after all that how did I manage to come face to face with myself, with the bloke I've really been all my life?

Some might say that God alone knows for sure. Not me, though: I have my own theory. I blame it on an occult power, an unseen malevolent hand which shapes the destiny of every one of us on the planet. The way I see it, God is a bit like me . . . or like the person I always thought I wanted to be. He created the Heavens and the Earth in six days and six nights, took a rest on Sunday, and reckoned a lot more to that than He did to creating. So, satisfied that His pension fund was fat enough to keep Him flush for the foreseeable eternity, He made one last final adjustment to the celestial plan (the creation of the electric buggy), took unto Himself the name of Arnold Palmer, and pissed off to Augusta, Georgia, USA, to play some serious golf.

The actual running of this place, He left to one of His earlier creations, someone . . . or something . . . He'd put together in the Void, before He moved upon the surface of the waters — incidentally, I was taught as a child NEVER to do that!

1

That's the trouble with architects the world over, and beyond in this instance. They're great on the drawing board, and most of them see the job through to completion, but invariably they get rat-arsed at the opening ceremony then bugger off for good, leaving someone else to do the troubleshooting, and leaving the poor bloody clients to live with the consequences.

There are no exceptions to this rule: not even God.

In His case, when it came to delegating the after-sales service, His human resources department (sorry, His personnel department; this was, after all, a long time ago) got it badly wrong. Today the mistake would have been spotted at the first interview; or if not, then as soon as they gave the candidate a psychometric test, he, it, would have given the game away. The application form alone should have done it; the fact that his, its, works number was 666 ought to have made someone tumble to it even before they got to the name: surname, 'Antichrist'; forenames, 'Satan The'.

But no; the lucky Devil got the job, the middle-management post he had always hankered after, and had always been denied when God was focused and on the ball, as opposed to later, when he was fishing it out of Rae's Creek. It wasn't that his Creator had anything against him; One takes responsibility for One's own mistakes, after all. It wasn't his appearance that had held him back either: after all, a crimson-clad, twelve-foot-tall, eight-hundred-pound hunchback, with talons instead of fingers, a body temperature which could fire clay pots, and eyes which literally are red-hot coals, all topped off with a pair of horns that would give a fourteen-pointer stag a Bambi complex might look out of place in today's sanitised, politically correct, beauty-obsessed society, but in the pre-dawn of creation he was just another bloke on the team-sheet. (In fact, I have always suspected that if Mr A could prove to the Scottish Football Association that he had as little as a single Channel Islander grandparent, he would be in our next World Cup squad. And I know for sure that England could have done with him in the centre of their defence in Euro 2000.)

It wasn't his attitude to Good and Evil that was the problem either. (The notion that God is on the side of the former is completely fanciful anyway, as a quick read through selected parts of the Old Testament will prove beyond doubt.)

No, the thing that held him back was his sexuality. Satan is always represented as a bloke, which biologically he is. However, it's not quite as simple as that, or as straight, one might say. For the truth is . . . he's gay. Yes, the Devil is a poof. Old Nick is a nine-pound note. Not, I rush

2

to say, that this maketh him a bad perthon. The problem is that with it, he has acquired a quirky, mischievous sense of humour, the sort which in a smaller, less formidable personality is liable to result sooner or later in a good kicking. From the start, God perceived this flaw in His precious work . . . the sexual clock wasn't His work, it was one of the first examples of evolution . . . and determined to keep him about the house, as it were.

But He didn't and as a result, this cosmic Kenneth Williams has been inflicting his notion of fun on mankind since before our species could stand straight. Some of the most momentous events in our history have been his idea of a joke.

The parting of the Red Sea, for example, took place not because he had decided to lead God's chosen people out of bondage in Egypt. (God has never heard of Moses, and, as He faces that intimidating tee shot across the water at Augusta National, wouldn't give a bugger about him, even if He had.) No, the fact is that it was all set up because S. T. Antichrist did not approve of the formal dress of the pharaoh's court. Too butch, he thought. On the other hand he was behind the toga. (The kilt was not his; he never messed with the Highland Scots.)

He had a great time in the Middle Ages too; there is a school of thought that the pan-European epidemic of witch-burning was no more than his revenge on a particularly terrifying primary-school teacher. Those of us who were educated in Scotland in the days of corporal punishment can understand that. The Dracula legend is another of his. A cover story, that's all, to cover a sexual cult whose practices would attract the attention of even the Turkish police force. Far from being the model for the vampire count, Vlad the Impaler was no more than a convenient fall guy, if appropriately named in the circumstances.

His games are around us, for all to see, his quirks, his foibles, his gay little jests. Appropriately, many of them exist in the world of architecture. The Leaning Tower of Pisa? Sydney Opera House? The City of Birmingham? The Sagrada Familia? The Scottish Parliament Building??

These days he even dabbles in sport and the performing arts. Who else could have invented *The Archers*? Or synchronised swimming? Or ice dancing? Or rhythmic gymnastics? Or Dennis Rodman? Or Gazza? Or the Sex Pistols? Or *Who Wants to be a Millionaire*? Or *Coronation Street*? Look at the Rolling Stones and ask yourself this: did Mick and Keith write 'Sympathy for the Devil', or was it dictated?

All of these truths only came to me after many hours of alcohol-

3

assisted meditation upon the many bizarre events which have turned my life upside down over the last few years, and which have come between me and my still-cherished ambition. I'm with God on this one; all I really want to do is play golf. Yet these days I can't find half an hour to hit fifty balls on the driving range.

Satan has a thing about golf too. You see he really liked God; he looked up to Him as a Father... which, in a non-biological sense He was... and he was really hurt when He turned his back on him, created azaleas and went off to roam among them for ever. (Even if STA did land a good job as a result.)

When he found Mary Queen of Scots whacking a ball around on Musselburgh racecourse, she was marked down for a very unfortunate life thereafter, and a very brutal end, as the accounts of her execution bear out. The old Devil was so pissed off that he even made her wig come loose when the axeman picked up her severed head.

He couldn't stop the game from taking hold, of course. Not even he can get in the way of a clutch of Scots caddies waiting in slavering ambush for the next busload of Americans or Japanese. But he has twisted it to his own ends, by making it such that it takes normal men and women and, over the course of a three-hour walk, turns them into cursing, spitting, vengeful, violently masochistic beasts. In a final act of vengeance he has also taken from them the ability to resist spending large sums of money which most of them cannot afford on increasingly complicated and expensive equipment which does them no bloody good at all.

I know, I know; occasionally a Jack, or a Gary, or a Seve, or a Nick, or a Tiger bursts from the throng to show that the game can be a thing of unsurpassed beauty, but in fact they simply demonstrate that God in His Paradise is not completely oblivious to the ways of mankind and is still capable of reminding Works Number 666 not to push his luck.

He hasn't done it with me, though; I still play off thirteen, and rising.

I don't know what I did to attract Mr A's attention. I thought I always tried to be as relaxed and laidback as I could, to do a good, sound dependable job, giving no one any bother, any hassle, not never, not no-how. Maybe that was it. Maybe I was too good at it and the master of my destiny decided that he wasn't having any more of it.

And that's where I come back to his special sense of humour. A Devil with less imagination would simply have given me piles, or eczema, or male pattern baldness; or if he'd really had it in for me, a crippling cerebral haemorrhage, or testicular cancer, something like that.

But no. What did that capricious bastard do to me?

He gave me Primavera Phillips, that was all!

2

On the face of it, my second wife has always seemed to be a sensible, straightforward, ingenuous woman. On the face of it.

I thought that for years. From the moment of our first meeting, when she walked into her flat and found me there, alone yet not alone, in most unusual circumstances, she struck me as just that solid no-nonsense person, an ultra-capable woman given neither to fear nor panic.

We fell in lust at first sight. Ever since then I've barely passed a day which in my old world would have seemed normal. Some might say that sharing a loft in Edinburgh with a green iguana named Wallace is not everyone's idea of normality, but it suited me at the time.

Not even our courtship was straightforward. We did our thing together, and, our lucky shamrock having made its presence felt at an early stage, went off to Spain with a bag of money and spent some time shagging ourselves insensible. Then Prim fell in love with someone else, at the same time as I realised that I wasn't a real person without Jan, the girl with whom I had grown up, and whom I had mucked around for several years.

They're both dead now, Prim's soul mate and mine. That old Devil had an invisible hand in Jan's death, that's for sure. As for the other one, I'm pretty certain now that he and STA were related. I should have guessed it at the time, but I was still an idealist then. I told myself that I believed in the basic goodness of the species. Now I admit publicly what privately I've always known, that the Seven Deadly Sins have a hell of a lot more pulling power than the Ten Commandments.

The night my wife Jan died, I was fifteen hundred miles away, in another city. And whom did I meet, right there, for the first time since we had gone our separate ways? Primavera Phillips, that's who.

In my innocence, I thought it was a kind of serendipitous coincidence. But I've seen a lot of evil since then and I don't believe that any more. I believe in Fate, but not that it has a kindly eye and a long white beard.

I don't believe that Luck is a Lady either. No, I see them for the single demon they are.

Okay, okay, okay. I've got my tongue in my cheek. I'm not the happy-go-lucky yuppie I once was, but if I have a saving grace it lies in the fact that I'm still Mac the Dentist's son, and that's all that a bloke could ever hope for. When my dad dies . . . if he ever does, because he's strong as an ox and never ill . . . then the Architect of the Universe will have a partner at Augusta, one who'll give him a few tips on those fast greens, at that. Someone once said to me, watching him hole a curly forty-footer on the difficult thirteenth at Elie, 'Your old man putts like God.' That was rubbish, of course; I don't care how long God's been playing, he can't be as good a putter as Macintosh Blackstone.

And don't get me wrong about Prim, either. She's not Jan and I'm not . . . him . . . but when I married her it was because I thought I loved her to bits. Sure she's a trouble magnet, but while she's been at my side I have also done things I had never even dreamed about, and come into possession of a right few million quid in the process.

So when she proposed that for our honeymoon we took an extended break in Spain, to give it a second shot together in happier and more settled circumstances, I worked out the odds against lightning striking three times and fell into line. (You'd think a guy who's won the lottery would have been less likely to disregard a long shot.)

There was nowhere else we wanted to go but the Costa Brava. This was not as simple as once it might have been, since we had sold the apartment which we had owned together in the historic village of St Marti d' Empuries. We had bought it at a knock-down price from a Dutch bloke whose wife had left him, and who flogged it way under value just to spite her. She must have got the message, for after a while she came back, and he asked us if he could buy it back.

He was amazed when we said that he could have it for what we paid him; but the truth was that the place was too full of ghosts for me . . . and for Prim, but I'll get around to that.

So we booked into the finest suite in a country house hotel called Crisaran, a medieval building which has been beautifully restored by its lady owners. We arrived in mid-November, checked in for a month, and barely left the place for the first week, doing mostly what honeymooners are expected to do – reading and watching television.

When we had had our fill of that, we climbed into our hired Mondeo and set out to visit an old friend. Shirley Gash, the ex-pat queen of L'Escala, isn't that old, actually. Somewhere in her late forties, one might say, but it would be irrelevant, for she is a woman in her prime . . .

8

a lot of woman. About six feet tall, blonde and gorgeous, with a figure that outdoes any screen goddess I've met since I made my first movie.

Miles Grayson's *Snatch*, co-starring his wife . . . Prim's sister Dawn . . . and 'introducing' Oz Blackstone, private enquiry agent turned wrestling announcer turned actor, had just opened in New York. Shirley watches CNN and Sky News like some people watch *Coronation Street* and *EastEnders*, so after brief congratulations on our marriage, there was only one thing she wanted to talk about.

'Was it a one-off?' she asked. 'Or are you going to do another? They say you're great in it . . . Well, not bad for a newcomer, anyway.'

I had practised self-deprecation in front of the mirror, but I still hadn't cracked it, so I guess my smile was more self-satisfied than modest. 'That's kind of them,' I responded, 'but you know what they say about beginner's luck. As a matter of fact, Miles has offered me a part in his next movie. I've said I'll do it; but that's as far ahead as I'm thinking.

'Forward planning's bullshit anyway.'

I looked around Shirley's new garden. She had sold the house in which she had lived when first we had met, for reasons similar to our own . . . to an Australian beer baron, she told us; now she was settled in a newly built bungalow, ostentatiously named Villa Balearic, and designed in what she described as Ibizan style. It was built on a half-acre plot in a street called Carrer Caterina, not far from the old Greco-Roman city of Empuries, and had a fine view across the Golfo de Rosas.

'Nice this, Shirl,' I said.

'Thanks.' If she'd had feathers she'd have preened herself. 'I only moved in a month ago. I had a big hand in the design.'

'That must have been a help to the builder,' Prim chipped in, so deadpan that not even I could tell whether she was kidding or not.

'Yes,' Shirley nodded. 'Although he never said.'

She looked from Prim, to me, then back again. 'So,' she demanded, 'where you gonna live now you've sold your old place in St Marti?'

'What do you mean?' we asked in unison. 'We live in Glasgow,' I added, 'with a better view than you've got . . . If you like buildings and bridges and lots of traffic, as we do.'

'Sure, but you belong here as well. L'Escala fits you two like a glove. Besides, we need a movie star here. We've got all bleeding sorts, Flash Harrys from all over Europe, but we're a bit low on showbiz. Go on, buy a new place, then we'll have someone to gossip about.

'Who knows, Oz, you might even become a tourist attraction. Before you know it the British Catalan Society will be organising bus trips past your house.'

I was flattered, but I had to laugh. 'One movie does not a celebrity make, Shirley.'

'Bleeding well does in L'Escala,' she countered.

'In that case we're well out of it,' said Prim.

'But you need to invest some of that money in property. Where else you gonna go?'

'How about Florida?'

'Too hot, and they've got alligators.'

'Barbados?'

'Hotter and the sanitation's lousy.'

'Rome?'

'Full of Italians.'

'Puerto Banus?'

'Puerto Anus more like. Come on Prim, you love it here, admit it. You too, Oz. You've got memories here.'

'Some of which we'd rather forget,' I suggested.

'Sure, but you've sold your apartment, just like I've sold my house.'

'Yes,' I agreed. 'Why did you do that?'

'Why do you think? After Davidoff went away, I just hated the place. I couldn't look at that summerhouse again without thinking of him, and without wondering what had happened to him. You don't know do you?' She fired her question too quickly for her effort at sounding casual to be convincing.

'No,' I lied quietly. I did, of course, but I couldn't tell her; not even her.

'Ahh,' she sighed. 'There was always a bit of the cat about him. I expect he just went off somewhere to die, just like an old moggie. I miss him, all the same. So that's why I sold up. Couldn't leave L'Escala though; so I found this lump of land and I had this house built. That's what you two should do.'

Shirley had made her point. We didn't get into a discussion right there and then, but that night, back at the hotel as we did justice to a bottle of cava before going down for dinner, Prim brought it up. 'She's right, you know,' she exclaimed, out of the blue.

'Who? Margaret Thatcher?'

'Yes, but apart from her. Shirley is. We should buy something else in L'Escala.'

'Yes, dear.'

She frowned at me. 'Are you humouring the little woman?'

'No, dear.'

'Well, what do you mean?'

'I mean okay.'

'Just like that?'

'Why? Do you want an argument? I can read that look in your eye, and I know that if we had one I'd lose. So I might as well agree with you and save the hassle.'

She isn't just a magnet for trouble; she can radiate it too, when she feels like it.

'Besides,' I conceded. 'I happen to agree with old Shirl. I do feel right here. And there's something else. Back in Glasgow we live in a place that Jan and I shared. Sure, I know you can hack that, but given our financial position it's only fair that we have a place that's ours alone.'

'Aww,' she murmured, slightly, unusually, stuck for a word.

'And finally . . .'

Prim laughed. 'Oh yes? You've got your smartarse look on. Out with it.'

'I looked around as we were leaving Shirley's. There's a place two doors along with a "for sale" sign, and I like it up there; I like the quiet. So I thought we might look at it tomorrow.'

3

And so we did. Next morning I called the estate agent, having mentally noted the number on his signboard, and next afternoon we met him on the road which runs towards the public entrance to the Ruins of Empuries.

It occurred to me as we shook hands that I hadn't spoken any serious Spanish for a while, but in any case he launched straight into his version of English. 'Goot morning, sir,' he began, getting off on the wrong foot by ignoring Primavera. 'I am Sergi.'

He looked to be around forty, a strapping bloke approaching six feet tall, big for a Catalan of that vintage. He had a heavy jaw . . . not quite in the Jimmy Hill class, but showing promise . . . which made all of his other features seem smaller. When finally he did turn to acknowledge Prim, I saw that his thick dark hair was held back in a pony-tail.

He reached into his pocket, fishing around for keys. I hadn't expected him to be wearing a suit . . . very few business people in that part of Spain wear jackets and the manager in any bank is usually recognisable as the guy wearing a tie . . . so I thought nothing of his designer jeans, but his heavy woollen jacket looked a bit flamboyant. It had a South American look to it.

'I sorry I ask to meet you here. It been such a long time since I visit this house, I forget how to find it.' He smiled, creasing up his little eyes. 'But I look before you come, so I know now where it is.'

'It's been for sale for a while then?' Prim asked him, in Spanish.

He looked at her, gratefully. 'Yes,' he told her. 'For seven months now. It has been empty for over a year.'

'Who is the owner?' I ventured in Castellano. Actually, I'm not bad at the national language, although most of the local tongue, Catalan, is a mystery to me. To put my communications skills in perspective, though, I once met an eight-year-old boy in L'Escala who spoke four languages and was fluent in three of them.

'He's a Frenchman,' Sergi replied. 'I don't know what happened. He just went away. A few months later I had an instruction to sell the villa, exactly as it stands. I get in touch with him through a lawyer's office in Geneva. Come on, I'll show you the place. The road from this side is rough; it's easier if we walk than drive all the way round.'

He led us up a short rocky alleyway which might have taken a car, but might have taken out its exhaust in the process. At the top of a short slope we turned left into Carrer Caterina, which happily is a proper tarmac street, with paving and everything, and found ourselves in front of Shirley's new Ibizan villa, its terra-cotta walls standing out proudly against the cloudless blue winter sky.

'This way,' said our guide leading us on, rummaging again in the pocket of his cardigan and coming out at last with a monster bunch of keys, just as we arrived in front of the house where I had seen the '*En Venda*' sign. There was a plastered brick wall facing the street, two metres high and solid. Once it had been white but it looked around ten years overdue for repainting. On one of the pillars, which supported its gate, there was a stone nameplate. It read 'Villa Bernabeu'. Sergi caught me peering at the mossed-over lettering.

'The owner is a Real Madrid fan,' he explained.

'No wonder he left town,' I murmured.

The estate agent's sign covered half of the double metal gate, hiding, I guessed, a sizeable patch of rust in the process. It took our lantern-jawed pal three minutes, and several failed attempts, to find the key which unlocked it. As he swung it open, my heart sank.

The house was on the crest of a slope, the front door approached by a weed-invaded driveway on the right of the plot, which led from the gate to the garage, then veered off to form a path. It was big enough, a two storey villa with a pillared entrance, designed by an architect who had either a rough idea of Greek style or had seen *Gone With the Wind*. Like the wall, it was plaster-clad, and in a similar state of disrepair.

The garden to the left of the drive was raised up; a short flight of stone steps led up to what seemed to be a terrace. It had a balustrade, which for some reason had been painted blue.

'The plot is two shousand metros,' Sergi announced, lapsing into lumpy English once again.

'*Dos mil*,' Prim repeated, getting him back on track.

'Yes, it's big. The land alone is worth twenty million pesetas; the price of the house . . . everything, including the furniture and the car in the garage . . . is fifty million.'

'Pardon?' I exclaimed.

'But I think they would take forty-two,' he added quickly.

'I think they might have to,' said Primavera as we walked up the driveway. 'Look at those shutters.'

I followed her pointing finger. Several of the slats of the wooden blinds, which covered all of the windows, were twisted and rotten, and some were missing altogether.

'As I said to you, I was told to sell the house in its present condition. I concede that it needs work done to it, but once you have spent the money, you will have something very good indeed.' He led us up to the front door; this time he was able to open it at the third attempt.

Even in the little light which spilled in from the doorway we could see that it looked much better inside. Sergi found the power box, in the customary place behind the door, and switched on the light. The house smelled musty, but that was only to be expected. To the front, the ground floor was one open area from wall to wall, with a stairway rising from the centre, seating to the left of the entrance, and fine oak dining furniture to the right. Two big open fireplaces, stone-built with thick timber mantelshelves faced each other across the huge apartment and a Sony wide-screen television, with a video player and a satellite decoder box stood in a corner of the living area.

He walked from window to window, opening each one inwards; they were floor length, with black-painted metal frames and small square panes. 'See,' he exclaimed, as if he had remembered that he was supposed to be selling the property. We kept our faces straight as the shutter nearest the seating area more or less disintegrated in his hands.

He rushed us through the rest of it: cloakroom, breakfasting kitchen, bathroom and laundry on the ground floor and, upstairs, four bedrooms, the front two en-suite . . . the master chamber with the biggest, most solid brass bedstead I had ever seen, and an oval Jacuzzi big enough for a football team . . . and opening out on to an upper terrace which ran the full width of the house.

As we looked down we saw that the spacious garden to the front was paved in stone, and dominated by a big rectangular pool, covered for the season by a blue tarpaulin, lashed securely to rings which were set into the ground all around.

'Twenty metres by eight,' our guide volunteered. 'That's big for a private pool.'

He paused. 'What do you think?'

I followed Primavera's gaze out over the Golfo de Rosas, and read her mind at once. 'We're interested,' I told him. 'But we want it checked out.'

If we had been at home, we'd have sent a surveyor, but that's not the

15

way they do it in Spain. Instead, we went to Shirley's builder, Vincens Siemens, who had a good reputation around the town, and asked him to give us a report and an estimate of what it would cost to refurbish it to a standard suitable for an international movie star and his consort.

It was less than we thought; the central heating system and plumbing were in good condition, and the bathroom fittings were all of the finest quality. The pump machinery had been renewed and the pool retiled less than three years before, by Señor Siemens himself, and so we were left to contemplate only rewiring, a new kitchen, replacement shutters and a complete redecoration.

Apart from the lumpy mattresses, the furniture was pretty good too; not antique, but old enough to have a comfortable feel to it. The car in the garage turned out to be a Lada Niva four by four, but you can't have everything.

Sergi's little eyes lit up when we told him we wanted to buy. They narrowed to slits when we said we had been thinking of offering forty million, but relaxed once more when we said that we would go to forty-four, for completion within the week. Three days later, on the second Friday in December, we did the deal before the local notary, a pleasant chap with a moustache thick enough to have swept a ballroom floor. Sergi acted for the seller, having been granted a power of attorney months before.

'Well,' I asked my wife as we stood, that afternoon, on the terrace of our new second home, 'have we done the right thing?'

'Let's hope so,' she answered. 'But time will tell. Come on; let's find out where the bodies are buried.'

4

We hadn't said a word to Shirley. Nor did we, until we had checked out of Crisaran and moved in, on the following Tuesday. It wasn't a problem; the place wasn't just furnished, it was fully equipped with linen, towels, crockery, cutlery, glassware, the lot.

I called her, mobile to mobile, and asked if she fancied a coffee. 'Sure. Where?'

'Two doors along.'

'You bleeding what!'

I was watching from the bedroom terrace as, within two minutes, she came striding into the driveway. It was a mild day, but she was wrapped in a long dark overcoat. 'Honest to God,' she bellowed, as I swung the door open and we stepped out to greet her. 'I drop one bleeding hint and look what happens. What if I was to say I fancied a new car?'

Primavera laughed out loud. 'There's a very nice Lada in the garage with four thousand kilometres on the clock; you're welcome to it.'

'Here,' I protested. 'That's a motor of character. I plan to drive that.'

'Ship it to Russia and break it up for spares,' said Shirley. 'That's my son's new business venture,' she added. 'He buys Ladas in Britain and France for peanuts, breaks 'em up and ships the parts across to a warehouse in St Petersburg. Making a bleedin' fortune, he is.'

'Do you see much of John these days?' I asked.

'No. He's too busy, with his Russian thing, with running the family company . . . although our manager does most of the donkey-work . . . and with keeping an eye on a pub he bought just outside Newcastle. The other Newcastle, I mean; the one in the Midlands.

'Last time he was over, though, round about Easter, he had a look at this place. I heard him mutter something about buying it as an investment. He'll be pissed off that you've beaten him to it; still, if he was serious, he should have been quicker off his mark.'

She stepped inside and looked around. The place was a mess, with two big cardboard crates, which until an hour before, had held a washing

17

machine and a tumble dryer, lying in front of the stairway, and the plastic coverings from four new mattresses strewn on the floor, waiting to be stuffed inside them for disposal. It was warm, though; there had been plenty of oil in the tank which fed the central heating boiler, and for good measure we had lit fires in each of the two great hearths, using dry logs which we had found piled in an Aladdin's cave of a brick shed at the back of the house.

'Let me get this straight,' Shirley said, slowly. 'You've moved in already?'

'Sure,' I told her. 'The place is liveable, the telly works, and we've had the old broken-down shutters taken away, and that rusty old gate's going too, once its replacement is ready. Vincens the builder has our new kitchen on order; he'll do that and the rewiring once we go off to start work on Miles's new movie. We have a painter starting work tomorrow, and we've even got a guy doing something to the satellite dish that'll give us British digital television.'

'Christ, you'll be in the bleedin' pool before the week's out.'

'Hardly,' Prim laughed. 'We'll need to fill it first. We have been thinking about putting in a heating system for it, but so far we haven't even taken the cover off.'

We installed Shirl in one of our new soft leather armchairs, and Prim poured coffee from a top-of-the-hob percolator, which we had found in one of the old kitchen cupboards. She looked around, nodding from time to time.

'Yes,' she proclaimed at last. 'Not bad at all. Get some nice pictures on the walls, and some nice rugs on the floor, put some nice lights on that big terrace around the pool, and you'll have a home fit for a film star.'

'Thanks,' I acknowledged. 'Do you know anything about the previous owner?'

'Well . . .' Shirley answered slowly, 'he was French, I know that much; also a friend of mine, who lives up here, mentioned him once or twice, after he went away. She didn't know his name, but she said she'd heard that he was a bit dodgy. Not that that means much; there are lots of mysterious people around here. Even me. Even you two.

'When John looked at the place he asked about him. He told me that all that Sergi bloke said was that he'd gone away; when John pressed him a bit more he got the impression that no one was quite sure where he'd gone to. Again, there's nothing unusual about that, not by L'Escala standards. People come and go all the time, and if they don't volunteer information they don't get asked for it. That's one reason I prefer it to

England. You're allowed a bit of privacy here.'

Our new neighbour drank her coffee, and demolished a pastry stick filled with chocolate, which I had found in one of the local bread shops. When she was finished, we gave her the grand tour of the house, then, like the good guest she is, she excused herself and left us to get on with settling in.

We had hired a firm of commercial cleaners to go through the house like a dose of salts in advance of our moving in, so from that point of view there was little to do. We finished laundering the sheets and towels, then filled the cardboard crates with the mattress wrappings, for me to pile them into the Lada . . . I really was taking a shine to the ugly, square, bus . . . and take them to the nearest rubbish skip. While I was gone the telly man, an English ex-pat, did what he had to do to our satellite dish and tuned in the decoder box which gave us illicit access to British broadcasting.

I came back to find Prim almost jumping for joy. 'We can get British radio,' she shouted as I stepped inside. 'It comes through the satellite! I can keep up with *The Archers*.'

I gave the bloke a serious stare. 'What the hell did you tell her that for?' I asked him. Both he and my wife grinned. I didn't know why they thought I was kidding, but they did. From somewhere close by, I thought I imagined a Satanic chuckle.

All the same, when he left I was ready to sit down for an hour's telly. It was almost five, and there was a review of the previous week's European football about to begin on Eurosport. Prim had other ideas. 'Is that it?' she exclaimed, in a tone which told me at once that it wasn't.

'What else is there?' I protested. 'You can't want to go out for a drink, can you? We've just filled that bloody great fridge with booze.'

'No. We'll go out later. But first we have to get that cover off the pool.'

'Gie's a break, love,' I pleaded. 'That thing must weigh a ton. There's a hell of a lot of it. Look, I'll get the painters to help me tomorrow.'

'They'll be here to paint. The two of us can manage it together, Oz; and Vincens said we should fill the pool as soon as possible, to get the motor running. It's a ten-minute job and there's enough daylight, so let's do it now.'

I gave up. Normally, I'd have muttered something about alternative uses for daylight, and taken her off to test-drive our new mattress, and that monster of a bed, but I'd had enough of that at Crisaran. (We have a technical term in Scotland for that condition. We call it Being Shagged

19

Out.) Or maybe my actions were being guided by A Higher Power? (No, on this occasion I was Absolutely Shagged Out.)

I followed her outside and went to work untying the ropes which held the big blue cover firmly in place. We started nearest to the house, which we assumed was the shallow end, working our way down the sides. The metal rings to which the nylon rope was lashed were set two metres apart, eleven of them down either side, with three along the top and the far end. They were screwed into the stone, so that they could be removed when not in use, thereby saving a right few broken toes.

The knots were tight. For a while I thought we were going to have to cut the damn thing free, until Prim had the bright idea of using a long screwdriver, which we had found in the outhouse, as a lever. With that tool, we finally managed to unfasten all the ropes at the shallow end, then one by one on either side, turning back the cover as we went, so that its weight would not pull it downwards into the empty pool.

Primavera's ten-minute job took us forty-five: by the time we were finished, it was practically dark. We stood at the deep end, the blue cover in a roll at our feet and looked down into our new pool. The tiles seemed to be navy blue, with a denim fleck through them, chosen to give a cool look and yet to attract the warmth of the sun at the same time.

It wasn't completely empty. Since it was last filled, rainwater had flowed or been driven under the cover, and had gathered down there below us. Looking at the sides I guessed that it was between two and three feet deep; it was dark, stagnant, impenetrable to the eye and, now that the tarpaulin was off, smelly.

'Shouldn't there be a drain?' Prim asked.

'Of course there's a bloody drain. It's probably clogged with leaves. I'll run some water in. That should clear it. If not, we'll add it to Vincens the builder's things-to-do list.'

The small room which housed the pool machinery was directly beneath the point where we were standing. I trotted down the steps to the driveway and opened it with a key on the big ring which I carried. Vincens had given me a quick run-through of the system, so I knew what to look for . . . starting with the light switch so that I could see what I was doing. I didn't bother about setting the filter at that stage, but went straight to the lever which controlled the flow of water, turned it on full throttle and switched on the pump.

Even in the pool-house I could hear it splashing on to the tiles. I waited there for a minute or two to make sure that it was running okay, then I grabbed the pole and net which stood against the side wall, at an angle because it was so long, thinking to use it to clear the leaves. As an afterthought, I pressed the button marked '*luz*', which over-rode the master clock of the pool lights.

Prim is not a screamer, other than in certain private circumstances, and then she does it quietly. But I wasn't even out of the small room when, above me, she let out a belter. 'Oz!' she cried. 'Oz!' Not frightened, I thought . . . she has never been frightened in her life . . . but startled, very startled.

I was up that stair in a flash; or would have been if I hadn't tripped over that bloody pole on the second step. I made it though, as fast as I could, stumbling and scrambling, grabbing hold of her, and turning her towards me.

'What's up?' I gasped.

She was calm once more; icy calm. A sure sign of shit flying off a fan. 'Look,' she ordered, glancing back over her shoulder.

I felt icy myself as I peered over the side into the pool; icy with apprehension.

The rushing water had done its work, the stagnant pool was clearing fast and the drain was unblocked. There was no doubting what the obstruction had been; no doubting it at all.

As I stared down; I came to a conclusion. It was based on pure speculation, but I was strangely certain nonetheless. The mysterious Frenchman hadn't gone far. Indeed, he hadn't gone at all.

5

I wish I could describe the expression on Ramon Fortunato's face when he saw who owned Villa Bernabeu. Yes, I really do, but, glib bastard though I am, it's beyond me.

Our living room was well lit, by four big wall fittings, one on either side of each fireplace. When the captain stepped in from the night outside and saw us, his jaw dropped, he turned several different colours in succession, and it was well over a minute before he could speak.

'Fucking hell!' he shouted at last. The regional commander of the Mossos d'Esquadra, the Catalan police force, has a remarkable command of the English language; for a guy from Albons, that is.

I hadn't seen Fortunato for a while; our acquaintance went back to my last extended stay in Spain when Prim and I had become involved in a business which had led to us a stumbling over a number of people in succession, each of them, coincidentally, somewhat deceased. As *muerto* as *cordero* as they say in Spanish. To his great credit he had accepted from the off that we weren't the sort of people who were likely to have been responsible for any of them.

Prim had got to know him socially rather than professionally, after I had left St Marti and gone back to Scotland to marry Jan. During that time, she eventually told me, she had carnal relations with a Spanish man . . . and why not, as she put it. I had never been entirely sure, despite her denial, and despite the existence of a wife, that it wasn't Fortunato that she'd shagged.

If that was the case, the memory of it didn't exactly overwhelm him right then. 'You are magnets for corpses!' he exclaimed, running his fingers through his thick black hair as I poured him a medicinal glass of Le Panto. Prim and I don't usually attack the brandy early in the evening . . . or late, for that matter . . . but we agreed that the circumstances justified the exception.

Looking back, in that moment, I realised that he was right . . . about Prim at least. In all my time with Jan, we never discovered a single body!

'Just a minute, Ramon,' my wife exclaimed. 'You can't say that. We came upon him, not the other way around.'

She walked over to him; he leaned down and kissed her on the cheek. Looking at the two of them, in a fleeting second, my suspicions were reinforced. There was something in the way he allowed his hands to rest on her hips that convinced me they'd been there before. Not that I got steamed up; at the time she had been well entitled.

I walked across, shook his hand and gave him the brandy. He hadn't changed much; medium height, solidly built, black-haired, olive-skinned. He was clean-shaven but looked like the sort of bloke who should be wearing a moustache.

'Don't go on to us,' I warned him. 'Talk to the estate agent. What sort of an impression will it give property investors if word gets around that in L'Escala there's a free stiff in every swimming pool?'

'Who sold you the place?' he asked, as he sat down on the couch.

'A bloke called Sergi, from an agency called SolVacances.'

Fortunato chuckled. 'That figures. He's a good guy, but not of this world. A bit like the man in the pool, but not in the same way.

'When did you buy it?'

'Last week. We moved in today. We're on our honeymoon.' I didn't have to volunteer that, but something made me. 'We sold the apartment a while back, but were talked into having another property here.'

He looked at Prim. 'I never thought I'd see you back here,' he said quietly.

'How else would you find your corpses?' she shot back with a grin. 'How's Veronique?'

'Very well. We had a little boy six months ago; his name is Alejandro.'

There was a silence; somehow I didn't feel part of it.

'So who's our pal out there?' I asked, to break it as much as anything else. I glanced out of the window, just in time to see two uniformed Mossos officers carrying a plastic coffin up the steps of the pool.

The captain looked up at me and shrugged his shoulders. 'How the hell should I know? He's not exactly recognisable. He's been out there for a long time, but this house has been empty for a long time too.' His face twisted into a bitter grin. 'That shows you how quiet it is up here; apart from the lady Shirley, no one lives in this street all the year round. Even at that though, the smell must have been bad for a while.'

'When you remember how the L'Escala drains get sometimes,' I muttered, 'who'd wonder about it?

'Come on,' I persisted. 'Is it the Frenchman? The guy who owned this place?'

'It could be him; but like I say, it could be anybody. It could be a tramp who crawled under the cover for shelter in the winter, then took a heart attack or something. Christ, I can't even be certain that it's a man.'

'Forget the tramp idea,' I told him. 'That cover was lashed down tight; no one could have crawled under it, or at least no adult. Wasn't there anything on the body to give you a clue? He was clothed, after all.'

'Hah!' Fortunato laughed, explosively. 'I tell you what Oz; I haven't heard the morgue wagon leave, so why don't you go out and take a look through his pockets? Go on, I give you permission.'

I thought I caught a challenge in his tone; it needled me so much that I actually moved towards the door. Then I thought better of it.

'No?' the policeman chuckled. 'Well not me, either. Let's leave it to the man who does the autopsy. He's paid more than I am; he can look through the pockets, and pick through the bones.' He held up his goblet; somehow he had managed to empty it. 'Meanwhile, I am still suffering from the shock of exposure to that thing, and to the cold night air.'

He wasn't wrong about the weather; when the sun goes down on the Costa Brava in the winter months it can turn bloody freezing, bloody quickly, however bright the day may have been. I poured him another Le Panto.

'Going back to the Frenchman,' I said, as I settled myself into an armchair. 'I got the impression back there that you knew who I was talking about. Right?'

He sipped his brandy, then gave me a funny smile. 'Name, Reynard Capulet. Height, one metre seventy-nine; fair hair, small scars on right cheek and on chin. Date of birth, June eight, nineteen fifty-seven. At least that's what it said on the Interpol file which I saw, and that's what it said on the passport he used around here. Monsieur Capulet crossed frontiers under several different names, and one or two different hair colours, too, I suspect.

'Technically, he didn't own this place . . . but you'll probably know that by now, from your transaction with the *notario*. It belonged to a company which he and his sister set up in Switzerland.'

'His sister?' Prim murmured. 'Sergi never mentioned her.'

'There was no reason why he should; I'd be surprised if he ever met her. Her birth name is Lucille Capulet, and as far as I know that's the only one she uses. She didn't come here, though. She lives in Geneva, and she runs the company through a lawyer.'

'I take it from the fact that Interpol have a file on him,' I said, 'and from your tone, that Mr Capulet is bent.'

'Bent?' For once Fortunato's English let him down.

'Crooked. Not straight. A criminal.'

'All three. Capulet is, or maybe was, a friend of the friends. He has contacts with organised crime in France, Italy, Spain and the United States. He has homes in Paris and Florida.'

'What was his business?'

'He was a merchant, you might say. He was registered, quite legitimately, in Monaco as an antique dealer. He bought and sold internationally; often he would act for individuals on an agency basis. They'd give him lists of what they wanted, and he would find the items and acquire them. He did very well.

'But there was a suspicion that he had another, more lucrative business. He may have been involved in the movement of goods from one country to another, usually, but not always, on an informal basis.'

'He's a drug smuggler?'

'Smuggler yes . . . or so the police believe . . . but drugs no, apparently. According to the Interpol file he did not deal in narcotics. He was suspected of smuggling cigarettes, alcohol and people; those three illicit commodities.'

'People?' Prim exclaimed.

Fortunato gave her a smile and a shrug. 'Sure. There's money to be made by moving people from one country to another; Moroccans into Spain, Chinese and Asians into Britain . . . Christ, Chinese everywhere . . . Africans anywhere in mainland Europe, and into the States.'

'But if you know all this, why wasn't he in jail?'

'No, we suspect all this. Nobody has ever been able to prove any of it. But maybe he is in jail, dear Primavera.' He seemed to caress her name with his tongue. 'Maybe he is in prison in another continent, under another of his names.' Outside, a diesel engine barked into life. 'Or maybe he's in a plastic box on his way to the morgue in Figueras.

'To answer your question, criminals like our French friend do their business on the basis of bribery. People are paid to be absent from their posts at certain times, or not to search particular consignments, or to develop sudden deafness should they hear voices coming from within a container as it is being unloaded from a truck or a ship. It's very difficult to catch them.

'Whatever the truth, he hasn't been seen anywhere for over a year, by the people whose business it is to watch him. On my way here, I checked with Interpol; in Lyon . . .'

I interrupted. 'I thought it was based in Paris.'

'That's what everyone thinks. No, it's in Lyon; Quai Charles de Gaulle. Christ, it even has a website. I used the telephone though; I called them when my men gave me this location, and asked about M. Capulet. They told me that he had dropped out of sight.'

'At around the same time the house was put on the market?'

'A few months before that.'

'Mmm. If that is him in the van, he might have had a problem when it came to giving the sale instruction to the lawyer.'

Fortunato frowned.

'So?'

'So if it is him, and he didn't authorise the sale, who did? His sister?'

'A good question. One of many Interpol may be asking . . . if it turns out that way.'

'How about his antiques business?' Prim asked.

'As far as I know it's still trading; but it was run by a manager for much of the time. Capulet needed it, you see, to make his wealth look legitimate.'

He finished his brandy. 'I must go,' he announced abruptly, rising easily from the couch.

As we walked him to the door, he looked down at Prim. 'It is good to see you again, my dear,' he said quietly, giving her forearm a gentle squeeze. 'I am happy to see that you seem to be happy.'

'You too,' she murmured.

He seemed to remember that I was there. 'I hope that we don't have to disturb you much more, Señor Oz. If your latest specimen turns out not to be Capulet, we won't. But if it is . . . well, that may be another matter.'

He shook my hand, kissed Prim briefly on the cheek once more, and stepped out into the night.

6

I did my best to put it out of my mind; honest. I might have succeeded too, had Prim not been clearly as preoccupied as I was trying to pretend I wasn't . . . if you see what I mean.

We made it all the way through dinner; big steaks, with fried red peppers, washed down with a bottle of Vina Pomeral. Maybe it was the brandy I had earlier, but eventually, as we settled down into our armchairs with mugs of coffee, it overcame me.

I looked at her, trying to smile. 'Remember what you said about you and the captain? Just good friends, and all that stuff?'

She nodded. When she reddened, I knew what she was going to say.

'That wasn't exactly true,' she exclaimed, then paused, and her eyes fell. 'Christ, it wasn't at all true!

'We had an affair, Ramon and I. It started a few months after you had gone back to Scotland, to marry Jan.

'I told you that I used to see him in Meson del Conde, in St Marti, remember. The first time he was with this nice young woman; he introduced her as Veronique, his wife. The second time she wasn't there. I was at a table in the square one evening, when he appeared and asked if he could join me.'

She shot me a glance. 'I didn't just jump into bed with him, you know. He sat down, and we began to talk: a lot, as it turned out. I told him about how you had gone, and why. He told me about himself, and Veronique. I hadn't realised that they were separated, when I met them before. That evening, he had been trying to persuade her to come back to him: with no success, at that point at any rate.

'At some time that second evening, I said that I was bored. About two days later Ramon called me. I had told him about having been a nurse, and without another word he had arranged an interview for me in the hospital in Girona. I saw him again after that, after I got the job, for a "thank you" meal in the restaurant. Afterwards I took him home to the apartment . . . and I asked him if he wanted to sleep with me.' She chuckled, bitterly. 'He was every centimetre the gentleman; he even asked if I was sure! I said, "Too right, I am!"

'That was the start of it.'

'How long?' I asked. I felt strange, like a voyeur, in a way. I was aware of the need to be calm and rational, yet surprised to find that I actually was. I knew I wasn't Prim's only lover, but, with one unforgettable exception, she'd never discussed any of my predecessors, or successors; not till right then.

'Five months. After a few weeks he moved in. We kept ourselves to ourselves at that point; I didn't mix with the British crowd at all, so as far as I'm aware none of them know about it.'

'He was gone when I met you again.' I realised that was an assumption. 'He was, wasn't he?'

She nodded.

'So what happened?'

'I got bored, and threw him out.'

'Just like that?'

She nodded.

'Why don't I believe,' I challenged her, 'that that's the whole story?'

She hesitated, looked down, and went an even deeper shade of red. 'I became pregnant by him,' she whispered, and I could see that her eyes were glazed with tears.

I haven't been struck dumb very often in my life, but score one on that occasion.

'Oh my,' I murmured eventually. It was all I could say.

'I had a termination,' she went on, in that same small voice.

'Why did you do that?' I asked, in a tone as quiet as hers.

'Because I didn't love him. And because he was still in love with Veronique; I knew that. He told me eventually that she'd been unfaithful to him. He assured me that he hadn't simply been using me to get even, but he could never make me believe that. Not quite. Honestly, I had told him to go before I even suspected I was in the club.

'When I did find out, I thought about keeping it, as one does. But it felt like nothing inside me and, try as I might, I couldn't summon up a single maternal urge. I was afraid, no, I knew, that if I went ahead with it, I'd never have been able to give it the love it deserved, the depth of love I had as a child. It would have been difficult for Ramon too, trying to make things work with Veronique, yet having a baby by another woman in the next village. So I kept my secret, saw someone at the hospital where I worked, and did what I had to do.

'Hell, I didn't want Ramon's child. Oz, the truth is, I didn't want anyone else's child but yours. Even then, though you had gone out of

30

my life for good, or so I thought. Ironic, isn't it?'

'You don't have to tell me about irony, love. Just tell me this. What do you feel for the bloke now?'

'Nothing,' she replied at once. 'He's a nice enough guy, but I never loved him, or anything approaching it. Okay, so he may have got involved with me to get back at his wife, but I'd nothing to complain about there. That was nothing to what I was doing with him, from the start. I was fucking to forget in a big way!

'What you have to realise, Oz, is that after you left, and after *he* died, I was here on my own, doubly hurt, feeling bitter and sorry for myself at the same time. I had no one to talk to, no shoulder to cry on. Shirley had troubles of her own at that time, and the rest of the people you and I had got to know here are all so much older than us.

'Then Ramon turned up, as if it had been planned. I needed someone like him as a friend if nothing else. But I decided that he'd serve a more practical purpose than that. Once I'd thought about it for a while . . . like an hour or two . . . I decided to screw you out of my life, boy; in our bed, too, yours and mine.'

She settled into her chair, and took a sip from her coffee, not looking at me; looking at anything but me. 'The trouble was,' she murmured, 'my tactic backfired on me . . . and I'm not talking about getting pregnant. When I was with him, there in the dark in the apartment, being ridden in our bed, and I was faking it for him, to make him feel a bit special . . . which he wasn't, by the way . . . the face I always saw was yours . . .'

'Not *his*?' I interrupted with a cruel emphasis, which I regretted, in the instant I saw her flinch.

'That couldn't be,' she murmured, 'not in that way, as you know well.

'No, even as I was banging Ramon, I couldn't erase you. It was your breath I felt on my neck, your prick I felt inside me, not his.' Prim ground the words out, bitterly. She sounded like a stranger. She was punishing someone, but I wasn't sure whether it was herself or me. 'It was dispassionate,' she continued, 'but I didn't want passion anyway. I was cold inside, frigid, but that's how I felt. Yet always, Oz, from the moment I helped him into me until the moment he slithered out again, I saw your face.'

She sat bolt upright and glared at me. 'And . . .' she shouted, making me start for an instant . . . then she stopped abruptly, as if afraid of voicing thoughts that might destroy everything. She slumped down again in her chair, her eyes misted suddenly.

I finished it for her anyway. '. . . and that's more than I can say? Or is it what you want me to say? That when I was with Jan, I saw you?'

'Well, did you? Were you thinking of me while you were fucking her?'

She had gone much further than she intended. I knew that, just as I knew that she couldn't help herself. Why couldn't I have left her that one secret, so I could hold on to mine? But no, once the ball was rolling it couldn't be stopped; and after all, it was good old Oz who had started it on its way down the hill. I tried to put a foot against it, all the same.

I looked at the ceiling, and whistled. 'Christ there's a shit-load of worms in this can. Let's put the lid back on it, eh?'

'We can't,' she retorted. 'You took it off with a tin-opener.

'No, you didn't think of little Prim while you were on the job, did you. Not once, I'll bet.' I opened my mouth, not knowing quite what I was going to say. She cut me off. 'No, wait. There's another begged question, isn't there.

'Are you picturing her now, when you're on top of me?'

I looked at her for a moment, blankly, afraid that this was something I couldn't control, afraid that it really would never be the same again. I didn't feel any anger towards her, only pain within myself; but that was nothing new.

'No: never: not once.' I told her. I leaned back and closed my eyes.

'Oh I see Jan, all right. Every time we go to Anstruther, where she and I grew up, I see her in the fields, in my dad's garden, on the harbour wall. I see her at ten years old, at sixteen, at her twenty-first. But I'll never see her at any older than thirty. How could I?

'I see her every time I walk into that kitchen where she died, and my blood runs cold.'

When I opened my eyes, I saw that she was staring at me. For the first time, I was showing her all of me, even the darkest corner of my heart. 'Yet you kept it,' she exclaimed. 'We live there now.'

'Sure we do. It's just a house.

'Prim, I'll see that fucking kitchen wherever I am, just as I'll see the inside of that wee room in the Royal Infirmary mortuary, where they showed me her body. So there's no point in selling the flat for the sake of it.

'Anyhow, that's the truth of it. That's as far as it goes. She's gone and you're alive and I don't mix the two of you up,' I ventured a grin. 'Neither horizontally nor vertically: honest. You want to sell the Glasgow flat? No problem to me.'

'I like Glasgow.'

'But not there?'

'Not especially.'

'That's it then. Done deal.'

She smiled back at me, faintly.

'Since it's all coming out,' I continued, 'has there ever been a time since then when you've pictured him, Davidoff, in the same way?'

It was Primavera's turn to examine the ceiling. 'Honestly?' she began. With some people that's a sure sign that what you are about to hear will be anything but; not with Prim, though . . . I thought.

'Not when I've been with you: anyway, you know that it wasn't physical with him . . . not completely, that's to say. He was my lover, yet I couldn't be his, not in the same way.

'Still there were times when I was alone, and I tried to imagine how it might have been if he had been there after you'd gone. I tried to convince myself that I could have made him whole again, and that I could have given myself to him properly, rather than taking all the time. I could never make it a happy scene, though. He wasn't immortal; he'd have died eventually, and the best I'd have got would have been to watch him. I think he knew that too, that's why . . .'

I nodded. 'Yes, I think he told me as much, that last time I saw him.'

We sat for a while, gathering our thoughts; gathering our breath almost.

'One last secret,' I said eventually, 'and then there are no more. Remember that time I went back to Scotland to see a potential client? I slept with Jan then. We couldn't help ourselves, but then we never could. That was when I understood how it was.'

'I know,' she whispered. 'I've always known that.'

I frowned at her, taken aback. 'How?'

'Same way you guessed about Ramon and me. I know you all too well.'

I beckoned to her. She rose from her chair, put down her mug, came to me and settled into my lap. I kissed her on each eye, tasting salt on her lashes.

'Well?' she asked. 'Feel any different knowing you're married to the village bike?'

'As long as you're not a tandem, I don't care.'

She giggled and slapped me on the chest. I felt myself rock-hard, and realised that I had been that way for some time, and that I wanted her, maybe more than I had ever done.

'It all needed saying,' I told her. 'Long ago, probably. I wonder why it wasn't?'

'We needed a catalyst. Something to start the ball rolling.'

I grunted in her ear. 'Some catalyst . . . your spurned lover.'

'What will be . . .' she murmured. 'Sauce for ganders, but let's not start that again. No, maybe we needed neutral ground too, somewhere that's ours and ours alone.'

'Maybe.'

I paused. 'One more thing I have to tell you.'

'Whassat?' she murmured.

'I love you, Mrs Blackstone.'

'Then take me to bed.'

'Ever faked it for me?'

'Never had to; honest.'

Afterwards, we lay in the dim light of a bedside lamp . . . an item to be changed, for sure, along with bedroom curtains that made the place look like every schoolboy's idea of a Paris brothel. 'I feel much the better for that,' I said, my grin from ear to ear.

'What? Our true confessions?'

'Them too. But I'll tell you this. If that's what happens when you find a body, I hope we don't discover another for a while.'

7

When Fortunato came back two days later, I did my best not to give him the slightest hint that Prim had told me about the two of them. So I don't know how he guessed, unless he caught something in my eye, or, more probably in Prim's. She was edgy from the moment that he phoned to check that we'd be in.

I gave him my best, 'Hail, fella, good to see ya,' greeting, and he responded, but as soon as Prim disappeared off to the kitchen to fetch the coffee, he seemed to change, to become completely un-copperlike, on the defensive. He spent quite a while admiring our new rugs, and a very nice repro cabinet which we'd bought the day before from the Masia Store, on the road to Girona, before he could bring himself to look me in the eye. When he did, it was as if he was quizzing me.

No way was I going to kick the subject off. 'Well?' I asked, trying not to sound aggressive.

'So you know?'

'So I know. So I didn't know last time you were here. So what am I thinking?'

Ramon nodded.

'Nothing,' I told him. 'She was a free girl then, to misquote Tom Petty; I was gone. You're part of her history. God knows I have enough of my own, so I can't take issue with hers.'

I let that sink in, but not for too long. 'I take it that Prim is history as far as you're concerned?' I asked him.

He looked at the cabinet again. 'Yes,' he answered quietly.

'That's fine then. The subject's closed, for good, as far as I'm concerned.'

The captain looked relieved. 'For me too, obviously. Thank you.

'You must meet Veronique some time, and Alejandro.'

I couldn't think of a worse idea, but of course he didn't know about Prim's child. So all I said was, 'Let's not rush that one.'

Bang on cue, Primavera returned with coffee on a tray. I suspected

35

that she had been listening, behind the door. 'So, Ramon,' she began as she handed him his, 'what's the news on our departed guest?'

'No good news,' he answered, mournfully. 'As you saw, the body was badly decomposed, but not completely. The pathologist estimates that it had been in the water for around a year, maybe a month more, maybe a month less. There was nothing on it to identify it, but you can forget my theory that it might have been a tramp. The cause of death was a single gunshot wound to the heart; the bullet was still there, lodged in the spine.'

'So it was the Frenchman, Capulet?'

Fortunato shook his head. 'I can't say that for sure. It's beyond visual identification, and the clothing gave us no clue. It's all designer stuff, a mix of Hugo Boss and Pierre Cardin. Could have been bought in L'Escala, could have been bought anywhere. There was no wristwatch, no jewellery.'

'What about dental records?' Prim asked.

The detective smiled, sadly. 'For that you have to have been to a dentist. This man had perfect teeth. No, I'm afraid there is only one way we can prove it is Capulet, and that's through DNA profiling. There's no material from him that we can use for cross-reference, so we'll need to take a blood sample from a close relative. He had no children, so that means his sister, Lucille.

'Yesterday I called my colleagues in Geneva and asked them for cooperation. This morning they called me back. She has not been seen at home since Saturday, and no one knows where she is. They've spoken to the lawyer who administered the company; she visited his office on Friday afternoon to check that the company had received your bank transfer for the purchase of this house, but said nothing about going away. I also have checked Capulet's homes in Paris and Florida. Each one was sold during last summer, and new people live there now. Quite a mystery.'

I glanced out of the window at our empty, uncovered pool. Ramon had asked us not to fill it for the time being. 'Where's the mystery? She's killed her brother, then cashed up and buggered off into the wide blue yonder.'

Captain Fortunato stared at me, bewildered. It was another of those rare occasions when his English let him down. 'Sorry,' I said. 'She's sold the company's assets and gone away.'

'You may be right. And that will not help me.'

'So what happens now?' Prim asked. 'Can we fill our pool?'

The policeman shook his head. 'Not yet, not yet. Your pool is now a murder scene; that makes this situation very awkward. It brings up matters of jurisdiction also.'

'How come?'

He looked up at me from the couch. 'When I met you for the first time, I was an officer of the Guardia Civil. Now I am Mossos d'Esquadra, but I have many of the same duties. Normally, the death of this man would be for me to investigate. However, if the body is that of Capulet, that could make things different. He was suspected of crimes which crossed the Catalan border, into other parts of Spain, and those would still be the responsibility of the Guardia.'

'I see where we could have a big argument. For the moment though, since we don't know for sure that it is the Frenchman who is dead, I am keeping hold of this business. I want to have my technical people look at your pool again. Also I want to search your house, to see if there is anything still here that might tell us something about the man's death.'

'But we've had cleaners in,' I said.

'I know, but it is still something I have to do. Better that it is me than someone from the Guardia, who does not know you.'

'Better the Devil you know,' I murmured.

'Excuse me?'

'I mean, yes; I agree with you.'

Ramon had been sure of himself, and us; there was a squad of officers waiting in a van, out of our sight in the street below. Prim and I decided that it was best for us to leave them to get on with it, so we took ourselves along to Shirley's.

She had been wide-eyed the day before, when he had told her about our bonus surprise in the pool. 'Bloody hell, Oz,' she had exploded. 'People leave some funny things behind them when they sell houses here . . . the punters who bought mine were left a model of the Tower of London that my late husband made out of matchsticks . . . but dead tramps is pushing it.' We hadn't let her into our suspicion that the body was that of the previous owner.

When we told her the hot-off-the-press news, that the guy had been shot, her jaw dropped so far I thought it was dislocated.

'Say that again,' she gulped eventually.

I did.

'Do they know who it is?' she asked.

'They think it might be our predecessor. He was an antique dealer but he was also in the import business, apparently.'

'You mean he was a smuggler?' She catches on quickly, does our Shirl.

'So they reckon. Not drugs, though. According to Fortunato, he dealt in fags and stuff. His name was Reynard Capulet.'

She looked at me steadily enough, only I thought I caught a flicker somewhere in her gaze.

'You said the police think it might be him. Don't they know for sure?'

I nodded. 'From what we saw the other night, he looks a lot worse than his passport photo. They're going to have to identify him by other means. The police in Switzerland are looking for his sister right now, so they can run a comparison test.'

'Ain't science wonderful?' she muttered.

There was no doubt about it; Shirley Gash seemed just a bit distracted. She was making a big effort to hide it, but she wasn't quite getting there.

Prim saw it too. 'What's up?' she asked. 'You didn't know this man, did you?'

She drew a deep breath. 'Yeah,' she admitted. 'I knew Rey Capulet: knew him fairly well, or so I thought. But I never, ever, knew that he lived up here. All your talk of a Frenchman, and I never made the connection. I thought he was Swiss, you see; he mentioned his sister in Geneva fairly often, so I just assumed.'

'How did you get to know him?'

'I met him one night in Bar JoJo, oh, it'll be eighteen months ago at least; first half of last year. He was with that bloke Sergi, from the agency in town. I was with some people from Conservatives Abroad. I had had enough of the bloody dominoes by that time, so I said hello to Sergi, and he introduced me to his pal.

'He seemed like a nice chap. We talked for a bit and that was all. Then a few days later, I bumped into him in the bank. He invited me to dinner in El Golf Isobel. A perfect gentleman, he was; bit younger than me, but what's that got to do with anything.

'I took him out to Kathleen and Carlos's restaurant . . . you know, La Clota . . . returning his hospitality, then we had a few more dinner dates after that. Never got down to any of the other, you understand, but it was on the agenda . . . mine at any rate. Mind you, he did talk about me going to his place in Florida, so it might have been on his too.

'Last time I saw him? Oh, it must have been a year ago.' She frowned. 'November, it was; early November. He took me to Mas Torrent . . . that was when he mentioned going to Florida, in fact. He said he was off to Geneva for a couple of weeks, to visit his sister. But he never came back . . . or so I thought. I never saw him again, anyway.'

'And you never knew he lived two doors down from here?' Prim asked.

'I'd no idea; we never got to the stage of him inviting me back to his place. I was still in my old house then. I'd only just signed up for the plot, and when Vincens showed it to me, Rey was off on his travels. So I never made the connection; all I was told was the same as you, that Villa Bernabeu was owned by some French geezer.'

'Did he never discuss his business?'

'Not much. He said that he came from a wealthy family and that he dealt in commodities. When someone says that to you in L'Escala, you can draw your own conclusions, but you tend not to ask any more questions. If Fortunato says that he was a smuggler, it doesn't surprise me.'

'Did he ever talk about other friends or business associates?' I caught Prim giving me an old-fashioned look.

'No. And Sergi was the only guy I ever saw him with, as far as I can remember.'

All of a sudden, Shirley shuddered. She seemed to shrink into herself, to become smaller, as the impact of what we had told her began to sink in. 'The police really think that was Rey in the pool?'

'It's a possibility,' I told her. 'They're a bit vague about the actual time of death, but it could fit with the time you saw him last.'

'God,' she whispered.

'Unlikely,' I muttered. 'He doesn't use a gun.' I winced as soon as I'd said it, knowing that she had heard. It wasn't something that the old Osbert Blackstone would have come out with. No, that crack was very definitely new Oz, worldly wise and maybe none the better for it. But Shirley didn't seem to mind; in fact she sat upright again.

'No, He doesn't. If you move in that world, I suppose you have to live by its rules. I wonder who he upset?'

'Maybe he didn't upset anyone,' Prim suggested, an hour later, as we walked back to the villa. 'Maybe someone upset him.'

I laughed out loud. 'What? So he shot him, dumped him in the pool, then left town and put the place on sale: with all furnishings and fittings?'

'Smartarse,' my wife grumbled.

'Come on. You love me really.' I remembered a moment. 'Here, why did you give me that funny look back there at Shirley's?'

'I don't know what you mean.'

'Sure you do. When I was asking her who Capulet's pals might have been, you shot me a right frown.'

'Ah that. Just for a moment I thought you were slipping into private eye mode.'

'Gie's a break, honey. I never was a private detective. I was a private enquiry agent; different animal altogether. I just got drawn into a few things, that's all.' I paused as another brick slipped into place. 'And always when you were around, come to think of it.'

'Don't blame me! You couldn't stop yourself. Well, just remember, whatever you called yourself, you're out of that business for good. You're an actor, and to prove it you're an Equity member. I will not . . . Hear me? I said I will not . . . have you getting involved with this business.

'If that was the previous owner in our pool, then he probably got what was coming to him. If it wasn't . . . So what? It's Ramon's job to find out who it was and why he was put there. It's got nothing to do with you. Hear me?'

'I hear you! I hear you! You just remember it too. You know, sometimes I think that it's no wonder I took to acting. My whole life's been a fucking movie since I met you, darlin'.' My blood went cold suddenly. I had pronounced that last word just like Jan used to.

Prim never noticed though. She was still chuntering to herself as we walked back into the villa.

'Hello there,' Captain Fortunato greeted us, clutching a mug of our finest Bonka coffee. (I've often wondered why they don't market that brand in Britain.) 'We have almost finished. You will be glad to hear that, so far, we found nothing out of the usual.'

'If you're happy, we're happy,' I said, being fairly keen to see the back of the bloke.

No such luck. 'Ahh, I did not say I was happy. I am a detective, and so I have the sort of mind that expects to find something out of the ordinary. When I do not, I become suspicious.

'When people buy a house in this town, it is not unusual for it to be sold with furniture and most of the fittings. Normally, the person who sells will clear out personal items, but there is usually something left behind, something which gives a clue about the previous owner.

'When you moved in here, what did you find? Were there clothes in the wardrobes?'

Prim shook her head. 'Yes, there were; men's clothing. Most of it casual. I chucked it all out.'

'Were there any papers in the drawers, anything at all? For example, were there any cards for restaurants, or for businesses in L'Escala? Were there any maps of the town? Were there even any matchbooks, or the little packs of sugar which they give people in cafés, and which everyone takes home?'

'No, there weren't. Not that I can recall. Can you, Oz?'

I thought about it for a while. 'No. I can't. I don't think there was a single piece of paper left in the house; other than books, novels and such, all of them French. I tell you something that struck me as odd. There was a telephone, but no directories. Why would somebody leave town, leave Spain, as far as anyone knows, yet take the telephone directory with him?

'And the tape? There was a telephone answering machine, but it was empty. There was no cassette in it, and none anywhere in the house.'

I looked at Fortunato. 'I see what you mean,' I told him. 'When we moved in here there was nothing that referred in any way to the Frenchman. It was as if the place had been stripped of anything that might, anything on which he might even have made a note, or scrawled down a phone number, an e-mail address, anything like that.'

'And yet his clothing was still here, his books . . .'

'And a stack of CDs,' I added.

'And a few cases of expensive wine . . . Unless you have bought the bottles which I found in the storeroom at the back.'

'No, we found them there too. So what does that tell you, Captain?'

No one can shrug his shoulders quite like a Catalan. It's a national trait, and one of the most expressive gestures I know. Fortunato's said it all. He didn't need to add, 'Everything. Nothing. Either the body is Capulet and the person who killed him has covered his tracks, or it is not, and he is covering his own.' But he did.

'What it means,' he continued, 'is that I think I do have to share this now, with my colleagues in the Guardia Civil. I hope they don't want to dig up your terrace, or your garden at the back, but you never know.'

8

Happily, they didn't. Three days later, on Saturday morning, Fortunato came back with a couple of them, stern-looking, thirty-something guys in olive green uniforms. They looked into the pool, as if they were thinking deep thoughts; they looked around the house; they looked into the outbuildings; they looked into the garage and the Lada.

Then one gave the other a Catalan shrug that would have scored high marks for both performance and artistic impression, and they left.

'Is that it?' I asked Ramon as they walked down the path. 'Is that the investigation? Don't they want to take our fingerprints for elimination? Don't you want to take them?'

'Do you want us to have them?' he laughed. 'Oz, Prim, those cleaners you hired were very good indeed. They wiped just about every print in the place.

'As for the investigation, one of my colleagues just said to me in Catalan, that if a gangster is killed, the most sensible thing to do is bury him and take him off the wanted list. Even if we're right and we have found Capulet, they don't care; certainly they want nothing to do with the investigation. That's all mine.'

'And what are you going to do about it?'

The amiable copper grinned. 'I believe that you have a saying in English, which does not translate into Spanish or Catalan. Fuck all. That is what I am going to do about it; fuck all.

'I don't even have a victim identification, until the Swiss or Interpol find the sister . . . If they even bother to look for her. Where would I start? There is no one on the missing persons list who matches the age and sex. No, I will keep samples for DNA testing, and I will bury the rest.'

He looked at me, searching my eyes. 'Have I surprised you, my friend Oz? Do I disappoint you?'

'You surprise me, for sure. And yes, you disappoint me. When we first met, I had you pegged as someone who understood the rights of the victim. That guy in the pool; whoever he was, whatever he did, somebody put him there. Somebody killed him. Doesn't he have a right to . . . justice?'

'Maybe he's had it,' the policeman shot back at me. Then he seemed to soften. 'Life is not a movie, Señor.' He shot me another quick smile. 'Yes, even I have heard of your new career.

'In the real world, all of us have to set priorities. For example, if that was a child you had found murdered in your pool, or a young woman violated, then this crime would have a very high priority indeed. In fact, my men and I are currently investigating the abduction and murder of a child, a young girl, in another part of the province. It is painstaking work, and we are under a lot of pressure from the newspapers and the politicians to find the beast who did it.

'If I took even one of my few detectives from that case and set him to work chasing the killer of a man who was probably a criminal himself, I would be crucified. The Spanish people do not care about French smugglers, but they do care, very deeply, about their own children.

'The truth is that I brought my Guardia friends here because I hoped they would take this business off my hands, but they are in the same position as me; overstretched.

'I'll deal with it when I am able. Until then, if you feel a personal interest, then you go ahead and investigate.'

Beside me, Prim snorted. Actually, it wasn't far short of an explosion. 'That will be right! We're on honeymoon, Ramon. And our detecting days are very definitely over.'

Fortunato smiled at her, softly, as if he had played the scene with her himself at some point in the past; as, probably, he had. 'In that case, my dear, fill your swimming pool.' He glanced at the men who were erecting scaffolding around the house. 'Paint your villa. Enjoy yourselves.

'You are here for Christmas, yes?'

'We don't know,' Primavera replied. 'We haven't decided yet.'

'I am looking forward to Christmas,' he murmured. 'It will be Alejandro's first; even if he will be too young to appreciate it. I know now I was never really happy till I had a son.' There was something in the way he said it, that made me wonder; as if he was telling her that he knew. Or maybe I'm simply paranoid.

'Make a fuss of him, then,' my wife told her former lover, making an effort to keep her voice light, but only succeeding in sounding unlike herself. 'He'll appreciate that.' I thought I caught a message in her tone too; maybe it was an unspoken apology. If it was, then certainly it wasn't intended for me.

44

'Sure he will.' I burst in to the middle of whatever might have been going on. 'Maybe we should have our boys here too; our nephews. We've got room for them and Ellie, if they fancy it.'

'I will leave you to your planning,' said the policeman. He chuckled. 'And please, feel free to investigate our late friend if you wish. Just don't find any more like him.'

9

My casual suggestion took wings. As the overtime painters finished their scaffolding, we talked and made a couple of phone calls.

My sister Ellen jumped at the chance to spend Christmas in our new house. Jonathan and Colin weren't old enough to vote, but there was no doubt about what they'd want. More than that, we decided that we had room for my dad and Mary, my stepmother, too . . . without creating parental rivalries, since Prim's folks were heading for Los Angeles to end the year with the pregnant Dawn and her megastar husband, Miles.

The master plan was completed when Mary insisted on cooking the turkey. Nobody does it better.

We had no intention of doing any more cooking ourselves than we had to, so in the evening we headed into L'Escala, for dinner in La Dolce Vita, at a table in an upstairs window with a view across the Golfo de Rosas. The pizza was world-class . . . I could live on pizza . . . but the place was busy and there was a queue for tables, so we didn't hang about long after dessert.

It was just after ten when we stepped out into the crisp, December night. We didn't feel like going home; instead, we went for a wander.

We had walked past Bar JoJo many times, but had rarely gone in. We probably wouldn't have that night either, only we saw Shirley sitting there, at a table.

I really don't know how to describe JoJo's. It serves as a local for many of the L'Escala ex-pats, but it isn't exclusively their club. It caters for young . . . some very young . . . and old . . . some very old . . . alike, and it is open at least six nights a week through the year, even on black Mondays in the dead of winter when there are no other lights showing in the old town. I'm not even going to try to describe JoJo herself . . . Dammit, yes I am. Imagine, if you will, that Rita Hayworth had been English and had lived a year or two longer than she did.

Shirley wasn't alone when we stepped inside; there were half a dozen other customers, plus Jo herself, and a set of dominoes lay scattered on each of the two tables. Clearly, there had been a hot time in the old town that night.

The proprietrix pushed herself up from her chair. 'Naich to see you again,' she said. 'What can I get you?'

The wrong answer to that question can lead to the land of very sore heads, but we settled for two beers. As we took them, and as Jo entered them into the notebook where she keeps everyone's tab, Shirley called across from her table. 'Hello you two. Your ears burning? I was just talking about you; so was everyone else, in fact. You're the talk of the town.'

The man on her right nodded, then took a quick slurp from a drink that looked as if it might have been lemonade, but wasn't. 'Aye, that's right,' he barked, in an accent from somewhere north of Birmingham . . . I've never been very good at telling Yorkshiremen from Lancastrians. I can't even remember which colour of rose is which. 'It's been right quiet here for a while. Still, it's nice to 'ave you back, for all that.'

'Nice to be back,' I said. I like Frank Barnett; he's a fixture in L'Escala, to the extent that when he dies there's talk of stuffing him. As a matter of fact, some people can't wait, or so it seems; I've heard them tell him to get stuffed on several occasions. He and his wife Geraldine left wherever it was around ten years ago for a brief stay in Spain, and have hardly been back since. He's a plain-spoken man, is our Frank; I didn't really appreciate the meaning of the adjective 'bluff' until I met him at a Catalan Society do.

'So,' he demanded, 'is it 'im, then? The French bloke who was chatting up Shirl; is it 'im?'

'Well if it is, it isn't, Frank . . . If you see what I mean. What we found in our new pool was a pile of bones and other stuff I don't even like to think about.'

He gave a deep macabre chuckle. 'Maggots, like?'

'Fucking crocodiles, mate.' He likes a story embellished.

'So the police don't have a clue then?'

'Nary a one. They think it's Capulet, but they can't prove it.'

'Not even in this day and age? Wi' all this genetic fingerprinting and stuff?'

'If you can find one of his toe-nail clippings under your bed, they'd identify him in as long as it takes to test it. But otherwise . . .'

He grunted. 'Under your bed, more like. I 'ardly knew the bloke.' He flashed me a wicked smile. 'Can't speak for the Missis, though. She likes a bit of French.'

'Gerroff,' Geraldine muttered, cuffing him lightly on the back of the head.

'They've looked under our bed already,' Prim told him. 'No joy. If you're ever looking for really good cleaners, we can recommend a firm.'

'Did you know him though, Frank?' I asked.

'Oh aye. Not very well, like I said, but I knew the bloke. He were in here once or twice.'

I must have looked surprised, for he continued. 'Yes, he were. Not a regular customer, like, but he came in once or twice.'

'Sure, with me,' Shirley interjected.

'Aye, but other times as well. Jo'll tell you, won't you, Jo?'

'Yes, that's right,' came a voice from behind the bar.

'You know that Moroccan bloke?' Frank asked.

'Which one among the several million?'

'Dark-haired guy.'

I searched my memory, but couldn't for the life of me remember when I've ever seen a blond Moroccan. 'Keep going,' I said.

'Thin bloke; tall for a Moroccan. He's got a fishing boat. Sayeed,' he bellowed at last. 'That's 'is name. The Frenchman were in here with him a few times. They made an odd couple, him well-dressed, smelling of aftershave and dripping in gold, and this other fella, well-enough dressed, but dead scruffy and looking like 'e didn't own a razor.'

'What were they talking about?' I asked him.

'I don't know, but it were private whatever it was. I said "Hello" to them one night . . . just like that . . . and the Moroccan looked at me as if he thought I'd been listening in. After that they clammed right up. So I just left them to get on wi' it. I were only trying to be friendly, that's all. Bugger the pair of 'em, that's what I said to myself.'

'How about Sayeed? Is he still around?'

'I suppose so,' Frank muttered, scratching his forehead above his light-framed glasses. 'I suppose he must be. Can't remember when I saw 'im last, though. Can you, Shirl?'

'The Moroccan? I wouldn't have a bloody clue,' she answered.

'How about you, Gerrie?' he asked his wife. 'Sayeed the fisherman. When did you see him last?'

She looked at him, only mildly interested. 'I don't know,' she complained. 'He's not the sort of bloke you'd miss, is he?'

Prim laughed. 'You're all missing him, by the sound of things; you've mislaid him completely.'

Defeated, Frank turned to the Oracle. 'Jo. When was Sayeed in here last?'

She pondered the question. 'Must be a year and more back,' she announced at last. 'Before he went to prison.'

'Christ,' I muttered, aloud. 'The story goes on. What did he get the nick for, Jo?'

She looked at me as if I was simple. 'Smuggling,' she answered. 'What else around here?'

'Ahh,' shouted Frank in triumph. 'That's it, I'd forgotten 'e got put away.'

'So what was he smuggling?' asked Prim. 'Drugs? Booze?'

'Nah, love,' said Jo, 'none of that; not Sayeed. He was caught with what most of these people smuggle.'

'Which is?' she asked, as intrigued as I was.

'Other bleedin' Moroccans; what else?'

10

When we woke next morning, we didn't give Sayeed another thought. Instead, we finally got round to climbing down into our pool and giving it a good scrubbing out . . . especially the area around the drain . . . then began the slow process of filling it. The painters were off that day, so we had the place to ourselves for once.

Once the bottom was completely covered, shallow end to deep, we added a load of chlorine, as advised by another English bloke we had met in JoJo's, after we had moved on from Frank's table.

'Looks okay, doesn't it?' I said to Prim as we stood by the steps, watching the sun sparkling on the surface.

'Mmm.' She nodded. 'I wonder how long it'll be before I can look into it without imagining I can see something on the bottom.'

'I wonder how long it'll be before it's warm enough to dive in to check.'

'The end of May, without a heating system; or so that man said last night.'

'Let's get one, then,' I proposed. 'Like they say in Glasgow, toffs is careless.'

Prim was pondering this when my mobile, which was clipped to my belt, played its wee tune. I let it sound for a second or two . . . I like Peer Gynt . . . then answered. It was my dad.

'What are you up to then, son?' asked Mac the Dentist.

'Nothing much,' I told him. 'We've cleared the last corpse out of the swimming pool, so we've just been filling it up.'

'Christ, coming from you I'd almost believe that was true.' I hadn't shared our secret with him. 'Weather okay? It's bloody awful here.'

'Aye, fine, Dad. Just the usual, you know. Shirtsleeve order, if you're in the sunshine and out of the wind.'

'Lucky wee bastard!' he snorted. 'It had better stay that way. I've got the flight tickets booked. We leave the Saturday before Christmas, once the schools have broken up, flying to Barcelona from Edinburgh through Amsterdam. Is that all right with you?'

'Damn silly question, if you've booked. But of course it is. Did you put them on my Visa like I told you?'

'Yes, I did. You could have made a mistake, son, giving me that number. But I put the hire car on mine, don't worry.'

'You're a daft old bugger then; we were going to pick that up too. Listen, I'll fax you directions from the airport nearer the time.'

I paused. 'So what else is new?'

'I'll tell you what is. I've had three different journalists on the blower trying to find you. They want to interview you before the premiere of your movie . . .'

'Miles and Dawn's movie, Dad.'

'Whatever. They all wanted to talk to you in advance, anyway. Wanted to know where you were. I did as you said, and put them on to the distributor's PR people in London.'

'I gathered that; I had a message from them yesterday on my mobile. I'm either going to see them when we come back for the Glasgow premiere next month, or the film people will fly them out here to meet me.'

My dad laughed. 'Do I sound incredulous?' he asked. 'Because I fucking well am. I cannot believe this is my son we're talking about. The same guy who used to be an ambition-free zone. So what do you do after the premiere?'

'I go to school.'

'Eh?'

'That's right. Miles was happy enough with the way I handled the first movie, but that was because the part was built around me. Before we start shooting the next one, he wants me to have some coaching, so he's hired a drama tutor to work with me one on one.'

'Wise man. He faxed me a couple of reviews from movie critics in the States. You get a mention in both of them; they actually sort of hint that you're no' bad . . . for a beginner.'

'If I was bad, Dad, I wouldn't have been there. Miles does no favours on his projects. He must have thought I was up to it.'

'And what do you think?'

'I enjoy it; and yes, I do feel comfortable. You're going to tell me I've been play-acting all my life, I suppose.'

'That I am. Your mother would say the same if she was here, God bless her.'

'Tell me about it. I can hear her saying just that, all the time. See you soon, Dad . . . Oh yes, and remember to bring your golf clubs.'

'Will do.'

I had almost hit the cancel button when he spoke again.

'Nearly forgot,' he exclaimed. 'Someone else called looking for you: Susie Gantry. She said she wanted to send you a card, so I gave her your new address.'

'How did she sound?'

'Okay. The spark seemed to have gone out of the lassie, as you'd expect, losing her man in the way she did; but she's a tough wee thing . . . She will survive, as the song says. She hasn't been in touch with you?'

'No.'

'Ach well, I expect she will. Give my love to Prim.'

He really did ring off this time. I passed on his greetings to my wife as I walked up to the other end of the pool to rejoin her, with lunch in mind. We were almost indoors when we heard the gate creaking open. I thought it must be Shirley, looking to borrow a cup of sugar or some such, but I was wrong.

As I looked towards the direction of the sound, a small, slender, brown-skinned girl stepped into the driveway. She carried what was either a small suitcase or a large vanity case, and was dressed in a heavy old-fashioned coat, the sort I'd have expected to see on someone twenty years older, but not on her. It flapped half open as I moved towards her and, underneath, I caught a glimpse of a flimsy cotton dress.

'Can I help you? I asked as I walked towards her, forgetting myself and speaking to her in English. She looked at me blankly, until I repeated the question in Spanish.

'I was told to come here,' she answered. The coat opened wider as she spoke, letting me see just how flimsy the dress was. It seemed to cling to her body, making it pretty clear that it was all she was wearing, other than a pair of shoes with platform soles and laces which wound their way up her legs to tie in front of her shins.

I sensed a wind-up in the offing; set up by Frank Barnett maybe, or by the pool man. 'Pardon?' I said.

'I was told to come here,' she repeated. I dragged my gaze back up to her face. She was very pretty, and certainly not Spanish, although I could only guess at her nationality.

'Oh yes,' I went on, still sceptical. 'And who told you?'

She frowned, her eyelashes flickering nervously. 'I was told. Sorry. There is a mistake.'

And then she was gone, as quickly as she had arrived, and as noisily, as the gate creaked closed behind her.

I walked back up the drive and into the house. Prim was in the kitchen, making coffee. 'Who was that?' she asked.

'If I had to guess, I'd say it was a call-girl; only she called at the wrong address.'

She raised an eyebrow as she looked at me. 'She'd better have,' she murmured.

11

For the next couple of weeks, we concentrated on settling in to our new home, and on getting things ready for the family coming at Christmas. The painters turned the place from a dirty white colour into a sunny terra-cotta shade, the new aluminium security shutters were fitted, and a wrought-iron gate replaced the pile of rust at the foot of the driveway.

We were even able to rejoin the world, when we had a computer system installed in a small room on the ground floor, which we had turned into an office.

One of my first e-mail messages was from Miles Grayson, our movie director brother-in-law. He told me that in spite of my perform-ance . . . his very words . . . *Snatch* was now officially a hit in the States, having taken over one hundred million dollars at the box office in its first month on release. Since I was on one per cent of the gross, that meant that I could no longer prevent Prim from going up to Figueras and buying the blue Mercedes SLK that she coveted. You know it; the one with yellow leather upholstery and the steel roof that retracts into the boot on sunny days.

Miles also sent me over the Internet a file titled 'Project 38'. I knew what it was before I opened it; the script for the new movie which we would be shooting in February. I printed it out on the morning it arrived and settled down to read it in one of our poolside chairs. The further along I got, the more nervous I grew.

My part in *Snatch* had been limited, tailored to fit an unschooled beginner like me. Originally I had been hired simply as a narrator, because my voice sounded right and it wasn't unknown to the public, thanks to my wrestling gigs and advertising voice-overs, But as the project had developed, and Miles had become used to me, a few on-camera scenes had been added. There was nothing complicated, nothing I couldn't handle with proper direction from Miles, and although my eventual impact on the movie turned out to be quite significant, in my heart I hadn't really felt like an actor, not even when I saw the rushes.

This was different; I knew from my first read-through of the script, a fifties drama set in the Chicago area, that this time Miles planned to stretch me. I reckoned that he was taking a big gamble, and I was grateful for the coaching sessions which he had booked for me in the New Year.

I was halfway through my second read-through when I heard a car pull up in the street outside. The new gate swung open silently and Ramon Fortunato stepped into the drive. '*Bon dia*,' he called out . . . 'Good day,' in Catalan. He looked up at the house. 'Very impressive,' he said, dropping into English. 'It's amazing what bright colour can do to a place. There's a town on the Costa Brava where the mayor has banned all the builders from painting new houses white.'

He whistled as he saw Primavera's new car in the driveway. 'Very impressive also. More than I can afford on my poor policeman's salary.'

'Bullshit,' I told him, watching him climb the stair to the terrace. 'You don't fancy being talked about, that's all.'

'I wish,' he muttered.

'So,' I asked, 'to what do we owe the honour, and all that?'

The captain shook his dark head. 'Nothing; nothing at all. I was just passing.'

I stared at him, unable to keep the smile from my face. 'What? You were just passing by, on a dead-end road, in the back of beyond?'

'I was visiting the ruins,' he claimed, but I didn't believe a word of it.

'Crap. You either want to tell us something, casually, or you want to find something out. You're a detective; I never yet met one of them who did something for no reason at all.'

Ramon surrendered. 'Okay, okay; I admit it. I am curious.'

'About what?'

'I am wondering whether you have been doing your own detecting, into the mystery of the man in your pool.' He glanced into the water. 'It looks good now that you've filled it.'

I held up Miles Grayson's script. 'Believe it or not, *Capitano*,' I said, 'I do have other priorities than doing your fucking job for you. I take it from that, that the crime on our premises is still not at the top of your list of things to do.'

He gave a short laugh. 'Not exactly. I caught the man who killed the child, though. He's in jail in Barcelona; having a very bad time, I hope. But since then there has been a jewel robbery in Figueras, and a large German-owned sailing boat has been set on fire in Ampuriabrava. They rank ahead of Señor Capulet also.'

'Well don't look to me for help, mate; not even in fun. Prim would kill me.'

'I don't think so,' he murmured. 'Prim is an unceasingly curious lady. For her life is one big question, or so it seemed to me.'

I didn't answer him. In fact I made a point of not answering him; I just let his words hang in the air for a while, as if they might remind him not to dig up Prim's past, not with me at any rate.

'We did find out one thing,' I told him, once I reckoned that he had got the message. 'Purely by chance, of course. We heard that he had a pal around here. He used to go into Bar JoJo in L'Escala, with a tall, thin, scruffy Moroccan fisherman called Sayeed . . . until he went to the slammer for running illegal immigrants into the country.'

'Is that so?' the policeman murmured. 'Did they go there often?'

'A few times, according to what we were told. Ask Jo if you want chapter and verse about it.'

Fortunato turned and ambled towards the staircase to the driveway. 'I might just do that,' he said. 'I think your body has just moved a couple of places up my priority list.'

12

My old man has spent most of his fifty-something years in Fife, so you might think that landing in a foreign country, then driving over a hundred kilometres to a backwater street in a strange town would be a major exercise for him. Not so.

You can see Edinburgh from some of the higher parts of the East Neuk, it's that close to the mainstream; yet there are villages tucked away in there, in their home county, that many Fifers have never heard of. My dad knows the lot, the whole place, like the back of his hand. As a Round Table member, and later, as a Rotarian, his speciality was the Treasure Hunt, point to point car chases with clues which lead competitors to the most obscure spots, following a trail which leads back to the starting point. This is invariably a pub with a large car park within walking distance, essentially, of the competitors' homes.

When Mac the Dentist put together a Treasure Hunt, they used to say that the farmers were favourites to win, because many of the points *en route* could only be reached in a Land Rover, but I know for a fact that he always did his research in his old Jaguar. You see he's a rare creature, a dentist who'll do house calls, on old or sick people whose only needs are running repairs to their dentures. I remember him telling me, once upon a time, about visiting a very old lady in a cottage near a hamlet called Carnbee. He discovered, in the course of conversation, that in all of the century for which she had lived, she had never been further from home than St Andrews.

Of course he offered to take her to Edinburgh, so that she could cross the Forth Bridge, at least, before she died, but she just looked at him and asked, 'And fit have they got there, son, that wid be ony guid tae me?'

Given that history, I never had any worries about him finding our new house. I simply faxed him a street map of L'Escala, with a big 'X' marking the spot and put the coffee on the hob at five o'clock on the Saturday afternoon before Christmas. Ten minutes later, a hired people-mover turned into our driveway, through the open gate.

59

At first, my nephews were unimpressed. 'Where's the beach?' asked Colin, the younger one, before he had even jumped out of the car. They had been to our old place, in St Marti, where they could run down a hill into the sea.

'Up there,' I told him, pointing to the terrace and the pool. 'We have our own. If you don't like it, you'll just have to get used to walking half a mile.'

Jonathan's the cool one. When he was a couple of years younger he was a toe-rag of a kid, but since his mum and dad split up he's taken his role as the senior man in the household very seriously. 'Nice house,' he said, just turned eleven and trying to sound sixteen . . . he didn't make a bad job of it either.

'Yes it is,' I agreed. 'Nice telly too. We've got BBC1; if you move yourself, you'll catch the football results in about half an hour.' He barely twitched, but I could tell from his eyes that I'd scored.

'Honest to God,' said my sister Ellie. 'You always were a self-indulgent bugger, even when you couldn't really afford it. There'll be no holding you now.'

We had a general hugging session in the driveway, Prim, Ellie, Mary, my stepmother, and me. While my dad started to lug bags from the car. I took one from him, and turned to pass it to Jonny, but he and his brother were gone, straight in front of the telly, for sure.

'Boys!' their mother bellowed but, like me at their ages, they were masters of selective deafness.

It was good to have the family there. For the first time since we'd moved in, Prim and I were able to show the place off. Looking back, I think that was the moment at which Villa Bernabeu began to feel like a home.

We were so domesticated that Prim took the girls straight to the supermarket on the edge of town, to finish off the shopping for the Christmas dinner. Dad and I gave the boys Cokes and a bag of pretzels as they squatted on the floor watching the early Premiership match reports, then sat down ourselves with a couple of beers.

'So you've landed on your feet again, son,' he chuckled. 'Did you get this for a song too?'

'If we did it was grand bloody opera. This is how the other half live, I'll have you know.'

'So what's wrong, then?' he asked, quietly.

I looked at him, genuinely astonished by his question. 'Nothing's wrong,' I protested. 'What the hell made you ask that?'

'Thirty-something years of fatherhood. I know you better than anyone on this planet, so when I ask you what's wrong, it's because I can see that something is . . . even if no one else can.'

'Even if I can't?'

'Even if, Christ, all those years when you and Jan were living those sham lives, do you think I didn't know you were deceiving yourselves? As soon as I saw you this afternoon, I knew that there was something chewing at you.'

I didn't have an answer for him. Nor, right then did I have one for myself, only surprise, for I've always trusted my dad's judgement. So I just took a swig of my Estrella and thought about it.

'It's this next movie, I suppose. I got the script from Miles the other day, and it's . . . It's going to be a lot tougher than the first one. I just hope I can hack it.'

'Mmm. I see,' Macintosh Blackstone mused. 'So all the experts, all the reviewers who've been saying how well you did in the first one, and what a natural actor you are . . . as if I couldn't have told them that for Christ's sake . . . they're all wrong, are they?'

'Maybe they are. The last part was made for me; maybe this one isn't. Maybe I don't fancy making an arse of myself in front of the world.'

I knew what was coming, well before he said it; we have that kind of telepathy, my dad and I. 'It's never bothered you before.'

'Ah, but this is bigger. And there's more than just me involved. If I blow this I'm blowing a few million for Miles.'

'He didn't have to cast you in the first place,' he pointed out. 'But he's got the same faith in you that everyone else has; more so, since he's prepared to put his dough behind it.'

He shook his head. 'Naw, son. You'll be fine. Deep down you know, it too. You sure there's nothing else?'

I pondered again. The body! Christ, of course; I hadn't told him about finding our friend in the swimming pool. Nor, I decided very quickly, did I intend to, and I would go out of my way to make sure that he didn't find out from anyone else. What a bloody meal he'd make of that! Several meals in fact, for he'd be dining out on the story for ever back home.

'No. I'm sure. Just as I'm sure you're right; I will be all right once the cameras start rolling. I really do like it, Dad. I'm not talking about the glamour side, either. I'm used to that from the telly work I've done, from being on the periphery of big Everett's rassling circus. No, I like acting; I enjoy the challenge of it, the lights and all the rest.

'When Miles put me in *Snatch*, I thought he was daft at first, but the

61

more I got into it, the more it began to take me over.'

I looked at him, as more truth came to me. 'You know what, Dad? I've tried for years to live in the normal world. Now I see that there's no such thing. It's all fucking mad, and the deeper you get into it, the further you go, the madder it gets.

'The wisest thing you've ever done was to stay at home, in the world you grew up in. Me? I started off just by moving to Edinburgh, no more than an hour from Fife, and look at me now. I've become wrapped up in a chain of events that got beyond my control long ago. The world is a lunatic's playground, and we're all his toys.'

'Rubbish. The world's your bloody oyster, son.'

'If that's so, I'm the pearl in it, waiting to be strung and hung round someone's neck. You know who had it right? That old lady you told me about; the one who saw St Andrews, and thought it was the Big Apple.'

My dad laughed, loudly enough for Jonny to frown at him over his shoulder. 'The Big Apple!' he exclaimed. 'The Big Raspberry, more like. And what does that make Enster? The Big Turnip! How about that? And L'Escala, what would you call this place?'

I was sucked into his game. 'It has to be the Big Anchovy, hasn't it?'

That was it for the serious discussion. We were through our second beers when the team came back with the shopping and when Prim announced that there would be no cooking done in the house that night.

My nephews are serious students of pizza and, as I mentioned, I'm not averse to it myself, so we took them to Pizza Pazza. It's on the beach in Riells, the newer end of L'Escala and it's a nice, recently built family restaurant. We'd only been there for half an hour when who came in with his nice, recently built family but Ramon Fortunato.

In Spain, the kids are barely out of the wrapper when they're taken out with their parents of a Saturday night; so it didn't surprise me to see a six-month-old loaded in the carrier which was strapped to the policeman's chest.

I waved them over and made the introductions; I didn't have any choice really. The ladies did the obligatory cooing over the baby, although it was obvious to me, if no one else, that Prim was a little more restrained in this than the other two. While they were doing that I took my first look at Veronique. She was very attractive; tall, slim, dark, well-groomed and, I told myself, unmistakably Spanish. She smiled at me, in a gentle way that told me a hell of a lot, not least that right at that moment she'd rather have been somewhere else than watching her old man's ex inspect her kid.

62

I caught the shrewd old dentist looking at her too; he wasn't just admiring her teeth.

It was as well that the Fortunatos' table was on the other side of the restaurant. I would have been happy simply to nod to them on the way out, had not the beer caught up with me. I was washing my hands in Pizza Pazza's palatial bog when who came in but the bold Ramon.

'Nice kid,' I said, as he went about his business.

'Thank you.' I was about to leave but he called me back.

'A moment, Oz. I wanted to ask you something.'

He sounded unprofessionally serious. I hoped we weren't about to go into any off-limit areas. 'The man you mentioned the other day; Sayeed the fisherman. Who told you about him going to prison?'

'An English guy in Bar JoJo. Or was it the lady herself? I can't remember, but they both seemed to know about it.'

'Yes,' said Fortunato. 'The story seems to be all over town. I can't find out where it began, but I do know this much . . . it is not true.'

'What do you mean?' I asked him, well hooked by this time.

'What I say. If Sayeed had gone to jail for smuggling I would not necessarily have known about it, since it would have been a Guardia Civil matter. But in the way of things, I would have heard something. So, I checked with them, and with the prison authorities; Sayeed Hassani . . . that's his full name . . . is not in prison, nor has he been in prison . . . Not in the last six years at any rate.'

'They got it wrong, then.'

'They did, but so did everybody else.'

'Eh?'

'I've checked around. I looked for his boat on the beach, where he pulls it up to save paying for a berth in the marina. It's there, but it's rotting. I went to his apartment; it's locked up, and the town taxes for the last year have not been paid. I asked the neighbours; none of them can remember seeing him this year.

'So I spoke to his brother, Abou. It was easy to find him, for he is in jail. He's doing three years in Barcelona for robbery. They were not close, but he was upset that Sayeed had not been to visit him for a long time. While I was talking to him, I leaned over and pulled a hair from his head. He thought I was crazy, that's all, or maybe that I was trying to frighten him. But I took that hair away and I used it as a comparison in a DNA test.

'And guess what, Oz?'

I guessed; and I got it right this time. 'The guy in the pool. It was Sayeed; not Capulet.'

He nodded. 'I thought you deserved to know that, since you were responsible for my finding out. There's more, too. The bullet that we found in the body is a heavy calibre, point four five. I discovered that at one time Capulet was a Swiss Army reservist, and as such, he was issued with a point four five Colt automatic.'

In spite of myself, I felt a bit of a shiver run down my back. 'So what are you going to do about it?'

'Find Capulet, if I can.' The policeman reached into his jacket, and took out a card, one of those that Pizza Pazza leaves lying on all of its tables for punters to take away and give to their friends.

'But first, there is something you could do for me.'

I looked at him and saw that he seemed to be blushing. 'If only to explain why we've been in here so long . . .' He held out the card. 'Could you give me your autograph?' He gave me a cringing smile. 'It's for my wife, you understand.'

13

Christmas Eve isn't quite the same in Catalunya as in Scotland; Spanish kids are given their presents on 6 January, the last day of the festive season, rather than on 25 December. There was no point in trying that on with my nephews, though, and especially with wee Colin. He had a focused look about him, and an air of suppressed excitement that seemed to be shooting off sparks.

Prim and I had put up the tree at the foot of the big stairway, and had decorated the rest of the house in traditional style, well before the team had arrived from Scotland, so there was nothing to be done in that department.

The ladies were working themselves into a controlled frenzy too, as they began the day-long preparations for a meal that would take two hours at most to demolish. As for my dad, he had bought Volume One of Chester Himes' Harlem Cycle at Edinburgh Airport and had settled himself in the gentle winter sunshine in one of our big deck chairs, not to be disturbed.

Since there was nothing for me to do, I decided to play the favourite uncle and take the boys off to see the Greco-Roman ruins of Empuries. The entrance to the great rambling site was less than a quarter of a mile from our front door, so I resisted the urge to take them for a hurl in the Lada, and instead we set out to walk there.

We hadn't got out of our street when an English voice called out to me. 'Hello there!' It came from inside Shirley's garden; I looked over the gate and saw her son. I had met John Gash before, in unhappy circumstances, and I had been unimpressed by a couple of things he had done, under the influence of his late and not very lamented uncle. But according to Shirl, he had got his act together and was doing a pretty fair job of running their family business, alongside his own ventures like the Russian spares job.

I was taken by surprise by his shout, since I had begun to think once more about Fortunato's bombshell the night before. Naturally, I hadn't mentioned it when we got back to the table; I still didn't want the family to know anything about the episode, and I didn't think that the new development would make Prim's evening either. Somehow, I had been more comfortable with the concept of Capulet being the bag of bones in the *piscina*. I mean, it was almost as if I knew him and, given his supposed line of work, his demise could have been classed almost as an industrial injury.

Call me illogical if you will, but the thought that it wasn't him . . . that it was a total stranger, if you like . . . made me feel a shade uncomfortable. For one thing, it meant that Capulet was probably still alive. For another, it raised the possibility that he had put the bloke there himself, before he disappeared. But would he really put the place up for sale with an accessory like that? I mean selling with furniture and fittings is one thing, but . . .

That was as far as I had got when Shirley's son and heir hailed me over her garden gate. 'It's Oz Blackstone, isn't it?' he boomed, cheerily as he strolled down the path to the high garden gate. The slope of the land wasn't quite as severe as ours, so he didn't see the lads until he had almost reached it. 'Oh, sorry. I didn't realise you had company.'

'Yes, these are my nephews, Jonathan and Colin. Jonny's the one who's partly turned into a human being; the other one's still just a wee boy.' Both of them shot me glares.

'You've put on a bit of weight, haven't you?' Mr Gash commented.

I might have been offended by such a personal remark, had it not been true. I'll never be Lennox Lewis, but since I started working out regularly with my wrestler chums, and built up a daily exercise regime, I've put on eight or nine kilos and turned some gathering fat into muscle in the process.

I shrugged my beefed-up shoulders. 'I suppose I have,' I agreed. 'How's it going with you, John?' I asked him, then answered my own question. 'Pretty well, I hear; according to what your mother says.'

'It's okay,' he agreed. 'The business is on a pretty solid footing. I'm more into importing than my father was. I've moved the manufacturing side up to the top end of the sector. There'll always be a market for traditional English high-quality furniture, and not just at home either. So I buy the cheaper stuff from abroad, taking advantage of the strong pound, and I sell the expensive stuff at home, and abroad to people who are so rich they don't give a damn about currency rates.'

Gash junior smiled thinly. 'I couldn't interest you in an over-stuffed Chesterfield, could I? Upholstered in the softest leather you'll find anywhere in the world.'

I sucked in a deep breath through my teeth. 'Nah. I'm a Fifer, John.

I earn in dollars, but I'll buy in euros. Makes much more sense.'

'Ah,' he said, with a hearty public school chuckle. 'No more buying British; that's what you're saying? I thought I saw a spanking new Mercedes going into your drive this morning.'

'Where can you buy a British car these days?' I asked him.

'What about a Jag?'

'Don't be daft, that's American.'

'Okay, a Lotus, then.'

'Malaysian.'

'Gotcha! Morgan.'

'Not if you want one NOW. We'll settle for the Merc, thanks and for the Z3 in Britain.'

I glanced up at him; I'd forgotten that he was a lanky lad, slightly taller than me. 'Shirley said you were going into the car business yourself, in a way.'

He gave that forced laugh again. 'You mean my Lada sideline. Just a bit of fun, you understand. Makes a pound or two though. It's a crazy concept isn't it? A car that's worth nothing in running order, but a small fortune once you take it to bits.'

I had to agree with him. 'I don't understand it, myself. I've got one. I inherited it with the house, and I've been running around in it. Maybe I'm a Russian at heart, but I like it.'

'They're not all dogs,' John conceded. 'The four-by-four is quite a decent motor.'

'Yes, that's what the previous owner left behind.'

'Ah yes, the late Mr Capulet. Mother told me about the nasty surprise that was waiting for you in your swimming pool. She was a little upset, I think, although she did her best not to show it. As far as I gather, the chap was paying court to her.'

I paused, wondering whether to reveal Fortunato's surprise. Finally, I decided that Shirley had as good a right to know as I did. 'She can cheer up, then,' I said. 'It wasn't him.'

As John Gash's eyes widened, I felt a tug at my hand. 'Sorry,' I told him. 'Got to get these lads on the move. Tell Shirley I'll explain later.'

14

'Later', turned out to be as soon as we got back from the ruins. She must have been watching for me from her window, for I had hardly turned into the street before she was out in the drive, as her son had been earlier.

I saw her coming and told the boys to go on ahead of me. They had enjoyed the ruins as much as I had known they would. Ever since his lucky escape after a fall in St Andrews Castle a few months before, Colin had been much easier to control; less liable to go crashing off to explore on his own, more likely to go along quietly, listening to what he was told.

'What's this John's been telling me?' Shirley asked breathlessly, holding the gate open for me. 'Rey's not dead after all?'

I didn't step inside; instead, I leaned against one of the gateposts. 'I don't know about that,' I cautioned her. 'Those weren't his bits in the pool; that's all I can tell you.'

'But the police have no reason to believe he's dead?' She sounded too eager for my liking. Shirl is pretty controlled as a rule, good at masking her feelings. I guessed that she had been more keen on Capulet than she'd admitted earlier.

'No, they haven't,' I admitted. 'But no one's seen him for a year, remember. All of his property has been sold; not just Villa Bernabeu, but the other places as well. As far as L'Escala's concerned he might as well be dead; he's not coming back, Shirley.'

I felt rotten as the gleam of hope vanished from her eye, all the more so, since I had put it there in the first place. 'No,' she sighed. 'I suppose not.' Then, as if with a great effort she perked up. 'Still,' she went on, 'it's good to know that he didn't end up at the deep end of his own pool. Do the police know whose body it is, then?'

'Yeah,' I said. 'Remember the guy we were talking about in Jo's that night?'

'What? Sayeed the fisherman? The smuggler who went to prison?'

'That's the one; Sayeed Hassani. Only he didn't get the nick; he got the bullet instead. It was him.'

'So who put him there?'

'The police are still working on that. They do want to talk to your pal Capulet, though, if they can ever find him. It begins to explain his disappearance, though. Maybe he had a fall-out with Sayeed, killed him over it and had to disappear as a result. Or maybe he had planned to disappear anyway and Sayeed was a loose end he had to tie off before he left.'

'Maybe it wasn't Rey at all,' Shirley protested. 'I seem to remember that Sayeed had a brother; a right bad lot he was too. Maybe they fell out. Maybe he did it.'

I knew that he'd have found it difficult from his prison cell, but I decided to leave her that one straw to clutch. 'Maybe he did. I'm sure the police are talking to him about that even now. But I do know that they're a lot more interested in finding Reynard Capulet than they were a couple of days ago.'

'Well bugger him if they do,' she said, tersely, yanking herself finally back into the real world. 'I thought he fancied me, I really did. Stupid old woman that I am.'

'That you are not,' I shot back at her. 'Why would he invite you to go to Florida with him if he didn't mean it? Of course the bloke fancied you. Who wouldn't?'

'You don't.'

'Who says?'

'Get away with you,' she laughed. 'I'm old enough to be your mother.'

'In that case I'd better keep you and my dad well apart.'

'Don't you dare! I have to meet the bloke who spawned you.'

I took my cue. 'Come for a drink tonight then. Make it around six thirty: we've got a table booked in Meson del Conde at half eight. Come with us if you like.'

'Can't do that,' she said. 'John and his girlfriend are taking me to Graham's, in L'Escala, for a meal, but I'll see you for that drink.'

'Fine. Bring John and . . . What's her name?'

'Virginie. No gags, please.'

'I promise. See you then.'

Virginie turned out to be a tall, elegant Italian girl . . . but aren't they all? . . . who spoke good English, although not very often. I couldn't make up my mind whether she was shy in such a hearty group of Jocks abroad, or just naturally aloof.

Jonathan thought she was something else: he couldn't take his eyes off her. As I looked at him, it struck me that I had known someone very similar. About twenty years back, I used to look at him in the mirror every day. I made a mental note to stay as close as I could to my older nephew for the next few years. I've been incredibly lucky in my life otherwise I could have turned into a real waster. No way will I let that happen to him.

John Gash, on the other hand, couldn't take his eyes off my car. The Lada was sitting in the driveway, still fresh from a total valet job a couple of days before, when the Villa Balearic Three arrived.

'You have to sell it to me, Oz,' he pleaded as soon as he saw it. Then he took a look at the mileage on the clock. 'The parts must look practically new,' he mewled as we stepped into the house through the open French window from the terrace. 'Worth a dollar fortune in St Petersburg. Tell you what; you give me that and I'll buy you a brand new Ford Fiesta.'

I laughed at him until I realised that he was serious. 'No,' I told him.

'Okay, then. How about a new Fiat Punto?'

I laid a hand on his shoulder and looked him earnestly in the eye. 'John, forget it. I don't want a new Fiat Punto; I want a used Lada Niva . . . and I've got one.'

'Please.' He looked to Shirley. 'Mum, help; tell him to sell it to me.'

'Sod off,' she advised him, maternally. 'You'll be wanting to buy his wife next.'

'There's more chance of him selling me than that bloody car,' Prim muttered, as she handed Shirley a glass of Segura Viudas cava.

'Maybe,' I conceded, 'but not to be broken up for spares.'

15

The car stayed put in the driveway for quite a while. In some parts of Spain they may take a more relaxed view of drinking and driving than we do in Britain, but Prim and I don't.

Once Shirley, John and Virginie had gone, my dad volunteered to drive us all to Meson del Conde for dinner in his rented people-mover. On another night we might have taken torches and walked there and back, but Ellie didn't trust Colin not to get lost in the dark. Neither did I, for that matter; he hadn't calmed down quite that much since the dungeon business.

The wee chap was hyper, like most kids his age on Christmas Eve, all through the meal and all the way back home. Then, just as I thought we'd never get him to bed, he suddenly came over all drowsy. Five minutes later, from sitting in front of the fire peering up the chimney for Santa Claus, he was out like a light and being carted off to bed by his mother.

'That was quick,' I said to my dad, as Ellie climbed the stairs with her younger son in her arms.

He tapped the side of his nose with two fingers, gangster style. 'Let you into a dark secret, son,' he muttered. 'See that last Coke I let him have when we got home? I slipped a bit of dark rum into it . . . Not enough to make him ill, you understand, but enough to do the job. The Coke masks the taste; that's why it's so popular with young boozers. Aye, Santa could come in a fucking helicopter now and it wouldn't waken the wee fella.'

'Jesus, Dad,' I hissed back at him, careful not to be overheard by Mary and Prim, who were making last-minute adjustments to the Christmas tree lights, 'that was a bit extreme, wasn't it?'

Mac the Dentist gave me a beatific smile, the one he uses when he bends over you with the high-speed drill in his hand. 'Maybe so, but it worked with you often enough.'

I felt my mouth drop open, and snapped my teeth together hard. 'You what . . .? You mean you . . .?'

'Aye, often enough. And your sister before you.'

'And did Mum know?'

His eyebrows shot halfway up his forehead as he looked at me. 'You must be joking. Ellie'd better not know either, nor Mary, or it'll be the parson's nose for me when they carve the turkey tomorrow. You remember it though. You might find that it comes in handy at some time in the future.'

I filed away another entry in the book of wonders which my dad had written for me all through my life.

'You fancy one yourself?' I asked him.

'What?'

'Dark rum and Coke. If it works on Colin, it should work on us.'

'Away and work yourself,' he said cheerfully. 'I finished with that stuff a while back, as you well know.' He paused. 'However, it is more than time for you to be opening that very fine bottle of Lagavulin that I brought you, all the way from Edinburgh Airport.'

We settled on that as our nightcap; the ladies turned it down and had a bottle of the Widow Cliquot instead. 'You know,' my dad announced, expansively, as we sat staring at what I still thought of occasionally as the Frenchman's fireplace, 'in my experience there are no bests, when it comes to Christmases. More than any other it's a moveable feast. Time moves on, we move on. People grow away, people go away; for the best and the worst reasons there are symbolically empty chairs at the table. You can't draw comparisons, because of that very fact.

'But every so often, there comes a Christmas which is truly different. This is one of them, one that none of us will ever forget.' He looked at me, and then at Prim. 'Thanks, you two, for making it possible; for giving it to us.'

He was right: it was different. It was the first time in their lives, even counting living in France, that Jonny and Colin had opened their presents outside, in the sunshine. They both slept until nine o'clock; I guessed that my dad must have spiked Jonathan's drink as well.

It was the first time that the rest of us had warmed up for Christmas dinner by drinking Singapore Slings round the swimming pool. Also, it was the first time that I had ever hosted a Christmas dinner, anywhere, with anyone. There was someone watching over us, of course; Mary and I felt it more intensely than anyone else, but once, as my dad said grace before the meal, I caught Jonny looking at me. His thoughts were written in his old young eyes, and they touched my heart.

I used to think that the time spent preparing for Christmas is way out of proportion to the time it actually lasts. Not any more. That was a different day, a special day, for all that my Dad says. Okay, it ended like all others, with the kids . . . not just the kids . . . watching the big movie on BBC1, but it was still a belter. I knew it for sure when Colin clambered up on me, just before Ellen took him off to bed, and gave me a great big hug. That's his highest accolade, and it's better than any award with 'BE' on the end.

Later on, Prim clambered up on me too. 'Hi,' I murmured. I had a slight buzz on and so did she. Somewhere in the background I could hear a noise; a rhythmic sound.

'Hi,' she whispered in reply. 'I'm still here, you know.'

For some reason, that turned my head upside down for a couple of seconds. I had to wait for my mind to settle down. 'What d'you mean?' I asked at last. That sound was still in the background, but its beat seemed a little faster.

'I mean that the only words you've said to me today . . . to me alone, I mean . . . have been "Merry Christmas", and "Thanks" when you opened your present. Is anything wrong, Oz. Is there anything on your mind?'

I squinted as I looked up at her in the soft light of our bedside lamp. 'Yes,' I said.

Her frown line appeared, between her eyes. 'What?' she asked.

'I can't work out where that bloody noise is coming from.'

The frown vanished, replaced by a grin and then a giggle. 'You know what Spanish bricks are like,' she whispered. 'I'd say that right now your dad is having a better Christmas than you are.'

I slid beneath the duvet, beneath her, partly to drown out the sound of my father and stepmother's coupling, and partly to attend to other business. 'That'll never do,' I said out loud but knowing that my voice would be muffled. 'Not for one minute more.'

16

Next day, though, I thought about what Prim had asked me. Something had been eating at me, but I couldn't figure out what it was. It wasn't her. No, I was pretty sure that I wasn't still dwelling on her liaison with Ramon Fortunato, subconsciously or otherwise. I've become pretty good at compartmentalising my life. In other words, that was then and this is now. There was no way, I told myself, that I was going to blame her for something that happened in the past, and at a time when, honestly, it was none of my bloody business. Honestly.

Had I something to prove as a result, though? Inside, did I believe that I wouldn't really be square until I'd given her a kid too? No, I'm more mature than that, and anyway we had agreed before our wedding that we'd have a couple of years as a free and easy couple before we went down the baby route.

So what was it that had been preoccupying me through Christmas Day?

It didn't really take me long to hit on it. I could feel a presence around the place, and I thought I knew whose it was. I'm not talking about the ghost of Sayeed Hassani, or anything melodramatic like that; the only real ghosts are those of people you've known and loved. The dead Moroccan was no more than a passing day's inconvenience.

No, the guy who was getting to me was Reynard Capulet. There were lots of things about his disappearance that I couldn't figure out. And right at the top of the list, sat a big question. Had he gone for good? Sure, the fact that he had left a stiff in his swimming pool before his disappearance did not suggest that coming back would be a good idea, and yet . . .

The guy had been paying serious court to Shirley Gash. There is nothing of the airhead about that lady. She's no romantic and her feet are as solidly on the ground as any I know. Yet whatever had stirred between them had affected her, beyond any doubt; and since Shirley has probably never been taken in by anyone or anything since she found out that the Tooth Fairy was really her father, I had to believe that the attraction was mutual.

So, with a burgeoning relationship which was clearly heading for the physical, given invitations to Florida and such like, something really cataclysmic must have happened for him to have taken out Sayeed, dumped him in his empty pool and disappeared. He couldn't have intended to come back. He must have known that selling the house would have triggered off a manhunt, with him as the prey.

On the other hand, maybe he had believed that everyone would assume that the body was his. Had he come up with a very clever plan not just to fake his own death but to leave an unidentifiable body behind as a convincer?

After all, the place had been left untended for months before the company, the nominal owner, had instructed the amiable and gullible Sergi to sell the place as it was. By that time, the corpse would have been unidentifiable. And the company was Capulet and his sister . . . who had conveniently disappeared herself.

So what had happened? Had he hatched a plot that would take him away from under the watching eyes of Interpol for good and all, or had he simply killed Sayeed in a quarrel and been forced to leave town fast?

However I looked at it, I didn't like it. I had half a mind to put the villa back on the market as soon as the family went back home, but I knew that Prim would have her say about that.

To take my mind off the puzzle, I decided to take the boys for a run in the Lada. They had never seen the Dali Museum in Figueras. I had a sentimental attachment to the place, and although Colin was a wee bit young, I reckoned that there was enough there to appeal to him.

I almost bumped into Shirley when I swung the big boat out of the drive, as she drove homeward in her Renault. 'Just as well you can hear that thing coming,' she said, as we sat window to window. 'I knew to leave you a wide berth.

'You two have a good Christmas?' she asked the boys.

'Yes thanks,' Jonathan answered, leaning forward in the front passenger seat. 'Uncle Oz is taking us to see the Dali now.'

'Good for Uncle,' Shirley laughed.

'Got to be back for six though,' I told her. 'Guess what? Bloody turkey again . . . curried this time.'

'Better get on your way, then.' She gave us a quick wave and we were off.

I was right about the museum. Colin thought it was great, especially the car exhibit . . . the one which fills with water . . . and the Mae West

Room. I kept that back until the end of the tour. 'Who's Mae West, Uncle Oz?' Jonny asked me. His wee brother didn't care; he just liked looking through the funny glass thing.

'She was a famous movie star in the last century... for a good chunk of the last century actually.'

'Like you, Uncle Oz?' Colin shouted. 'A film star like you?' There was a queue to view the exhibit; the couple in front turned and gave me a curious, blank look. I thought they were English, till I heard him muttering to her in German.

I had to laugh. 'No, wee man; not like me in the slightest. Mae West was a very naughty lady. I'm a very well-behaved man.'

'That's not what Mum says,' my younger nephew shot back. 'She says you were as bad as me when you were my age.'

That's loyalty for you, I thought.

'Listen sunshine,' I told him. 'Every dodgy thing I ever did, I learned from her. You can tell her that too.

'Come on. It's time we were heading back to L'Escala.'

There's a handy car park less than two minutes from the Dali Museum, an ugly concrete thing, but it's hidden out of the way. I loaded them back into my Russian off-roader, and out into the narrow, twisty streets which led towards the outskirts of town. The Lada was beginning to pall on me. It handled okay, but its stiff suspension was pretty tough on the back. I had to drive fairly slowly, for I didn't want Colin bounced around by too many potholes, so we were ten minutes late when we made it back to L'Escala, and turned up into the woodland road which led back to Villa Bernabeu. Darkness was falling fast.

We had gone fifty yards along, very slowly, for the tarmac is badly buckled in places by big tree roots, when I heard a crack. 'What was that?' I asked.

Jonathan, sitting beside me, looked over his shoulder... for all the rough ride, Colin was out like a light in his seatbelt, dreaming of Mae West for all I knew. 'I think the side window's broken,' Jonathan said.

'Damn it,' I swore, as we approached the villa. 'Must have kicked up a stone. The road's bloody awful here.'

I turned into the driveway and closed the automatic gate behind me with a remote. Colin was wakened when I stepped out of the car; I could see the woozy look on his face as he stretched in his seat. I could see it clearly through a round hole in the passenger window; that, and something else too.

In the opposite window, there was an almost identical hole; round, with spidery cracks radiating outward from it.

'There's one here too,' Jonny called out, unnecessarily.

My heart was thumping as I unfastened Colin's seatbelt. Call me a panic-merchant if you like, but by now, I think I know a bullethole when I see one.

'What happened to the car?' Prim's voice came from the terrace, behind me, as I lifted the wee chap out.

'A stone chip, I guess.' I forced a laugh. 'It almost looks as if someone took a shot at us,' I told her, meaning her and the kids to take it as a joke, but I made the mistake of looking into her eyes as I did so.

I had to tell her the whole story after that, everything Fortunato had told me; that it was Sayeed, not the Frenchman in the pool, and that the bullet which had killed him had come from a gun similar to his.

'Jesus,' she whispered, looking out of our bedroom window as I finished, down at the moonlight reflected in the pool. 'So what happened tonight? What happened to the car? You really think that someone took a shot at it?'

'No,' I answered, truthfully. 'I think that, maybe, someone took a shot at me. I reckon someone's seen the car driving around and thought that Capulet was back in town. The windows are smoked glass remember, from any sort of distance it would be difficult to tell who was at the wheel. It could be that our friend didn't just leave a body behind. It could be that he left an enemy as well.'

I suppose I should have been shaking in my boots as I finished my story: yet I wasn't. Neither, from the look of her, was my wife . . . although she wasn't actually wearing boots, but soft leather moccasins. The fact is, since she and I met we've been in stickier situations than that; one thing we've learned from them is that there's nothing scary about the past. Once it's happened, it isn't dangerous any more.

'What are you going to do about it?' she asked. 'Tell Ramon?'

'Probably. I'll call him later. Before that, I'm going to see John Gash. He wants the Lada; he can have the Lada. The sooner that thing's in bits, the happier I'll be.'

17

I didn't keep any secrets from John. No, I told him what I thought had happened, and I said that if he still wanted the bloody car he could have it, on condition that once it was in his mother's garage, it did not go out again, other than in a large crate. I told him he could stuff the Fiat Punto, though; I settled for two and a half grand cash.

I also settled for a nice new Chrysler Voyager, a great big seven-seater with windows so dark that, in emergencies, the local priest could have used it as a confessional. It also had a black paint job. When I brought it back from the dealer in Girona three days after Christmas, my dad took one look at it and asked me, 'What's that? A fucking hearse? Why didn't you have "Funeral Director" painted along the side?'

Of course, none of the family knew the real reason why I had sent the Lada along the road. Not even Jonny's fertile mind had worked out the significance of the two simultaneous holes in the side windows. All I told them was that I had been self-indulgent for long enough and that if John Gash could make a buck out of the damn thing then good luck to him.

'You're not self-indulgent, you tell me,' my dad grunted, as he looked at the Voyager and the Mercedes parked side by side in the big garage. 'What do you call those then?'

'Tax deductible, Dad,' I answered. 'That's what I call them.' The best investment any upwardly mobile young man can make . . . at least after he suddenly and unexpectedly finds himself seriously rich . . . is in a top-class tax adviser.

I suppose I should have called Fortunato right away to tell him about the Lada business, but I didn't. When I called at his office in Girona next day, after I had ordered the Voyager, they told me that he was on leave for the rest of the week. I don't know why, but I didn't feel like asking Prim for his telephone number.

Anyway, after a couple of days, I had persuaded myself that my imagination was working overtime and that the 'gunshot' which had drilled the Lada's windows was far more likely to have been a local vandal with a very strong catapult and a bag of ball-bearings.

So, instead of triggering yet another police investigation . . . or having Fortunato simply laugh at me . . . I concentrated on preparing for the Hogmanay party which Prim and I had decided to hold. As the only Scots couple in L'Escala, we felt more or less obliged to fly the Saltire.

We had invited a number of friends from the British community in the town, plus a few other people we had got to know during our previous stay. I didn't expect Prim to have put the Fortunatos on the list, but when I saw their names there, I said nothing about it. I was surprised when they brought Alejandro, but I don't suppose I should have been; as I said, Spanish parents are much more relaxed about their infants than we Brits are about ours.

We overruled Mary when she tried to insist that she would do the catering. Instead, we hired local people, a middle-aged couple who ran a restaurant in the summer months and worked privately . . . and for cash . . . during the rest of the year. (It has occurred to me often that much of the personal taxation system in Spain operates on an optional basis.)

They set up a buffet for forty from ten p.m. onwards, plenty of seafood, cured ham, casseroles, and salads. We also asked them to provide the wines; a smart choice since they came up with a couple of really good regional vintages that were new to us.

One of the advantages about seeing in the New Year in Spain, or anywhere else in Europe for that matter, is that you can do it twice. As is the case with many other things British, our time is out of step with the continent.

When the witching hour came, we tuned in TV3, the Catalan channel, and watched the celebrations in the Plaça de Catalunya in Barcelona, complete with the countdown to 1 January. We drank our toasts, wished everyone a Happy New Year, kissed a lot . . . then tuned in to BBC1 via the digital satellite and an hour later did it all again.

At some point between the two midnights, I found myself face to face with Veronique . . . if she was a Brit I'd have called her Veronique Fortunato but, in Spain, wives retain their own surnames. Alejandro had fallen asleep and had been parked with Colin in the boys' bedroom, Jonny having been given a late pass until one a.m. local time.

'So what's your other name?' I asked her, idly, in Spanish . . . It's not the best opening line, but it was all I could come up with at the time. 'Sanchez,' she replied, in English. 'My Catalan name is Veronique Sanchez i Leclerc; formally we call ourselves after both our parents.'

I nodded; I knew that from my first time there. 'So the names over your front door are Ramon Fortunato and Veronique Sanchez?'

She smiled. When she did, her brown eyes seemed to take on a deep amber glow. 'Almost. Vero Sanchez is what everyone calls me.'

'Where does the Leclerc come from?'

'From Niort. My mother is French.'

'Ah, like the previous owner of this place. Did you know him?' As I said it, it occurred to me that I was doing something most Jocks hate. It happens all too often, though. You're in London or Paris or L'Escala or wherever and you're introduced to some English prat who says, 'Oh, you're Scottish are you? Do you know so-and-so? He's Scottish.' Dickhead, Blackstone.

'Sorry,' I said at once. 'That was silly. France is a big place, and this town's full of French people, even at this time of year.'

She made nothing of it, other than to give me a look, which I took as pity for my lack of social graces. 'That's true,' she answered, 'but also British, as I can see tonight, and Germans, and Dutch. There are people of many nationalities living here now. We are even beginning to see some who, ten years ago, would not have been allowed to leave their own country, even if they had the money.'

'Poles, East Germans? I suppose so.'

'Yes, but Russians as well. There are quite a few already up and down the Costa and every year brings more. This is something which worries Ramon; he says that anyone from Russia who can afford to buy a house here is probably a criminal.

'He is concerned about what may flow from that. He says that they can kill each other in Russia if they wish, but not here in Spain.'

'Come on, Vero. Not everyone in Russia's a crook.'

'No. The poor people are honest. But I was in Girona Airport one day and I saw tourists there who were going home to Riga, in Latvia. They were all under forty, the women were all beautiful and they all wore very expensive clothes. It was a big plane, too. I think my husband is right to be worried.'

At that moment, John Gash's voice carried across to me. I thought of his sideline business. *Maybe Shirley should worry too*, I thought to myself.

'You and Ramon seem very happy, for all that,' I ventured.

She looked up at me, a shrewd look in those dark eyes. 'Yes, I suppose we are,' she answered quietly. 'You know, I guess, that it was not always so.'

The door to the past was open. A simple, 'No', would probably have slammed it shut again; would have been sensible, too. But . . . say no more.

'Yes, I know. I'm happy that it's worked out for you.'

'And I for you. I know all about you, of course. Ramon told me about you and about why you went back to Scotland, when you lived here before. Then, a few weeks ago, I saw a magazine article about you, and your new career. It said what happened to your first wife. That must have been terrible.'

I nodded. How many times have I done that now? I don't think I'll ever be able to talk about it with strangers.

Vero filled the silence. 'Still, I am happy for you now, that you and Prim are back together.'

'I'll bet you are.' Mouth first; brain second. *God*, I gasped inwardly, *What if she doesn't know!*

But she did. She looked at me, and then, for all her dark complexion, she blushed. 'Ah, I am sorry. I didn't mean that at all.'

'No, I'm sorry; that was a stupid thing for me to say.'

She shot me a quick, awkward, grin. 'It is true, though. Your wife is a very attractive lady, and my husband is a typical Spanish man. I am very pleased to see her married.'

'That doesn't always guarantee anything.' No, I will never have a future in the diplomatic service; I'd forgotten the reason she and Fortunato were apart when he'd been shacked up with Prim.

She went an even deeper shade of red. 'Shall I cut my tongue out?' I asked her.

That quick, guilty smile showed again. 'We do seem to know everything about each other, don't we?' she murmured. 'And about our past lives.

'I'll tell you the truth, shall I? Ramon can do what he likes now, and it won't break my heart. I have my son. That's why I took him back.' She sipped her wine. I don't know if she realised that she was smiling.

'When I heard from an indiscreet friend in the clinic about Prim being pregnant . . .' It was her turn for consternation as she realised that maybe I didn't know.

'It's okay,' I assured her.

'I'm sorry that I mentioned it.'

'It really is okay. I didn't think anyone else knew, though.'

'Remember where you are; L'Escala.'

'True. Does Ramon . . .?' I began. At the time I wasn't sure why I asked her that.

'No. I'm sure he doesn't.' I breathed a little easier. 'When I heard about it, though, I was jealous of her for the first time. I admit it. That wasn't the only reason why I took Ramon back, but it was the main one. I agreed to patch things up and try again, then as soon as I could I had his child. Now? We're happy enough, as you said.

'Our separate affairs are well behind us now; there's no old temptation in my way.' She glanced across at Primavera who was standing near the television with my dad, arms linked. 'Nor, I am happy to see is there in his.'

Her eyes caught mine again. 'But what about you? Are you jealous of Ramon?'

'He's here tonight as my guest,' I pointed out. 'So no, I'm not.' As if to emphasise it, I gave her the party line. 'When it happened it was none of my business, and it still isn't.'

I hadn't been aware of moving, but now I realised that we had drifted into the further corner of the big room, away from any possible eavesdroppers. I realised also that talking to Vero Sanchez i Leclerc gave me a distinctly odd feeling. There was a degree of intimacy between us, the nature of which I'd never experienced before. We were in a room full of people, among them our spouses . . . shouldn't that plural be 'spice'? . . . and yet I felt furtive, as we stood there, quietly baring our souls to each other. To my surprise, I felt guilty too. I wondered about that, until a constriction within my jockey shorts told me exactly why.

Thank you, Alejandro, I almost said out loud as they baby's cry came from upstairs. There's nothing better than a howling baby for dismissing Mr Stiffy, especially if his mother caused him to creep up on you in the first place.

Ramon broke off from a group of Brits, leaving Frank Barnett in mid-joke. 'We should go home now,' his wife said as he approached.

'Yes,' Ramon agreed. Just at that moment, there was a commotion around the television. The gathering parted and I could see the floodlit shape of Edinburgh Castle. It was 'Happy New Year' time again.

18

However happy we all think we are on high days and holidays, there's no door that we can step through to leave reality on the other side. (Well, actually, there is, but they don't sell return tickets.) We were reminded of that eight and a half hours into the new year when the phone rang by the side of our bed.

'If that's my sister...' I heard Prim muttering drowsily as I floated back up to the surface. 'Bitch. We agreed that I would call her tonight.'

She picked up the phone, and answered with a slightly threatening 'Yes?'

About three seconds later her face changed. Her free hand went to her mouth in an instinctive gesture, and she frowned more deeply than I'd ever seen. She didn't say much, just four more 'yes's, each one quieter than the one before. Finally she nodded, and murmured, 'I'll call you back when I've done that.'

I stared at her, waiting, as she replaced the receiver. 'That was Miles,' she told me; her voice was steady, but I could tell she was having to work at keeping it that way. 'Mum's in hospital, in Los Angeles. She perforated a stomach ulcer last night. They've operated and that's no longer critical but, during surgery, they spotted some other lesions. They removed them and sent them for biopsy; the hospital's path lab is closed because of the holiday, so it'll be a couple of days before they can run tests.

'But it could be malignant. Oz, Mum could have cancer.

I was sitting up by this time; I took her hand and gave it a quick squeeze. I've seen Prim in a couple of crises, and in each one she was unbelievably strong. But this was different; this was her mother she was talking about. I drew her to me, feeling warm wet tears on my shoulder, feeling the tremors of her quiet sobbing. I knew what she was thinking. I've been there myself with my own mother, and there was no happy ending then, for sure.

It didn't last long, only a minute or so, then she was back in control.

She looked up at me, embarrassed as she dried her eyes with the back of her hand.

'What did the surgeon say?' I asked her.

'According to Miles, he said there was a chance that the growths will turn out to be benign, but he wasn't hopeful. That's exactly what I'd expect from an American surgeon. Say or do nothing that you might be sued over later.'

I blew out a big sigh as I thought about what had happened. 'Elanore Phillips, of all people,' I murmured. 'I can't believe it. She's always seemed unsinkable to me.'

Prim chuckled, throatily. 'Like a galleon in full sail, flying battle flags. That's how I've always seen her, at her best.'

'I didn't know she had an ulcer,' I said.

'Neither did she. But it doesn't come as any surprise to me; she isn't exactly a nouvelle cuisine chef.'

'So how's SuperDave?'

'Dad's okay. He's with her at the hospital. She's still in intensive care, but that's normal, post-op.'

'And Dawn?'

From the way she glanced at me; I knew the answer to that one. Prim's sister is a lovely, incredibly talented girl, but no film director, not even her husband, will ever cast her as a vampire slayer.

'Miles is worried about her . . . worried about the baby, really, I suppose, although he'd never say that. He asked me if I'll go over there to be with her.'

'Of course you will. I'm coming too.'

Prim shook her head. 'No, you're not. You can't run out on the boys and your dad.'

'But Dave might need some support as well,' I protested.

'Miles is his son-in-law too. He's there already. Anyway, my father's a lot tougher than he looks.'

She bounced out of bed and stood, looking down at me. 'So am I, for that matter. I can take care of Dawn and him, if necessary. Not that it will be; it's entirely possible that these growths are just simple polyps, and that all Mum will have to cope with is recovery from her surgery.'

'Yeah, sure, but what if . . .?'

She cut me off. 'In that unlikely event, they'll throw the full arsenal of anti-cancer weaponry at her. They'll scan her for metastases, then treat, or take preventive measures as appropriate. Even if she has got stomach cancer, the survival rates are better than in most other types.

'You really want to help me?' she asked.

'Of course.'

'Right. Get on the Internet, find the next flight from Barcelona **to** Los Angeles and book me on it.'

It's astonishing what you can do these days. By the time Prim came downstairs in her towelling robe, her hair still wet from the shower, I had booked her on a flight from Barcelona to Charles de Gaulle, then on to LAX, first class on the transcontinental leg.

'Well,' she demanded. 'Haven't you even logged on yet?'

'And off. You pick up your tickets from the Air France desk at Barcelona, then check in straightaway.' I glanced at my watch. 'Your flight leaves in just under seven hours. That gives you two hours to get ready, and me two hours to waken up so I can drive you there.'

'Where?' asked Jonathan from the staircase. He was bright-eyed; looking at him, I made a mental note to drink Pepsi at our next party.

I told him where we were going. 'Can I come?' he asked.

'No. You and Colin have to stay here and help your Granddad.'

'Help him do what?'

'I haven't a bloody clue, but from the last I saw of him, whatever he plans to do today, he's going to need help.'

19

Prim's sudden departure for California knocked me completely off balance for a while. The family was the main reason why I'd stayed behind in Spain, and yet with her gone, I felt odd with them around; not uncomfortable exactly, but ill at ease. I had run out of interesting things to do with two pre-teen nephews, my dad and I had played all the golf that Mary and Ellie would allow, and so I was quietly relieved as I stood at the end of the driveway on the fourth of January, waving them off as the hired people-mover turned out of Carrer Caterina, bound for their flight home.

By that time, the Elanore situation had resolved itself: not for the better, but at least we all knew what she faced. The bad news was that the lesions removed from her stomach by the LA surgeon were indeed cancerous. The better news was that a full body MRI scan, carried out as soon as she was cleared to leave intensive care, had revealed no secondary growths, or metastases as Prim had called them in medic-speak.

In a rare show of his power and influence, Miles had flown in one of the top oncologists from the Mayo Clinic to supervise the diagnostic procedures. She had pronounced that, with a precautionary course of chemotherapy, our mother-in-law stood an excellent chance . . . not of a cure, for a cancer specialist will rarely use that word . . . of long-term survival.

Prim's relief had flowed out of the telephone when we had spoken at seven that morning. 'Do you want me out there now?' I'd asked her.

'No; it's not necessary. Anyway, Miles says that he'd rather you used the peace and quiet to get on with mastering the script. I'm going to stay on here for a while, though, until the treatment is well under way, to help Dawn understand what's happening to Mum.'

'How's she handling it?'

'You know my sister; she was terrified at first. But she's not so bad now; once we had the diagnosis and prognosis she got a hold of herself.

Christ, Miles is worse than she is; it's his first child too, and the way he's acting you'd think he was going to have it himself.'

So that was it. I had my orders from the boss . . . from both my bosses in fact, Prim and Miles.

The trouble was, I am still a high-handicapper at the acting game and, like all high-handicappers, there's a limit to the amount of time I can usefully spend on the practice range without a pro around to take my game forward. However, we were talking big money, and a lot of responsibility, so I was responsible about it. From the day the script arrived, I had committed myself to starting work on it at nine thirty every morning. Apart from a day or two over the holiday period, I had managed it too; yet, invariably, I was wasted by midday.

It was the same on the day the family went home; only it wasn't.

There have been times in my life when being alone has been my natural state. A flatmate does not count as a companion, especially not when he's a green iguana named Wallace.

I'm not talking about being lonely; loneliness is something completely different. It's possible to be lonely in a room full of people you love. There have even been times, intimate times, when I've been with Prim and yet I've been swept by a feeling of loneliness. Mind you, it doesn't do to let it show.

This was different, though; it was the first time that Prim and I had been apart since the night before our wedding, when she had followed established bride protocol by sleeping at her parents' place, and I . . . Ah, now that is, most definitely, another story, and one which she'll never know.

It was different also in that I was on my own in Villa Bernabeu.

Until that point, the moment when my brain cried, 'Enough!' and I put my script away for the day, I had never felt the slightest unease about our new home. You may have thought that, at the time, I was a shade blasé about the stiff in the swimming pool, but my life leading up to that point had been so bizarre that when it happened, I dealt with it as just another occurrence. Since I met Primavera Phillips, I've seen a few dead people; my first wife among them. I've even seen one or two of them being killed, close up.

Since I met Prim . . . Only now she was gone and, as I stood on the terrace and peered into the pool, I felt a slight shiver and imagined for a second that I saw something on the bottom. I turned and looked up at the villa, and had the distinctly deranged impression that it was looking back at me.

I can say honestly that I don't remember ever having panicked in my life. I did faint once, but I had an excuse. No, I've had a few scrapes and a few scares, but I've never bottled out of anything. I came pretty close to it then, though, under the gaze of that bloody house.

Then I thought, *This is silly*, and pulled myself together. 'You can take that look off your face right now,' I barked up at it. And, I'll swear, it did. I guess that houses are not used to people speaking sharply to them.

I pressed home my advantage. 'I'll tell you what's going to happen to you, pal. Your fucking name's being changed for a start. Villa Bernabeu, indeed! I'm not even a bloody Real supporter. You're going to be Casa Nou Camp from now on.'

I knew, as I said it, that I meant it; my friend the iron forger was in for a visit as soon as his holiday was over. I knew also that if being afraid of a house is silly, giving one a loud-voiced bollocking in broad daylight crosses the frontier into the land where the happy whistlers live.

So I went indoors, made myself a coffee, and brought it back out to the terrace. As usual, the sun was shining, and the temperature was in the low teens Celsius, or fifties in old money, as my dad says, so I settled down on a lounger to drink it. As I sipped it, I closed my eyes, feeling the gentle warmth on my face, and, without willing it, began to think about Primavera.

I recalled every detail of the moment that I met her. How she looked as she walked into the hall of her flat, at the end of a two-day journey; tired but not weary, crumpled but not unkempt, without make-up but still beautiful, and with a light in her eye which told me, 'This woman is different. This is someone to whom things happen.'

Despite an unfortunate incident with a traffic warden, it was indeed lust at first sight, for both of us; I know that now. Before either of us knew it then, we were in over our heads, I more so than she.

Had it not been for the malign influence of S. T. Antichrist, and a couple of his agents, it might have been over almost as soon as it started. I might have been living with Jan and our two point four kids in a nice suburban house in Glasgow, doing my boring job and earning decent if unspectacular money.

If it had worked out that way, I'd have seen Prim as an interlude in my life, that's all, and I'd have ended up as the happiest man in the world. But there is no such creature; STA won't allow it. I'm in tune with the German philosopher who believes that some people are temporarily less unfortunate than others, that's all.

Primavera was there when my happy life went to rat-shit. When I tried to piece things together again, she was there for me too. I didn't see her as part of the Dark Plan but, as I lay there, I did begin to admit to myself that she had been the easy option, a crutch I had been all too keen to grab and lean on, one that I was leaning on still.

As I lay there thinking, I understood that her departure hadn't simply thrown me off balance. It had made me realise that I didn't know any more who Oz Blackstone was, or even whether he was, in his own right. Everything in my restored existence, the winning lottery ticket which had been based on her parents' birthdays, even this weird new career of mine, this acting game, had come from or through Prim.

Whatever they said after the event, I knew damn well that if Miles Grayson hadn't happened to be married to her actress sister, no way would he have cast a part-time wrestling announcer and voice-over artist in one of his projects. The fact that his publicity department has orders never to refer to our relationship is proof of that.

'Will the real Oz Blackstone please stand up,' I said, aloud once more.

'Will any Oz Blackstone please stand up,' a voice replied. I opened my eyes and sat bolt upright.

It was Susie Gantry.

I shook my head and squeezed my eyes shut, expecting that when I opened them again, she'd be gone. But she wasn't; she stood there, short, trim, tits like racing airships, shown to their best advantage in a red woollen sweater, thrusting out from her fur-lined black leather jacket as it hung open.

I felt disorientated for a moment. I swung off the lounger and pushed myself to my feet. 'Susie . . .' I heard myself mumbling.

'Surprise, surprise,' she chirped, in her slightly nasal Glaswegian accent, oblivious of my confusion. 'How's my favourite yuppie, then?' She swung her bag into a more secure position on her shoulder, stood on her tiptoes, and kissed me on the cheek.

'Astonished,' I answered her. 'What the hell . . .?'

Her expression changed, dramatically and suddenly; cheery, chesty Susie turned before my eyes into a wounded robin redbreast. A frown creased her eyes in a way I'd never seen before, and her pretty face fell. 'Oz, I'm sorry,' she exclaimed. 'Have I got it wrong? Yes, I have, haven't I? But when you and Prim put that note in your Christmas card, with your new address, and said you'd be pleased to see me early in the New Year, I thought I'd just turn up out of the blue, to surprise you, like.'

94

She chewed her lip for a second or two. 'Silly Susie, right enough.' Her chin trembled and I could see how fragile she was. I gathered her up in my arms, lifted her clear off her feet, and kissed her on the forehead.

'Silly Susie nothing!' I said firmly, setting her down gently. 'It's me that should be sorry. I was miles away there. Welcome to L'Escala. Sit down there and I'll make you a coffee.' She raised an eyebrow; I remembered that sign of old. 'Or I could get you a drink . . .'

'A beer would be nice, thanks.'

I decided that I needed one myself, so I uncapped two Sols from the fridge and carried them outside.

'Thanks again,' said my visitor. 'I'm fair parched.'

'How did you get here?'

'I flew to Barcelona yesterday, stayed overnight in a hotel and got the fast train to Girona this morning. Took a taxi from there. The driver had a hell of a job finding this address; eventually he dumped me at the big roundabout coming into town. I went into the fruit shop there and asked for directions.

'Lucky for me there was an English woman there . . . elderly, long dyed hair, dressed sort of gypsy style. She heard me mention your name and said she knew you. She gave me a lift. A right character, she was.'

'You're not wrong there,' I laughed. 'I'll take you to her bar some time.

'You got a suitcase?'

She jerked a thumb over her shoulder; I saw it sitting at the top of the driveway, a great big black thing on wheels, with a handle.

'So where's Prim?' Susie asked. 'Down the shops? Having a lie-in?'

I glanced at my watch. 'Probably still asleep,' I told her. 'She's in Los Angeles.'

She gave a small scream. 'Oh my God,' she exclaimed. 'I've really done it, stupid wee bitch that I am.'

'Don't be daft,' I told her quickly, in case she got emotional on me again. I explained the situation with Elanore, painting the rosiest medical picture that I could.

'Oh dear,' she sighed when I was finished. 'I'd better go, hadn't I? I'll check into a hotel and fly home as soon as I can.'

If it had been anyone else, I'd probably have left it at that, but not with Susie. She and I had been to the same place emotionally; she had lost a partner, and her scars were a lot fresher than mine. She didn't have all that many friends, and I didn't fancy the thought of letting her

95

go back to Glasgow on a downer, embarrassed and with her tail between her legs.

'No you bloody won't,' I told her. 'We invited you, and you're staying. For as long as you like . . . How long is that, by the way?'

'My return flight's booked for a week on Sunday.'

'Fine. Chances are, Prim will be back well before then.'

'If I stay here she'll be on the first plane,' Susie murmured.

'No she won't.'

She gave me a faint smile. 'But what will the neighbours say?'

I laughed. 'This is L'Escala, kid, and you've been in town for an hour. They're saying it already. Come on, I'll show you your bunk.'

I picked up her suitcase and carried it into the house, then upstairs to the main guest bedroom at the front. Before the family had left, Mary and Ellie had insisted on changing all the beds. I was glad now that I had let them. For all it was unexpected and unorthodox, I was glad of Susie's arrival too. There would be no brooding with her around. Mind you, I still had to break the news to Prim.

'I like the new pad,' she said, after I had given her the grand tour round the place. 'I wish I could find one like it in Glasgow.'

'So build yourself one.' Susie had taken over the running of her father's construction group; after a sticky start she was making a damn good job of it too.

She wrinkled her freckled nose. 'I could think of twenty good reasons why I don't; every one of them a degree Fahrenheit.'

I left her to unpack, then, when she was ready, took her to lunch at a place in the country, a nice traditional farmhouse restaurant called Mas Pou, where they don't get upset at all if you skip the main course and have a couple of starters instead. The house red there is very local, very new and fairly strong. Susie took a liking to it at once.

'Are you two ever coming back to Glasgow?' She dropped the question without warning, as soon as she had finished her omelette cake.

'Sure we are, Susie,' I told her. 'I don't know how much time we're going to spend there in future, but we're not going non-resident or anything drastic like that.'

'So you're not going into tax exile then?' She smiled as she said it. The red had relaxed her; the surface tension that she had displayed earlier seemed to have gone altogether.

'No way. I'd rather pay tax than become a nomad. We'll still be around. We might sell the flat, though.'

She looked at me in surprise. 'You serious?'

'I think so.'

'Give me first refusal, then.'

'If you want, but why?'

'Ach, I've got to get out of my place, Oz. It's just full of Mike.'

You find your own truth in bereavement. I don't know a hell of a lot about life, but I do know about death, and that there are things for which we can't plan, and through which we have to find our own way.

'Funny,' I told her. 'That's exactly why I chose to stay on in my apartment . . . because it seemed full of Jan.'

'And is it still?'

'No. It came to me eventually that it never really was. I'm full of Jan; that's the truth of it.'

'And how does Prim feel about that?'

'They get along.'

She looked at the empty carafe; I caught the waiter's eye and ordered another, only a half this time. 'That's nice for you,' she said. 'But Mike wasn't like Jan. I want to scrub him off me, to put every trace of him behind me.'

'Moving house might not be the answer,' I warned her.

'It'll do for starters. Let me know about the flat when you've made your mind up.'

I took her for a drive when we left the restaurant, taking advantage of what was left of the short winter day. We looked at Pals, and then at Estartit, which was slightly less winter-dead than usual. Finally we called in at Torroella del Montgri, where Susie bought herself a nice leather jacket . . . red, of course, to match the sweater . . . in a specialist shop I showed her.

It was dark when we got back to the former Villa Bernabeu; late enough in the day for me to phone Prim. I called her on her mobile, rather than on Miles and Dawn's home number, figuring, correctly as it turned out, that she might be at the hospital. She was at her mother's bedside, so I got to speak to Elanore.

'How are you feeling, Mother Phillips?' I asked her. I'd never called her that before, but it had a Victorian echo, which seemed to fit her.

'I've never been shot,' she answered, 'but I imagine that afterwards it feels a bit like this.' She sounded tired, but there was still a booming tone in her voice that made me feel good. 'They're going to give me some chemicals tomorrow. Once that's under way, there might be a chance that these fussy daughters of mine will clear off and get on with their lives.'

Prim came back on line. 'Family gone?' she asked.

'Yup.'

'So you're on your own.'

'Nope.' I told her about Susie arriving and merging with my half-dream. She was fine about it; I hadn't expected her to be otherwise, but still . . .

'I could move her into Crisaran, if you like,' I suggested.

'Don't be daft,' she retorted. 'You're not going to stick her out there all on her own. How long's she staying?'

'About ten days.'

'Right; all being well here, I'll fly home on Sunday. Dad's staying on for the duration, so he can keep an eye on Dawn, and let Miles concentrate on work. How's the script going, by the way?'

'Steadily.'

'Keep at it. Can I speak to Susie?'

'I think she's in the bath.'

'Okay,' Prim chuckled. 'Just don't be scrubbing her back!'

The thought had never crossed my mind, until my wife put it there.

We ate out again that night. I knew that Susie liked seafood, so we went to the fishermen's bar in the new marina complex, to pig out on prawns and monkfish. I would have moved the wine choice a bit upmarket, but Susie saw a bottle of Penedes rosada, nestling in an ice bucket two tables along, and asked if we could have some of that.

The table talk was easier than at lunchtime. Susie told me about her construction company, the Gantry Group, which was running well, it seemed, now that she had slimmed it down, and proved herself in the eyes of the business community and of her bankers. She tried to surprise me by telling me that she had given Joseph Donn a non-executive directorship. She failed though. Old Joe's her only living blood relative, her natural father, for Christ's sake, although his isn't the name on her birth certificate; for all the bust-ups they've had in the past, there's nobody she could trust more.

I have trouble keeping count of my own drinks, far less anyone else's, but it did occur to me that Susie's intake during the day had been pretty formidable. She was holding it better than I'd known, too. When we'd finished dinner, she reminded me of my promise to take her to Bar JoJo, and since I had left the car at home in favour of a taxi, I had no good reason for wriggling out of it.

As it turned out, we were the only customers . . . well, it was still short of midnight . . . apart from a couple of guys whom I could hear but not see, playing pool in the back room. Jo treated Susie like a long-lost niece, and even poured her some of the best brandy, unbidden.

'You heard any more about that upset you had?' she asked me as she handed me a beer.

'Not lately,' I answered. 'I'm trying to forget it.'

'Was it the Frenchman then?' I was surprised; I thought the jungle drums would have sent out the message.

'No, as it happens. It turns out that it was another of your customers, Sayeed.'

'What? The fisherman? Him as went to prison?'

'He didn't go to prison, Jo. He got a death sentence.'

Susie was intrigued. 'What's this?' she asked me.

'A bit of local difficulty, that's all. I'll tell you about it tomorrow.'

'No! Tell me now.'

'Tomorrow!'

By the time the taxi arrived to take us home, she had forgotten all about it. By that time it had got us there, she had probably forgotten her name into the bargain. One minute she was okay, the next she had crashed, right there on the back seat of the white car. I suppose I shouldn't have let her drink as much, but I've never been my sister's keeper, literally or figuratively. As a matter of fact, in my childhood it was the other way around.

I had to carry her, more or less, up the drive, into the house and up the stairs to her room. I sat her on the edge of the bed, knelt down and pulled off her ankle-length boots. She gave me a woozy smile, then a giggle. 'The rest you do yourself,' I said.

'Easy,' she mumbled, then slowly toppled backwards. I swung her legs up on to the bed and left her to it.

My alarm read forty minutes past midnight. I undressed, got into bed and picked up a book; my dad's Chester Himes. He had finished it and left it for me; half-cut though I was, the magic Technicolor prose got to me at once.

Next thing I knew, the alarm was showing seven minutes past three. The bedside light was still on, but the book was on the floor. I reached over and snapped the switch off, as I did so I thought I heard a faint sound.

In Spain, the night is full of noises; I dismissed it, until a few seconds later, I heard it again. It was a squeak, more than anything else.

Then it turned into a kind of shuffle; and next, a soft bump. I got out of bed, knocking over the table lamp with my elbow in the process. 'Shit!' I swore, and again, as I half-tripped pulling on my boxers, which I had left on the floor earlier.

I wasn't even halfway to the door when there was another sound, long and continuous this time, a bumping, tumbling noise. It ended in a thump, and a soft, short squeal, then there was silence.

I stepped out into the upper hall and switched on the light. There was nothing there, but the rug, which ran along to the left of the stairway, to the point where it opened on to a wide landing, was twisted and crumpled in places, as if someone had staggered their way along its length.

I strode to the top of the wide flight of steps and looked down. The ground floor was in darkness, but there was enough light spilling down from above for me to make out the form which lay motionless at the foot of the stairs.

I jumped on the right-hand banister and slid down; it was the fastest way I knew to get down there.

Susie was lying on her back, motionless, her eyes closed. Her red hair was damp with sweat, and was plastered across her forehead. She had managed to get out of her clothes, apart from her black push-up bra. I was relieved to see from the way her chest rose and fell that at least she was still breathing. I stared at her for a moment, trying to think what Prim would do in these circumstances, and, as I did, she moved. Her eyes flickered open; she looked up at me, trying to focus, but she was badly dazed and confused.

I decided that I had better give her some reassurance, before she could start to panic. 'It's all right, Susie,' I said, as calmly as I could. 'It's Oz. You're in my place in Spain, remember? You've had a bit of a fall, that's all.'

She let out a whimper, and began to cry, softly, small, sad sobs. I wondered if this was the real Susie Gantry, lying before me, lost and lonely in the dark, with her sparky exterior stripped away. I felt desperately sorry for her.

'Lie still for now,' I murmured. 'I know a bit of first aid. Relax, now; just let yourself go, and tell me whether anything hurts.' Her right leg was bent at the knee, awkwardly up under the other. I touched it, gently. 'How about there?' I asked.

'No,' she whimpered. 'That's okay.' I took her by the right ankle and straightened the leg, letting her lie more comfortably.

'My shoulder, right shoulder. That's sore.'

I felt my way from the joint along the collarbone, squeezing gently as I went. She didn't scream and everything seemed in one piece.

'I think that's okay,' I told her. I reached across and smoothed her hair back from her eyes. She winced as I touched her and I saw a vivid red mark on the right side of her forehead.

'Sore,' she whispered.

'I think you banged it.'

'Where am I?' she asked.

'At the foot of the stairs. It looks as if you fell down them.'

'No!' She looked more distressed than ever.

I pressed on with my injury check, trying to put her at her ease. 'I want you to take a deep breath.'

She did as she was told, without showing any fresh signs of discomfort. 'Okay, let it go.' She gave a great sighing sound. 'Good. If you had rib damage you'd have felt it there. Now, I want you to move your arms and legs one by one; lift them up and put them down again.' I nodded approval as she checked each limb. 'Now make a fist with each hand, then unclench it.'

By the time we had finished the fear had gone from her face. 'Oz,' she murmured, so softly that I had to bend over her to hear her, 'can I ask you something?'

'Sure.'

She smiled. Just a wee crack in her face, but a smile nonetheless. 'Have I got any clothes on?'

I tried to stay matter of fact about it. 'Not so's you'd notice,' I told her. 'It's probably just as well that you were too pissed to undo your bra . . . even though it spoils the view . . . otherwise you might have squashed your tits on the way downstairs.'

She started to laugh, then winced and put a hand to her forehead.

'Lie there,' I said, 'I'll get a sheet to put over you, then I'll carry you back up to bed. It's safe to move you now.'

'Don't bother with the sheet, just help me up.' She grabbed my arm and tried to haul herself into a sitting position, but struggled. I got my arms underneath her and lifted her clear of the floor.

She put her arms round my neck as I rose carefully to my feet. 'You're stronger than you look,' she said, with a degree of surprise which hurt my feelings.

I carried her upstairs back to her room. The door was ajar, and the light from the hall let me see the bed clearly enough; the duvet was turned back, almost neatly. I laid her down and pulled it up to cover her.

At once she rolled over, putting her back to me. 'Undo that for me,' she asked. She meant her bra. 'I don't think I can reach the catch with my sore shoulder.'

I flicked it undone quickly, expertly even. She slipped out of it, awkwardly, tossed it out of the bed, then turned towards me again, pulling up the duvet to cover her chest as she did.

'Thanks Oz,' she murmured. 'Can I have a drink?'

'I think you had enough last night.'

'Go on, just a wee one. I feel really shaky.'

I gave in. I went downstairs, poured her some Le Panto from the decanter and brought it to her. She looked at me gratefully and took a sip. I sat on the bed, beside her. 'What happened?' I asked her.

She frowned, then winced from the pain of the lump on her forehead. 'I don't know. I really don't.'

'What's the last thing you remember?' I asked.

She thought for a moment. 'I remember you pulling my boots off, then I remember looking up at you downstairs. There's nothing in between.'

'You don't remember getting up? I heard you in the hall.'

'I don't remember at all.' Then she began to cry, for real this time. 'Oz, I'm just so frightened. It's so bloody difficult.'

'What is, love?'

'Everything.' She finished the brandy in a swallow. 'Just everything.'

'But you get through it.'

'Do I? Do I really?'

I smoothed her hair again, and took the goblet from her. 'You get some sleep now, kid. You've had a shock, that's all; that and a bad fall. You'll have a few bruises in the morning, but a few hours' kip and you'll feel better.'

I stood up, but she grabbed my hand. 'Don't go, Oz. I'm really scared; I think I must have been sleepwalking. What if I do it again?'

I had to admit that there was some logic behind that fear. So I sat down again. 'I'm sorry,' she said, plaintively. 'I'm a wimp, I know, and it's a hell of a thing to ask, but stay here with me, eh?'

Call me daft if you will . . . and you will, I know . . . but there was something small and fragile in her expression that got to me. 'Okay,' I conceded, crossing my fingers in the hope that Prim would understand. I went out to the hall and switched off the light, then closed the door and slipped under the duvet, beside her.

'Thanks,' she whispered. I felt the warmth of her as I lay there awkwardly in the dark, practically hanging off the edge of the big bed to make sure I didn't touch her, listening to her as her breathing softened, and grew slower, in time with my own.

20

I hadn't intended to drop off, but I'd had a few drinks too. When I woke, it was daylight. The room was warm and one of us had thrown back the duvet during the night. Susie was still sound asleep: she was lying face down, with her bum half uncovered. Her right arm was thrown across me, and her hand was inside my boxers.

I gave some thought to this predicament. In fact I was still thinking about it when she stirred beside me, and her eyes flickered open, registering instant amazement as they met mine across the pillows. I watched her as she remembered where she was and what I was doing there. It only took a couple of seconds, but her expression was priceless while it lasted.

She had barely surfaced before Mr Bendy . . . it's always had a mind of its own, and absolutely no self-control . . . stirred and began The Change, under her hand. She realised where it was and drew it back quickly, then rolled on to her side and looked at me.

'We didn't, did we?' she asked.

'Naw. I think you must have been wandering in your sleep again, that's all.'

She shot me a mischievous look. 'Pity,' she drawled. 'That's another of your hidden assets.'

I propped myself up on an elbow and glanced down. The way she was lying, and the way that my boxers were arranged, I saw that there were absolutely no secrets left between Susie and me. I pulled the duvet up again, quick. Naturally, I considered getting up and out of there, but walking to the door would have been awkward, or embarrassing, or both.

'Just something that happens to us chaps in the morning,' I said, lightly.

'Wish it happened to us girls,' she shot back.

'You're feeling better, then?'

'I don't know what I'm feeling. Well I do, but that's not what you're asking, is it? About last night, I still have no idea. I know that I was drunk as a monkey, but I've never chucked myself down a flight of stairs while I've been under the influence.'

I began to wonder whether she still was under the influence, thanks to that medicinal brandy I'd given her after her fall.

'I do act funny when I have a drink, though. I get very randy for a start; the real me comes out.' Her voice was higher than normal. A corner of her mouth twitched, and she blinked, several times.

'I'm a selfish, manipulative, wee bitch, you know,' she exclaimed, sounding just a wee bit strident. 'At least that's what Mike told me once, and he should have known. He was all of that, the bastard, and in spades, wasn't he just?' Her mouth was set hard now, and her eyes were narrow; there were tears behind them.

'He was mine, though, Oz; he was my bastard. Wasn't he?'

'No, Susie,' I told her truthfully. 'He was his own; or he thought he had to be; that's why he did what he did. He saw a chance to have it all, and he took it.'

As she gazed at me, her face creased with a wicked smile. 'If it was good for him, then, it's good for me.'

Lightning fast, she threw an arm round my neck, closing the space between us, and kissed me. I was taken by surprise, and I was off balance, so I couldn't prevent myself from being rolled on to my back. She slid on top of me, way up on top, reaching down with her free hand. At first, I thought she was trying to rip off my boxers, but there was no need. They were no impediment at all.

I know that I could have picked her up and thrown her across the room, even as she thrust me inside her; no, I know that I *should* have done just that. But some things happen so suddenly and so unexpectedly that you don't react logically, or morally, or anything else . . . you just react.

In this case, I can only remember feeling myself getting bigger and harder, until I seemed to explode, at the very moment that she started to come on top of me, thrusting and gasping, drawing her orgasm from my life-juice as it pumped into her. Then, with a last, climactic shout, she collapsed, spent. It must have taken only seconds, that was all, the whole frantic act; yet the sudden violence of it left me stunned.

For a long time, afterwards, Susie couldn't look at me. She just lay there, astride me, as I slowly subsided, clutching me tight, with her face buried in my chest, baptising me with her pent-up tears, which had finally found release. I lay there, numb, looking up at the ceiling. I felt like an idiot, which I was. I also felt something I had never even imagined before. I felt like a victim.

106

There was no point in acting like one, though. She slid off me eventually, down on to the bed once more, her back to me this time. She was still shaking with her silent sobs. I heard her whisper something.

'What is it?' I asked her.

'I'm s-sorry,' she cried out. 'I told you I was a selfish, manipulative wee bitch, didn't I?' Whether she was or not . . . and Prim would have agreed with her, that's for sure . . . she wouldn't have been helped by me telling her that. I put my hand on her shoulder, the one she'd hurt in her fall, and rubbed it gently.

'Okay, okay,' I said, quietly. 'You've been through a terrible time, Susie love. You're not going to make me call you names.'

'Make love to me again, then,' I heard her mumble.

'No, I'm not going to do that either.' Instead, I put my hand between her shoulder-blades and eased her over until she was lying face down, turned away from me still. I could see that the muscles of her back and neck were bunched and tight, and so I began to massage them, slowly but firmly, drawing the tension from them. There was a bottle of her body lotion, unpacked the day before, I assumed, and lying by the side of the bed. I picked it up, squeezed some down her spine, and began to rub it gently into her shoulders, her back, her buttocks, her legs. As I worked, she began to moan softly, as if I was soothing more than her muscles.

Once I had worked my way down to her feet, I turned her over, with her arms spread wide. She didn't speak at all; she just lay there, eyes closed as I oiled her shins, her thighs, her belly, her big full breasts. All the time, she continued to make her sound of pleasure, and to move, very slightly, beneath my touch, matching its rhythm.

When I was finished, she opened her eyes, and looked up at me for the first time. She looked cleansed; that's the only way I can describe what I saw in her eyes. I leaned over and kissed her on the forehead, and she smiled.

Lazily, she stretched her arms above her head, then brought them down to rest on top of her thighs, her hands framing her diamond of bushy red hair. As I looked at her, I felt myself stirring again; and my lower brain began to engage itself. Then something caught my eye, something I had missed until that moment.

Susie's skin is porcelain white, like that of most natural redheads. On each arm, just above the bicep, I saw a wide purplish mark, round, almost like a bracelet. 'What are those?' I asked. I must have sounded sharp, for her smile vanished at once.

107

I sat back down on the edge of the bed, and lifted her right arm, gently. I leaned down to look at the mark, then drew her over on to her side so that I could have a better look at its twin. 'Sit up, Susie,' I said. She did, awkwardly, her back bent forward. I looked at the marks again. 'Now stand up for a minute.'

Again, she did as she was told, looking puzzled but without a word. I stood behind her and put my hands on top of the marks, fingers reaching round her arms; then I gripped them and lifted her up on her toes.

'Ouch,' she exclaimed, 'that's sore.'

Curiosity got the better of her at last. 'What are you doing?' she asked.

I relaxed my grip, lowering her, but kept my hands in place. 'In the last few days, has anyone touched you like this, lifted you up in this way?'

'No, of course not.'

'Aye, but somebody has, wee one. You've got bruising on your upper arms, nearly all the way round, just where I'm holding you. Someone, or something, has grabbed you hard enough to leave marks.'

'Could it have been you last night?'

'It wasn't. I picked you clean off the floor, remember.'

She looked over her shoulder and up at me, puzzled. 'What are you thinking?'

'I'm not certain yet.' I slapped her gently on the bum, in a way that would have to cease and desist from now on.

'You go and have a shower, and get yourself dressed. I'll do the same. I have to think about this.'

21

I thought long and hard about the whole business as I stood in the shower. Okay, she'd been hurt, she was dazed, she was frightened and, if she'd been sleepwalking, I'd been right to share her worry about her safety, but for God's sake, there's looking after, and then there's *looking after* . . .

I guessed that Susie had been giving serious thought to what had happened as well. Her face is oval, strong-featured, and cheerful, normally, but when she came into the kitchen it was almost tripping her. 'What do you fancy for breakfast?' I asked her.

She looked at me as if I'd offered her a choice between hanging and electrocution; maybe it was just the start of a hangover after all. 'Coffee,' she said slowly. 'Just a nice strong cup of coffee, that's all.' She was dressed in tight tan trousers, and the same red sweater she'd worn the day before, a hell of a long way from sackcloth and ashes. As for me, if I'd had a hair shirt I'd have put it on, rather than my Ralph Lauren polo.

The old-fashioned percolator was completing its simple steam-driven process, even as she spoke. I filled her a mug, handed it to her, and pointed to the fridge. 'Milk's in there,' I told her, as I poured my own.

We sat on either side of the breakfast bar, letting the heavy silence build up as each waited for the other to say something. I cracked first.

'Aye,' I muttered, 'the things you do for your friends, eh.'

She looked into her mug, as if she wasn't sure whether to laugh or to start crying again, so I let her off the hook. 'I'm sorry, Susie. I should never have put us in that situation. I should have known better, but when you asked me to stay with you, I thought, well us being pals and all, and you being scared, well I thought . . .'

Her eyes came up and held mine. 'I know,' she said, 'and when I wakened up and saw you there with your dong hanging out of your boxers, I just thought well, us being pals and all . . . Don't tell me you never shagged a pal before.'

She shook her head. 'Please, don't say any more, Oz. Stop apologising all the fucking time! Leave me with the illusion that you might have fancied me just a wee bit.'

'Hey,' I protested, 'don't get mad at me. How do you think I feel? My wife . . . whom I love dearly, by the way, and who told me not even to think of putting you in a hotel . . . is away, and what do I do? Probably the daftest of the many daft things I've ever done in my life. Yes, I was worried about you after what happened, but why didn't I sleep in a chair outside the door?'

'Good question.'

'Because it never occurred to me, okay? I thought . . .'

Her brown eyes flashed. 'You thought, what the hell, it's only wee Susie, she's no danger. Christ, but you are good for a girl's morale! Couldn't you even *pretend* you fancied me? I'm not shy about it. I wanted you . . . no, shit, I needed you . . . and I had you. Know what? I'd do it again too, only I wouldn't want you to lower your standards any more.'

Somewhere, my brain registered that Mike Dylan had been right about her; she was really good at being manipulative. 'Susie, don't give me that,' I shot back at her. 'Listen, if I was in the market for a shag, you'd be the first person I'd ask. It's not a matter of whether I fancy you or not, or whether I find you attractive. Of course, you're fucking attractive! You've got a body on you that would give a jellyfish a hard on.

'But allow me a bit of guilt here! Allow me a bit of self-recrimination. Prim'll be back on Monday and I've got to figure out a way of looking her in the eye.'

She reached across the bar and patted my hand. She was smiling again, but there was a hard edge to it. 'You'll manage, Oz my son. From what I remember, you've managed it before.'

'Jesus!' I gasped. 'That was below the belt.'

'It was true, though, wasn't it? You know something? Jack Gantry might not have been my natural father, but he raised me as if he was. Heredity isn't everything; upbringing counts for much more. The old Lord Provost used to say to me, "You know, kid, there's one thing that'll stand between a man and his conscience every time. But he'll never admit it."

'Maybe it's time you did. You like women, Oz. You could have married Jan when you were both twenty-one, but you put her on the shelf so you could screw your way through Edinburgh. I know; she told me. Not in so many words, but she told me. You haven't changed now, and you never will. Sure, you can wring your hands for the sake of it, you can have your guilt, and you can have your self-recrimination; but let's have some honesty here as well. You could fuck the daylights out of me for the rest of the weekend and still look Prim in the eye when you meet her at the airport.

'Oz, my dear, you are a serial shagger. You always have been and you always will be. Face the fact.'

I don't know why . . . no, that's a lie, I do know why . . . but when she said that, I closed my eyes and saw a face; not Jan's, not Primavera's, not hers, but the olive skin and dark eyes of Veronique Sanchez i Leclerc.

'I'll make it easy for you,' Susie went on. 'I'll be gone by Sunday. I honestly don't want to bust up your marriage, and I'm not as smooth as you. I know how perceptive Prim can be.'

She took a good swig of her coffee. 'Strong stuff this. I can feel my brain beginning to work again. So let's go back to what you were on about upstairs, just after you . . . on your own initiative, by the way, not mine . . . gave me that very enjoyable full body massage. What were you on about?'

'Yes, please,' I said. I was more than happy to change the subject. 'First off, tell me this. Do you have any history of sleepwalking? Do you often go to sleep in one place and waken up in another?'

'Never,' she replied firmly. 'I've crawled into bed often enough, like last night, but I've never ever crawled out of it.'

'Okay. Now, what do you remember about last night?'

'From when?'

'From the beginning.'

'I remember we had a couple of beers and went out in a taxi.'

'What did I do before we went out?'

She frowned. 'Went for a slash? I don't know.'

'No, immediately before we went out; at the front door.'

'Ahh. You set the alarm.'

'Right. Go on.'

'We went to that fisherman's place and had a meal, and a bottle of nice pink fizzy wine. Torres de Casta, it was.'

'Very good. Before we left, you went to the ladies. Were you okay there?'

She raised her eyebrows, and smirked at me. 'Everything was a perfectly normal colour, if that's what you mean.'

'No, you daft bitch. Did you slip, did the bevvy get to you, did you flake out?'

'No. I did what I had to do, then came back to join you.'

'Right, next.'

'We went to that wee bar, to see the nice old dear who gave me a lift. I went on to the brandy.'

'I went to the gents again while we were there. When I was away, did anything happen? Did you fall off your bar stool or anything?'

'Certainly not! While you were away the two guys who'd been playing pool came through, paid Jo for their drinks, and left. Then a German couple came in. Then you came back.'

'Then?'

She sighed and smiled, blushing slightly. 'That's it. I remember you coming back and sitting down beside me, and finishing another big horse of a brandy. Then it all got very vague, until I was looking up and seeing you and my bum was feeling cold on the floor. Thinking back, the first thing I thought was that I'd fainted and that, yes, I had fallen off my bar stool. I was puzzled though; 'cos I knew I'd been wearing knickers when we went out.'

I felt myself frowning as I looked at her. 'Think really carefully, Susie. Can you remember dreaming, even?'

She concentrated. I waited for almost a minute. 'You know,' she murmured, eventually. 'I think I can. It was a funny dream. You were in it. You were standing in a big dark room; you were holding my boots in your hands, of all things. I knew I had to get your attention; I tried to shout to you but I couldn't. I tried to run to you, but I couldn't. I could feel someone dragging me in the opposite direction and all the time you were getting further away.'

'How was he pulling you?'

She looked at me. 'By the arms,' she whispered. 'Oz, does that mean anything?'

I pushed myself off my chair and walked across to the back door, which was at the end of a small hallway. Susie followed me, without being asked.

I showed her a panel set in the wall. 'That's a second control panel for the alarm system. It's old technology, but it's sound. You can set it, or disable it, back and front. You can do it manually, or with a remote; once it's set, the whole ground floor is covered, and all the bedrooms that aren't programmed out. Just now, that means yours and mine. I always set it at night, Susie; always with the remote as I go upstairs. Just as I always lock all the doors, then and when I go out. The shutters are all secured by bolts on the inside, but even if they weren't, the windows have sensors. The only way to get into this house quietly when the alarm is set is by coming in through the back or front doors and switching it off.

'I realised this morning that when I came down to see to you last night, the alarm didn't go off. I checked it; it had been disabled. Then I checked all the doors, and the windows, just for luck.' I grabbed the handle of the back door, turned it and swung it open.

'It was like that,' I told her. I didn't have to draw her any more pictures. She stood there, looking up at me shocked.

I put my hands on her shoulders, to steady both of us, maybe. 'Susie, love,' I said. 'I don't want to frighten you, but . . . I don't think you were sleepwalking last night. I think someone broke in here, took you out of bed and chucked you down the stairs.'

I felt her start to shake; her chin quivered. 'Why would anyone want to do that?' she asked me, in a small voice.

'I don't know. I really don't.'

She looked up at me in a strange way; there was fear in there, but something more than that. Her shivering grew more violent, and I had the distinct impression that she wanted to say something, but couldn't find the words . . . or was afraid to find them.

I got it at last. 'No!' I shouted. 'No, Susie, I promise you it wasn't me. I'm the good guy here, honest.' I pulled her to me and hugged her, as if to emphasise my innocence.

She pressed her face into my chest. 'Sorry.' I felt her say it as much as I heard it. 'I know you didn't, or wouldn't, really. It's just that when I came round, I saw you and when you said that . . . I just had a terrible thought.' She laughed, nervously. 'Too many movies, I guess, and with you being in them now and all.'

She slid an arm around my neck, pulled herself up on her toes, and kissed me. Her lips were full and moist, and she seemed to taste of honey; her tongue flicked mine. I should have pulled back, but instead I felt myself draw her to me. I tried in vain to think of mistletoe. It was still Christmas, after all. 'Susie,' I murmured, as our mouths managed to unweld themselves.

'Funny, innit?' she said, in a voice that matched her taste. 'We've had sex, but that's the first time we've ever kissed.'

'And the last, eh?' I tried my best to smile.

'We'll see,' she answered, teasing, as she took her arms from my neck and linked them round my waist. And then she was serious. 'I'm sorry I got scared then, Oz. Christ,' she exclaimed suddenly, 'I'm entitled to be, though.

'In a way I'd rather it *was* you that was the homicidal maniac! At least I know you. The thought that there's a complete stranger out there who's got it in for me . . . that does give me the willies.'

113

I eased myself out of her grasp and guided her back to the kitchen, then I poured the last of the coffee and steered her though to the living room. She sat beside me on the big soft sofa, big hair, big chest, legs pulled up under her. 'What's been happening in Glasgow since I've been away?' I asked her. 'Have you been making any enemies?'

She shook her head at once. 'No. Since Mike . . .' She hesitated for a second. 'I've just been running my business; that's all. I haven't had any social life, and I certainly haven't been screwing any other husbands. There are no wronged women after me, if that's what you mean.'

'It wasn't, but anyway, let's assume that it was a man who got in here. Whoever left those marks on you has hands at least as big as mine. Tell me; what sort of deals have you been doing lately?'

'Deals? I'm a builder, not a corporate lawyer.'

'Semantics. What projects have you got on the go?'

Susie threw her head back, gazing upwards. Her thick red hair fell back; she had small ears, I noticed for the first time, surprisingly delicate features for such a robust girl. The skin on her neck, above her sweater was fine as well, soft, milk-white and absolutely unlined.

Her eyes locked back on to mine, making me start, in spite of myself. 'Since I closed the Healthcare division,' she began, 'the Gantry Group's a lot easier to run. I can keep track of it all, no problem. Our financial control's a lot better, thanks to Jan's work. The books all balance; nobody's been into the till and put themselves in danger of exposure.

'Let's start with the housing division. Remember that big conversion project with the old church in the middle of Glasgow? That's finally under way; the councillors fell into line. I've got private housing estates at various stages of development in Milngavie, Whitecraigs, Houston, Bothwell, Troon, and Lanark, and a land bank to follow all that. I'm also doing a big refurbishment project for a housing association in Barlanark, funded by Scottish Homes and a couple of banks.

'Then there's the construction division. I'm working on a retail park development on the south side of Glasgow, on a small factory estate in Mossend, and on a specialist hospital . . . geriatric . . . in Stirling. I'm building a new section of dual carriageway on the A1 in East Lothian, and a lump of trunk road in South Ayrshire. Plus I've also just tendered successfully for a project to build a private industrial park in Cumnock.'

'Do you think you might have any aggrieved rivals?' I asked her.

'No. I know my only competitor in that bid. He wasn't trying too hard; he'd have been overstretched if he'd won it. He was really only in it to help me. I'll scratch his back some time to make up for it.

'Finally,' said Susie, 'there's what I called managed investments. I had intended getting out of that sector. In fact I've sold off all the group's industrial estate holdings, all our tenanted factories, to one of the big pension funds. But one of my private banking consultants came to me last May looking for funding for a major golf course, country club and housing development, promising me big returns on my capital, and fast, too; like double it in two years.

'It looked good, but there were a couple of big downsides to it, so my natural reaction was to say no, and I did, at first. But my adviser told me who the other investors were; serious people with good records, all of them. So I decided to go with their judgement and put a chunk of money into it.'

'How big a chunk?'

'A lot less than I got for the estates; only a couple of million.'

I whistled; I knew from Jan's work with the Gantry Group, just how big it was on paper, but I hadn't really thought about it. I think of myself, and Prim as being fairly seriously rich, one way and another, but I realised that we weren't in the same league as the redhead on my couch.

'What were the downsides to the investment?'

'One was that I didn't know the guys who were running the project, but my consultant checked them out and said that they were okay. They're a couple of entrepreneurs from Manchester, apparently, called Jeffrey Chandler and William Hickok. The other drawback was that the project isn't in Britain.'

'Where is it?'

'It's in Spain; not all that far from here, in fact. Near a place called Oyastraight, or something like that.'

'You mean Ullastret.'

'What?'

'That's how you pronounce it. Remember yesterday, and where we had lunch? It's not that far away.'

'Whatever. To tell you the gospel truth, Oz, that's one reason why I decided to come to see you and Prim; so that I could go and see the place and check it out.'

'Why? Isn't it kosher?'

'No, as far as I know it's fine, but it's taking longer to get off the ground than I'd hoped. They were supposed to break ground last September, and they reported that they did, but apparently the excavators turned up some archaeological treasure or other, and the government put a hold on work.'

This sounded like a familiar story; I'd been in Spain long enough to have heard others like it. What I had never heard of was a golf course development in Ullastret . . . most other places, but not there . . . but then I had been away from the Costa Brava for a while.

'How much of the project are you in for?'

'One third.'

'And where's the money?'

'We had to lodge it in Spain. It's being held by something called the Banco Provincial, in Barcelona.'

'Who knew you were coming over here, Susie?' I asked her.

She gave another pondering frown. 'Let's see. Joe knows, Ann Hay, my deputy chief executive, she knows, and I told Brian Murphy. He's the consultant who brought me the deal in the first place.'

'How well do you know Murphy?'

'Well enough. He's never lost me any money and he's given me some good introductions.'

'What did you tell Ann Hay and Murphy, exactly? Where did you say you were going?'

'I gave them your address, and I told Brian to make arrangements for me to visit the development next week sometime. I was planning to get you to take me.'

She broke off. 'Oz, I don't like where this is heading. Are you thinking . . .?'

'. . . that what happened last night was linked to this project? It's the only local connection I can come up with.'

'But if someone was trying to get me, why would they do it like that. Why not just throttle me as I slept, or something like that?'

I shrugged my shoulders. 'I don't know. But I'm sure that if this is linked to your project, the guys wouldn't want it coming back to them. I'd guess that maybe the idea was to kill you by chucking you down the stairs, so that either it would be written off as an accident or I would carry the can.' I gave her a quick reassuring smile. 'Too bad for them you turned out to be bouncier than you look.

'I also think,' I continued, 'that I might have interrupted the guy before he could do you any more serious damage . . . if he meant to.'

Susie finished her second mug of coffee. 'I should bugger off out of your road, shouldn't I?' she said. 'Otherwise I'm putting you in danger.'

Maybe I should have taken my chance and gone along with that, but I couldn't. 'Bollocks to that,' I told her, firmly. 'If, and it's a big fanciful if, last night was linked to your trip out here, and if someone is out to stop you from looking into this development, you're safer with me now than anywhere else. They've tried. They've failed. They're not going to chance coming back here again for another shot.'

'But I can't just sit here,' she protested.

'No, you can't. There are a few things we're going to do. First and foremost, I'm going to put strong bolts on the inside of the front and back doors. They can pick all the locks they like, but they won't get past those silently.

'After that, I'm going to talk to a pal of mine,' I felt myself slipping into Action Man mode. I should have been even more worried by that, but I wasn't. 'Susie, this development must be run through some sort of company, set up and registered in Spain. Do you remember what it's called?'

'No . . .' she said slowly. 'I left my file back in the office, all I brought was a note of the location of the place. But Brian Murphy'll know. I'll ask him.'

'That's the last thing you'll do. Phone your secretary, and ask her to look at your file for the name of the company and the address of the bank.'

'We're closed till Monday.'

'Phone her at home. Get her into the office. You got a mobile?'

'Not here. It isn't enabled for Europe.'

I grabbed a pen and pad from the coffee table and wrote down my number. 'Give her that. Tell her to call us on it. Meantime, let's get going.' I jumped up from the couch.

'Where?'

'To the *bricolage* in L'Escala. We need to buy bolts, remember?'

22

Susie's secretary must live close to the office, because we had only just left the ironmonger on the Passeig Maritim in L'Escala when she called back on my mobile. I answered it as I climbed in behind the driver's seat of the Voyager, then handed it across.

'Yes, thanks, Clara. Hold on till I get a pen. Right. Spell it again. Yes, I've got that. And the bank? Spell that too. Got it. The weather, it's nice and sunny here, and quite warm for the time of year. Is it? Oh, too bad. Yes, see you soon; week after next.'

Susie handed me back the phone. 'She says it's pissing down in Glasgow right now.'

'I wish you were there. Don't you?'

She scowled at me. 'You mean rather than here making your life a misery?'

'Aye, put it that way if you like. But I really meant that you'd be safe in Glasgow.'

'Sure you did. Anyway, the answer's no. I told you, I'm a selfish, devious wee bitch.'

'Manipulative.'

'What?'

'You're a selfish, manipulative wee bitch, remember?'

'Maybe so, but I prefer devious. And it's still no. Apart from the falling down stairs bit, I like being here taking shameless advantage of you.'

'Susan, chuck it, please.'

'Making you uncomfortable, am I? Am I making you feel guilty because you don't feel guilty enough?'

I looked away from her; I'm uncomfortable when someone can see right to the heart of me.

'Come on. What have you got there?'

She looked at the diary in which she had scribbled her notes. 'The company is called Castelgolf SA. The Banco Provincial is in Plaça Catalunya in Barcelona.'

I started the car. 'Where are we going now?' she asked, glancing at the bag with the bolts and the new power drill, which lay on the back seat. 'Are you going to do your boy-joiner act?'

'Not yet. We're going home, yes, but I'm going to make a phone call, and then we're going to Barcelona. It's barely gone ten; we'll be there by one o'clock, easy.'

If I had thought to programme Ramon Fortunato's direct number into my mobile, we needn't have gone home at all. Since I hadn't, I had to look it up on the card that he'd given me, the one which I'd left lying in the kitchen. Happily, he was in his office. He even answered the phone himself.

'*Hola* Oz,' he said, cheerily. 'Good party the other night. Thanks again. What is it? I don't have anything new on Capulet, if that's what you were wondering.'

I had debated with myself whether to tell him about Susie's non-accident, but had decided to keep it to myself for a while, mainly because I wasn't sure I could trust him not to tell Prim about it. If anyone was going to do that, it had to be me.

'No, it's not that,' I answered. 'I need a favour. A friend of mine from Scotland has put a fair chunk of money into a leisure development here, and she's concerned about lack of progress. I wonder if you could check whether your people know anything about the company involved, or the people behind it.'

He sighed, heavily and wearily.

'What's up?'

'It's not the first time I am asked a question like this, Oz. I've been asked it in French, in German, in Italian, and yes, in English too. Gimme some names.'

I looked at Susie's note. 'The company is called Castelgolf SA. The two guys who own it are Jeffrey Chandler and William Hickok; there might be someone called Brian Murphy involved as well.'

Fortunato chortled at the other end of the line. 'Those are good ones, *amigo*. Like in the movies. Jeff Chandler and Wild Bill Hickok, yes? A couple of cowboys.'

Jesus! I almost said it out loud, but caught myself in time; I didn't want to alert Susie right then.

'In cases like this, if they are not straight, the names are never genuine. If those are real, I will bring out my old Guardia Civil hat and eat it. Where is this development supposed to be?'

'Ullastret.'

'You're joking with me again, yes? There's nothing near Ullastret.

Leave this with me; I'll get back to you.'

I sat there, on my kitchen bar stool, pondering. Eventually, I picked up the phone again and called a London number. 'This is Mark Kravitz,' the answerphone told me. 'Leave a message.'

'Mark,' I told it, 'this is Oz Blackstone. Can you call me back on . . .'

'Oz,' said Kravitz, bursting in on me, 'it's you. Sorry about the machine; I screen all my calls. What's up, mate?'

I kept my voice low; Susie was hovering around in the living room, waiting for me to finish. 'I've got a problem,' I told him. 'No details, but someone's trying to harm a friend of mine. I have a couple of aliases I need checked. All my Special Branch contacts are used up; I wondered if you had access.

'I'll pay you, of course. Usual rate, whatever that is, no matter how much time you have to spend on it.'

'Fair enough. Shouldn't take too long, hopefully. What are the names?'

I told him; Mark obviously isn't as big a film buff as Fortunato, because he didn't react. 'It's a property scam,' I added, 'out here in Spain.' I gave him my home and mobile numbers.

'I'll get back to you. I might have to grease someone. That okay?'

'If it's not actually illegal, sure.'

'Fine. I'll be in touch.'

As I was finishing the call, Susie appeared in the doorway. She had changed into a beautifully tailored, very expensive business suit; suddenly she looked very high-powered indeed. 'You about ready?' she asked, impatiently.

'Yeah. Let's take the Mercedes, eh. You look as if you're dressed for it.'

23

I always take the *autopista* when I go down to Barcelona. The drive along the Costa Brava is nice, but neither one of us was in tourist mode. We both had an interest in nailing the so-and-so who had broken into my house and attacked Susie, while the girl herself was brimming with suspicion that her golf investment might be a two-million-pound pig in a poke.

'You think I've been swindled, Oz, don't you?' she asked as we picked up our ticket at the Orriols motorway entry.

'I hope not. But I know Ullastret; I was there last week in fact. There are some old Iberian ruins there, complete with museum. I took my nephews to see them. Okay, I wasn't looking for a new leisure complex, but I don't remember seeing anything remotely like it, nor any billboards advertising it.

'On the other hand, it could just be well away from the road. The story about tripping over some relics during excavation is certainly plausible enough. You're walking on layer upon layer of history in this part of the world, and they're keen on preserving it.'

'Maybe I should have invested in a museum instead,' Susie snorted.

'That would probably have been a better bet; less risky, that's for sure.'

She reached across and thumped me lightly on the shoulder 'Go on, you; cheer me up.'

'That's what I'm here for. Tell me, have you met these guys, Chandler and Hickok?'

She frowned at me, so hard that I almost felt it. 'Of course I have. I'm not so stupid that I'd entrust that sort of money to someone I've never met.

'They gave a presentation of the project to the three investors before we signed up. Brian Murphy arranged it; he was there, together with various architects, brokers and financial advisers, and the guys themselves.'

'What were they like?'

'Impressive. Both about forty, one of them, Hickok, had quite a strong Manchester accent; the other one was smoother, bit of the public school about him. The presentation was very professional; they ran through their CVs, then the architect ran through the project, explained how it would be phased and how it would be sold. It made sense to me as a builder. They needed a lot of money up front, they said, because the Spanish insist on developers building the golf course first, then the housing which will have paid for it ultimately.'

'Did they tell you how you were going to get your money out?'

'The plan was that when the course was built and the first housing was sold, they'd float the company on the Spanish Stock Exchange, with a market value of not less than fifteen million sterling. The backers would double their investment and the executive directors would split the other three million in shares, plus they'd continue to manage the business.'

'What's Murphy's take?'

'Ten per cent of the investors' profit: six hundred thousand.'

'What is he investing?'

'Nothing that I know of.'

'Good deal for Mr Murphy.'

There was nothing but silence from the passenger seat.

We drove on down the road in the whisper-quiet sports car, and soon hit the *peaje* north of Barcelona. As we drove on, having paid with a card at one of the auto-booths, Susie pointed to a huge walled building off to the left of the road. 'What's that?' she asked.

'That's a rest home for retired property developers.' She gave me a blank look. 'They call it Barcelona Prison.'

Most cities these days are nightmares for motorists, and normally Barcelona is well up among them. However it was still the holiday season, and so the traffic was well short of gridlock. One thing that the city does have in its favour is plenty of off-street parking, much of it below ground. I knew of a well-guarded subterranean multi-level garage on the edge of Plaça de Catalunya, and headed straight for it.

The sun had disappeared behind heavy clouds when we stepped out of the car park, and the temperature had fallen by several degrees. I had brought a heavy leather jacket, but Susie was cold, so we made a beeline for El Cort Ingles, where she bought a nice designer overcoat. While she was doing that, I asked a floor manager if he knew where we could find the Banco Provincial. He gave me precise directions. Without them, we'd probably never have found it before it closed, for it wasn't actually on the square itself, but in a small passageway which led off it.

124

Susie walked up to the door and pushed it. 'Damn!' she swore. 'They're shut.'

I shoved again and heard a buzz as a cashier inside released the lock. 'Security conscious,' I told her. 'Not unusual though.'

We stepped inside and I looked around. It looked like a pretty typical Spanish bank, not the kind you'd expect to be handling a significant corporate account. None of the staff wore uniforms; the women were smartly dressed in the same style as Susie, if less expensively, while most of the men wore slacks and sweaters. The counter was open, without security glass. I walked up to the first available teller and asked, in Spanish, if we could see the manager.

The girl, for she was no more, looked doubtful and replied in Catalan; I'm not much good at that but I worked out that she had said that he wasn't available without an appointment. '*No, en Castellano,*' I told her, trying to look business-like. '*El jefe, por favor.*'

She gave in and left her position; I watched her as she approached, a shade nervously, a man at the back of the staff area. He gave her a black look, but came towards us, unsmiling. '*Si señor, yo soy el jefe aqui. Que pasa?*'

I nodded towards Susie. '*Por mi amiga, hablar Ingles?*'

'A little,' he said. 'You wish to open an account with us?'

'No, thank you. But we do wish to enquire about an account here.'

As I've mentioned, no one shrugs better than a Catalan. They use the gesture so often and so well that it is almost a language of its own. The manager's was a classic; it said, *Piss off*.

He emphasised it. 'Sir, if it is not your account then I cannot tell you anything about it. It is not your business.'

'Listen,' Susie snapped at him. 'It's got a big chunk of my money in it, so that makes it my business.'

I put a hand on her shoulder to quiet her down. I could read the guy; there was a chance that he'd talk to me, but he'd never back down to a woman in front of his staff. 'Let me explain, señor,' I said. 'My friend is a substantial investor in a company which, we are told, maintains its account at this branch. She has become nervous about her money . . . it is a lot, as she says . . . and so wants to make sure that the account actually exists.'

I won't say that he softened, but at least he stopped to think about what I had told him. I watched him rub his chin for about thirty seconds until finally he shrugged again. This one said, *I'll go along with this guy for a while*.

'Come into my office.' He pointed to a door to the left of the counter, then turned and walked away. A few second later the door opened and we were shown into a dull, sparsely furnished private room, and offered seats on the punter side of his desk. A nameplate faced us; Josep Lluis Peyra i Nunes.

'Okay,' Sr Peyra said briskly, 'What is the name of this company?'

'Castelgolf SA,' Susie told him, then spelled it out for him.

Like everyone under the sun these days, me included, he had a computer on his desk. He clicked its mouse a couple of times, then played with the keyboard. As he was doing this, I watched his face, not his hands. I thought I saw a slight twitch of his right eyebrow.

Finally he swung his chair round, to look at Susie, not at me. 'No, señora,' he pronounced. 'That company does not have an account here.'

She went noticeably pale. 'How about the directors? Could it have been in their names; Chandler and Hickok?'

'Señora, I cannot look through all my customer files . . .'

'Wait a minute,' I said, fairly heavily, forcing him to turn his attention back to me. 'Did that company ever have an account here?'

When he broke eye contact, he gave me my answer. He confirmed it with the tiniest shrug. This one said, *Okay, you got me.*

'Yes, it did. But it is closed now.'

'How much was in it, who were the signatories and when was the money moved out?'

He tried to look at me as if I had asked him something preposterous. 'Señor, I cannot tell you any of those things,' he laughed.

'Would you rather tell my other friend?' I asked. I produced Fortunato's business card from my pocket and handed it to him. 'Be sure that if you don't give us some answers, he will be here to ask you.'

The manager studied the card for a long time. 'Listen,' I said. 'I understand that you might be concerned about the effect on your bank of the publicity attached to an incident like this. But we are talking about a lot of money, and we are not just going to walk away. We are going to find out what we want to know. Please, let's do it the easy way.'

He gave one last shrug to himself as much as to us. This was his *What the hell!* model. Then he looked at the screen once more. 'The account was opened in June and closed in November. The opening balance was one billion, six hundred and fifty-six million pesetas, and it was almost the same when it was closed; it gathered twelve million pesetas in interest during the time it was open. There was one large payment made from it, of ten million pesetas, and a couple of smaller ones.

'The money was transferred electronically to a bank in Nassau, in the Bahamas. The authorised signatories on the account were the people you mentioned, Señor Chandler and Señor Hickok. There was also a third signatory, Señor Josep Toldo; he has an office where we send all the account details.'

'What's his address?'

'I cannot give you that; that I can only tell your policeman friend, if he ask. This man, Señor Toldo, he is a lawyer, and if you go to see him he may think that I sent you. He could make a lot of trouble for me.'

I understood that, so I didn't press it. I was well chuffed with what we had got out of him as it was, and tracing the lawyer wouldn't be hard. My elation lasted till we stepped back out into the narrow street and I saw the expression on Susie's face. It looked like a stone mask. She might not have blown the entire Gantry fortune, but being taken for two million is going to hurt anyone.

'Do you know what happened to me last month?' she asked me, tugging her new designer overcoat closed tight against the cold. 'A magazine in Edinburgh voted me Scottish Businesswoman of the Year. A fat bloody lot they knew, eh?

'Business failure of the year; that's more like it.'

I slipped my arm around her waist and headed her back towards El Cort Ingles. 'Come on, wee one,' I said, in what I hoped was my best 'cheer up' voice. 'There are other people involved in this too, and they were supposed to be pretty smart. Are you bankrupt? No you're not . . . Not by a long shot. Are your shareholders going to demand your resignation? You *are* your shareholders.

'The worst that's going to happen is that you've generated a capital loss to offset against a capital gain somewhere along the way.'

She snorted. 'Huh. You'll be singing "Always Look on the Bright Side of Life" next. I believed them, Oz. I really thought I was a business whiz kid. Now I know I'm anything but, and soon the whole world's going to know about it. D'you think the newspapers aren't going to find out about this?'

'Get your PR people to handle it. They'll get you a decent press.'

'Maybe, but everything I'm trying to forget will get raked up in the process; my Lord Provost, Mike, maybe even the fact that Joe's my real dad.'

'No way anyone's going to find that out. Jack Gantry's name's on your birth certificate, isn't it?'

She conceded that point as we stepped back into the hypermarket and took the lift up to the top floor cafeteria.

127

We found a table with a fine view across the city and ordered lunch, plus a bottle of Vina Sol. Susie had decided that the hair of the dog was a must. As we sat and sipped it, waiting for our food, she looked at me. 'What do you think, then? What do we do now?'

'First, you call Ann Hay or Joe. Tell them what we've found out and have them contact the other investors . . . they've got to be informed. Then we turn my friend Captain Fortunato loose on this man Toldo.'

'Captain Fortunato? Your friend?' She didn't even try to hide her surprise.

I didn't bite. 'Why shouldn't he be?'

She gave me a long look.

'You've heard of him, though?'

'Yes. Prim mentioned him to me once.'

'What did she tell you about him?'

She eyed me up, unsure about me, unsure of what I knew.

'Oh, you know; girl talk.'

'What? Like when I left her they had a fling, but it collapsed when she found that she was in the club? That sort of girl talk?'

'Mmm,' she murmured. 'She finally told you, then.'

'Finally,' I said. I didn't like the thought that Prim had told anyone, even Susie, before me.

'You don't mind, then?'

'It was none of my business then; it's none of my business now.'

She looked at me again, out of the corner of her eye. 'You don't mind, then?' she repeated.

'Of course I fucking mind!' It burst out of me in a shout that startled the woman at the next table, never mind making Susie jump; I lowered my voice. 'We come back here on our honeymoon, and one of the first people we meet is a guy whose kid she had aborted. This might be amiable old Oz you're talking to, but there's a limit.'

'So how come you say he's your friend?'

'First because I concentrate very hard on not thinking about it, and second because, apart from the fact that he had a wife at the time, there's nothing I can blame him for. I can't blame Prim for what happened either, only myself, but I don't like the way I found out about it.'

'Does that mean that you're going to tell Prim about what happened this morning?'

'It might.'

'Bullshit.'

I glowered at her.

'That's it,' she teased me. 'Show me those hairy eyebrows. You've just proved something I've suspected for a while. No wonder you're a hit in the movies.

'You're a natural, sunshine, a consummate actor. Amiable old Oz, as you called him, is a part you've chosen to play; the saintly youth that everyone loves and who can do no real wrong. But inside you're just as tough as the next guy, and probably a hell of a lot tougher. When it suits your book, you can be really brutal, but you get away with it because people look at you and think "Oh, but it's nice smiley Oz, so it must be all right."

'For as long as I've known you, I've been waiting for you to drop your guard, and now you've done it.'

I carried on looking at her, not smiling, not blinking. 'You're talking about someone I don't recognise,' I told her.

'If you could hear the coldness in your voice, you'd recognise him. "We all wear masks, kid." That's something else the Lord Provost said to me. "Most of us look in the mirror without knowing who we really are, deep inside." He did, though; he could see his inner man. His problem was that he didn't realise that, deep inside, that man was a monster.'

'And what about Susie Gantry?' I asked her. 'Who's she?'

'I'm like you,' she answered at once. 'On the outside, I'm light and cheerful and user-friendly; a lot of my business success is built on that, I'm sure. I'm everybody's flavour of the month. But behind it all, I'm hard and cunning and ruthless and, sometimes, not very scrupulous.

'I've only ever met one person who I reckon was the same however you looked at them, inside and out.'

'Who was that?'

'You have to ask? Jan, of course. She had no secrets from herself, or anyone else.'

I thought about that; she had none from me, of that I was sure. 'And Prim?' I asked her. 'What about her?'

'That, my dear, you have to find out for yourself.'

There was a bustling beside us, as the waiter arrived with our Catalan salads. I was grateful for the interruption. Susie hadn't made me angry, but she had made me feel very uncomfortable. I'm not a great Burns student, but I do remember the line about seeing ourselves as others see us. I had a feeling that what she was saying was all too true.

We didn't speak as we ate our starters, not until the waiter had taken away our plates. 'I'm sorry,' Susie began.

I held up a hand to stop her. 'No,' I said. 'I feel like you're taking me

129

on a journey of self-discovery here. I might as well carry on till the train gets to the station.'

My mobile rang as I spoke. It was Fortunato. 'Yes, Ramon,' I answered, to let Susie know who was calling.

'I have found out about your friend's company,' he told me. 'It is in the official register, okay. The holders of the shares are the people you mentioned, Hickok and Chandler; there is a third also, but he has only one share; a formality, you understand.'

'I understand. He's a lawyer and his name's Josep Toldo.'

'How do you know that?'

'We've been to the bank, and had a talk with the manager.'

'Ahh. Yes, Señor Toldo is the administrator of the company. He has an office in Girona; I have heard of him before, some good, mostly bad. If you are wanting to set up a business here, it is as well that you have some Spanish involvement. If you want someone who will not ask too many questions, you want someone like him.

'What did the manager tell you?'

'He said that the money's gone, and the account's closed. It was moved on more than a month ago. You should find out whether Toldo knew that it was being transferred. If he did, he could be in trouble.'

'Maybe. I would like that.'

'What else did you find out about the company?' I asked.

'There was very little to find. I had my people ask around in the town of Ullastret, and in La Bisbal. Toldo and the two Englishmen approached a farmer last year and offered him ten million pesetas, merely to explore the possibility of building a golf course on his land. He thought they were crazy, so he said okay.

'They brought designers along, and they brought another Englishman, a Mr Murphy, to meet him. Everything was very good, very enthusiastic, only they did not pay him the money. He had to ask Toldo for it, but eventually a transfer was made, last summer. That was the last he heard; there has been no digging, nothing; no visit from the people in the town council who approve these things, or from the Catalan government, which has a say also. This is not surprising, because no plans have ever been put forward.'

'I get it,' I said. 'They showed the investors the agreement with the farmer, and the model of the project. They set up an account in a small unsophisticated bank in Barcelona and lodged the invested capital, six million sterling. Then they moved it on, and spun a story about the project being delayed by an archaeological investigation, to keep the investors at bay for a while.'

130

'You are sure of all this?'

'Yes. Someone knew that Ms Gantry, my friend, was coming out to visit the development. Last night they tried to stop her.'

'How?'

'That doesn't matter right now. I'll give you the detail another time. But it does tell me that at least one of these guys is still around.'

'Then the sooner I pull Toldo in the better. I need your friend to make a formal complaint, Oz, but we can do that later.'

'Sure. I'll bring her to your office in Girona tomorrow.'

I looked across the table as I put the phone back in my pocket. 'There you are, kid. The wheels of justice are in motion.'

'That's good. Did you say I get to meet the nice policeman tomorrow? That's a dubious pleasure, after the way Prim described him when she told me about him.'

'What d'you mean?'

She fluttered her eyelashes at me. 'Well, dear, you know how we girls spill the beans to each other when we start . . . Or maybe you don't.

'I got the impression that she was pretty smitten by him; I know that she was really hurt when he left her to go back to his wife. He sounded to me like a bit of an arsehole all round. I mean, the least he could have done was stick around until after the termination.'

'You what?' I couldn't stop myself reacting.

'Ahh,' Susie exclaimed, with a hint of something I couldn't place, 'she didn't tell you that bit. I guess that's why the guy's still your friend. Apparently, when she told him she was pregnant, he insisted that she had an abortion; he more or less arranged it, in fact. And as soon as the appointment was made, he packed up and went back to his wife.'

The whole story must have been written on my face. 'She didn't tell you that much, did she?'

'No. She told me that he still doesn't know about the kid. She also told me that he was pretty mediocre under the duvet as well,' I added, bitterly.

'I don't know about that. She never told me otherwise, I promise you. And I can understand why she said what she did. She probably thought that if she'd told you the whole story you'd have filled him in.'

'Who, me?'

'Yes you!' she gave a short, explosive laugh, which startled the lady at the next table again. 'Mike told me once about the time you and your wrestler pal were attacked by a couple of hoodlums in London, and what happened to them.

131

'Knowing that, if I'd been in Prim's shoes, I'd have been worried about your reaction.'

'Who me?' I repeated.

'You really don't know yourself at all, do you?'

'I guess not.'

I shook my head, picked up the Vina Sol, and filled my glass to the top. 'Congratulations,' I mumbled, 'you've just earned yourself a shot at driving the Mercedes.'

'Oh dear,' said Susie, with no hint of remorse that I could pick up. 'I have spoiled your lunch, haven't I?' She lifted up my hand from the table, and kissed it, quickly. 'I didn't mean to, really.' I yanked it back from her and turned my head away, to stare out of the panoramic window of the cafeteria.

'Enough,' I snapped, then changed my mind. 'No, not quite. Is there anything else you know about Prim, or about me, for that matter?'

'I know she loves you. I know you think you love her.'

'Think?'

'You love you, Oz. Let's face it, you're a fucking egomaniac.'

I turned back towards her. 'And you're a fucking poison dwarf, you know that?' I think I was probably snarling. 'I should have let that guy bounce your head off the floor a couple more times before I came downstairs.'

She smiled at me, sweetly. 'Yeah. But I'm really getting you hard, am I not?'

She was right.

I left my Vina Sol on the table. All of a sudden I wanted to drive back myself. And so I did: fast.

If there's a speed record for the *autopista* A7, I must have broken it. There were times when I was fairly certain that the Merc's wheels were clear of the ground. I looked at Susie's knuckles as we swung into the exit lane at Sortida Five. Her fists were clenched tight, and they were bone white.

We hadn't spoken all the way from Barcelona, and we stayed silent for the rest of the journey home. As I drew the car to a halt in the driveway and pulled on the brake, Susie jumped out, and ran to the front door. I was perverse enough to go to the back, and unlock that.

She followed me into the kitchen, but I kept on walking, round and up the wide stairs. Still she followed me. I stopped at her bedroom door; it was open. I picked her up, carried her inside and threw her on to the bed. She tore at my clothes, I tore at hers; we broke the speed record for getting naked as well.

Foreplay was a type of golf as far as we were concerned. I covered her and we took each other as hard and as roughly as we could, but not quickly, pulling back just in time, slowing, stopping even, until we knew we were both ready. When we did let go, it was perfect; savage, screaming, exultant; I thought I would never stop as I came into her.

I did though, even if I'm still not sure when. Eventually, I was aware that we were eye to eye on the pillow. 'Tonight,' Susie whispered hoarsely. 'You're going to fuck me in that great big brass bed of yours.'

I didn't argue. I knew who I was now; I knew what I was.

After a while, I got up and went downstairs, naked, to fetch us a couple of beers. As I passed the telephone answering gadget, I noticed that its light was flashing. There were two messages. The first was from Shirley Gash, inviting me and my house guest to dinner that evening, eight thirty. The second was from Mark Kravitz.

'Oz, I turned something up. Call me back; I don't trust cell phones.'

I grabbed a pen and pad and called him from the kitchen, sitting up at the breakfast bar. 'Mark. Whatcha got?'

'Hey, you sound businesslike,' he said.

'No, I'm just cold. The weather's turned and I'm not exactly dressed for it.'

'Move to California then. Okay, I had a pal of mine . . . no names, obviously . . . feed your two punters into the Big Computer. Jeffrey Chandler is an alias of one Victor Fowler. He's also been known at various times as Ronald Colman and Leslie Howard. Seems to have a thing about mid-twentieth century movie actors.' He laughed. 'You never know; forty years from now there might be a conman calling himself Oz Blackstone.'

'What makes you think there isn't already? Go on.'

'Okay. Fowler's a long-term and successful fraudster. He's done one stretch for it, but that's all. Mind you, in his younger days, twenty-odd years ago, he served five for manslaughter. His speciality is corporate fraud; sets up dummy projects and takes silly rich people for lots of money.' He stopped; there was a silence. 'You all right?' he asked.

'Sure, sorry. Something distracted me for a moment.'

While he was speaking Susie had appeared in the kitchen, wearing a white tee-shirt . . . a very short one. Without a word, she had dropped to her knees, crawled under the breakfast bar and gone to work in her own special way. I tried to push her away, but she dug her nails into my thighs and hung in there. I've had guns pointed at me a couple of times, but I don't think I've ever felt more vulnerable than I did right then.

'Fowler's whereabouts are currently unknown,' Kravitz continued.

'He pulled a scam in his Leslie Howard persona a couple of years back, and took a very embarrassed oil sheikh for three million.'

'Ohhhh,' I said.

'Yeah, a big score,' said Mark. He thought I'd been impressed by the number.

'William Hickok, is also known as William Bonney . . . Billy the Kid to you . . . George Parker . . . Butch Cassidy to you . . . and Harry Longbaugh . . . the Sundance Kid to you. A cowboy fetishist, clearly. However his real name is Arthur Hardstaff . . .' For a second or two that name very nearly made me laugh. I thought I was going to have to call him back.

'He's not in the same league as Fowler, but he's worked with him a couple of times before. He won't again, though.' I sighed with relief as Susie came up for air, and a swig of beer. Again, Kravitz thought it was a comment. 'That's good news, is it? It isn't for Mrs Hardstaff, though.

'She found him in his garage last month. He'd topped himself with the car exhaust, or so the police assumed at first. When they did the postmortem, the pathologist determined that he'd been knocked unconscious by a severe blow to the back of the head, and left there to suffocate.

'No clue who did it, though.'

'Tell your pal . . .' Susie dropped to her knees again. I had to stifle a gasp. The beer had chilled her mouth; and the sudden shock sent a tingle right up my spine. 'Tell your pal,' I forced myself to continue, 'to put Fowler at the top of his list. Jeff Chandler just got away with a six-million-pound fraud in Spain. I guess he didn't fancy sharing it with Wild Bill.'

'Do you think he's out there, where you are?'

I came up with a very quick answer to that question. 'I think he was, up until last night, but things didn't quite go as he expected. I'd be very surprised if he's within a thousand miles of here now.'

'Wow. Can you give me details of that?'

'Tell your guy to get in touch with Captain Ramon Fortunato, of the Mossos d'Esquadra in Girona.'

'Thanks. That's us square for this one, mate.'

'Fair enough. What about the third name?'

'Murphy? There's scores of them, but not a Brian among them. He's clean as far as the criminal intelligence network is concerned.'

'That'll come . . . as a relief to a friend of mine.'

I replaced the phone, and took Susie by the hair, with the vague intention of pulling her to her feet. Then I thought, *What the hell, there are worse ways to spend a Friday*, and let her finish what she was doing.

I've always been amazed by the amount a good packer can get into a single, albeit large, suitcase. When she came downstairs at eight fifteen, my 'house guest', as Shirley had called her, was in another new outfit. This one was a cherry-coloured, silky-velvet dress, off one shoulder, its hem just below the knee. It clung to the contours of her body in a way that suggested that it was wearing her, rather than the other way around. The bump on her forehead had disappeared entirely, and she had covered the bruise which remained with some sort of foundation. Her lustrous hair was piled on top of her head, and she had picked dark eye make-up and crimson lip gloss to set it all off.

She had gone upstairs just after five to grab a couple of hours' sleep, and a bath. Now, restored, she looked sensational, and very, very dangerous . . . As indeed, she is. I wondered just what our hostess was going to make of her, although the newly self-aware Oz didn't care all that much.

I didn't feel tired at all. Far from going for a kip, like Susie, I had gone into the gym I had set up in a room in the outbuilding and lifted some weights, then done some serious exercising, following a programme which my friend Liam Matthews, the GWA World Wrestling Champion, had drawn up for me. I don't think I've ever worked harder than I did for that hour, that evening. It wasn't just self-punishment; the part in the new movie was fairly physical and I wanted to be at my best for it.

Afterwards, I showered. I was towelling myself off when the phone rang. I picked it up in the bedroom; it was Prim. 'Hi,' she said, breezily. 'How are things?'

'My thing's fine. How's yours?'

'Missing yours,' she laughed. 'You sound on top form.'

'Never been better, my darling. Have you sorted your return flight?'

'Yes. I can't get out of LA till Monday. All going well I get back on Tuesday morning, at ten past eleven. Can you pick me up then?'

'Of course.'

'How's Susie?' she asked.

'Resting,' I told her. 'I took her to Barcelona this morning.'

'Yes, but how is she now? I mean, is she showing signs of getting over Mike.'

'Hard to tell. She's a bit withdrawn, sort of quiet. I'm having trouble getting her to talk at all.'

'Don't force it, then. If she wants to unburden herself, she will, in her own time. Got to go now, I'm off to see Mum again. Love you. Bye.'

Now, as I looked at Susie, the thought of her unburdening herself made me smile.

'Mmm,' she said, 'you look pretty tasty.' I had changed into Burberry jeans, a crisp white shirt and a wool and cashmere blazer.

'You should know,' I muttered.

'Ha ha.' She took my arm and turned me, so that we could see ourselves in the full-length mirror, which our predecessor had placed beside the front door. It's a classic vanity thing; one last check to make sure that one looks perfect, and all that. We did, too. There was something about the guy who gazed back at me, something about his expression, that I didn't recognise. I couldn't put my finger on it; he just looked . . . cool.

Susie reached across to my breast pocket and pulled the white silk handkerchief so that it showed a little more. 'There,' she whispered. 'Now you look just like a movie star.'

'Hey, kid. I am a movie star.'

'I know. That's one reason why I decided to add you to my trophy cabinet.'

'When did you take this decision? This morning?'

She smiled at me, through the mirror. 'No, no,' she chuckled. 'A while before that; I don't know when exactly, but at some point a wee voice in my conniving wee head said, "I'm going to have his body".'

'I must admit, though, I thought it would have been harder than that.'

I gave her my best 'offended' look, and she laughed. 'Sorry. More difficult, I should have said.' She patted my chest. 'Like a rock, my darling, like a rock.'

We slipped on overcoats and walked the hundred metres to Shirley's house, along the dimly lit Carrer Caterina. I'm sure she twigged right away, as she opened the door and saw us there, but she's too good a hostess to have let anything show.

I introduced Susie, 'our best friend from Glasgow'. This was only half true, at best; she sure as hell wasn't Prim's friend any more, even if Prim didn't know it. As for me, I wasn't entirely sure of my new relationship with her, but I was fairly certain that it wasn't going to last long.

I was surprised to find that Shirley was alone. 'John gone home?' I asked her.

'Yes. I had hoped that he would have stayed till the weekend at least, but he and Virginie left this morning. Now I've got that bloody car you sold him taking up half my garage. He started to strip it, but decided that it was too big a job for him. Gawd knows how long he proposes to leave it there.'

'Does Virginie live with him?'

'Sometimes. She's fairly new on the scene, so I think they're still sorting themselves out in that respect.'

'Where does she live when she's not with him?'

'In a place called Divonne-les-Bains, so she told me; it's in France, somewhere.'

'How did they meet?'

'At a furniture show in Paris, according to John. The way he tells it, he saw her, fell in love with her, and just swept her off her feet.'

'Aww,' said Susie, 'isn't that romantic? I'm just waiting for someone to do that to me.'

Shirley ushered us into her living room, disappeared into the kitchen and came back with three gin-and-tonics on a tray. 'I don't know about you,' she exclaimed, 'but in the last couple of weeks, I've had so much cava, I've got bubbles coming out my ears. So I thought we'd have a real drink before dinner tonight.

'So how's Prim's mum?' she continued, briskly. I had bumped into her three days earlier and had told her about the emergency in California.

'She's coming along. She did have a malignant growth, but the surgeon's confident that he got it all. They're going to treat her to try to prevent any spread of the disease, and after that, we all live with our fingers crossed for a while.'

'Prim staying out there for long, is she?'

'She'll be back on Tuesday, I'm glad to say.'

'Me too,' Susie murmured, coyly. 'My idea of a surprise visit backfired on me, and no mistake. Oz has been great though. He's been showing me the sights; he took me to Pals yesterday, and to Barcelona this afternoon.'

'If you're stuck for something to do tomorrow, there's a Catalan Society cocktail party, at Frank and Geraldine's place. Three o'clock, a thousand pesetas per skull, and bring a raffle prize. JoJo's organising the drinks.' She looked at me. 'That's how I knew you had a house guest, by the way. She told Geraldine you were in last night . . . they came into the bar just after you'd left . . . and she called me this morning.

'The jungle drums beat fast in this place, as you know. She said that you'd been in with a redhead, and wondered who it was.' She smiled. 'I told her it was your sister. That seemed to satisfy her.'

'I'll put her right tomorrow if we go to this do. But wait a minute; you've met my sister. You know she isn't a redhead.'

'Yeah, but if I hadn't told her something, then the story of Oz and the mystery woman would have been all over L'Escala by now. And who knows? Some bugger might have phoned the British tabloids. There are people everywhere who might try to make a quid by selling a story like that.

'You're a celebrity now, my young friend; people are interested in you. You want to remember that.'

She had a point; I couldn't deny it. 'Thanks for telling Gerrie a convenient porky, then.'

'*De nada.* I knew there would be an innocent explanation, anyway.' She laughed. 'You and Prim have a hell of a history, but not even you could get off your mark that fast.'

'Should I be offended at that?'

'You wouldn't have the brass neck to be offended, not after what you did to that girl when you lived here before. Going off and leaving her like that. I've never told you this before, but I thought that was really cruel, Oz Blackstone.'

'Okay, but you don't know the whole story. It was mutual.'

'You might have told yourself that at the time, but don't go believing it now.'

I tried a Catalan shrug, but it didn't work. 'Maybe,' I said instead, 'but at least she didn't sit here pining for me.'

Shirley gave me an appraising look.

'It's all right,' I told her. 'There are no secrets between Prim and me. She's told me everything about that time.'

'Has she now?' our hostess chuckled. 'Good for her. I don't suppose there's a point to getting even with someone if they don't ever know about it.

'She really did too; especially with that Steve Miller bloke, so-and-so's son, the car salesman. She thought he was a creep, yet she went off to Madrid with him for a week. I asked her why; she told me to work it out for myself. It wasn't too difficult. You couldn't stand him, so that was why she did it.

'Then there was the Spanish guy, what's his name?'

'Fortunato?'

'No, before him. After Steve, after that young fellow from St Albans . . . only twenty-one, he was . . . and after that racing driver from Sussex. He was a waiter in one of the restaurants in the old town;

smarmy, oily chap, always chatting up the female customers.'

I knew him. But before I had a chance to dwell on him, Shirley went on. 'You might not think so, but Fortunato was good for her. She was really off the rails after you left, but the policeman straightened her out, even if he was messed up himself, with his wife having left him for our mutual friend.'

'What?' She had lost me now.

'Didn't you know that? Mind you, Prim might not have known his name then. She never met him; I know that. It was Reynard Capulet. The policeman's wife left him and went to Paris with Rey.'

I gave a light laugh. She didn't know it, nor I imagine did Susie, but all the way through Shirley's revelation I was honing my acting skills. 'She got the short straw then,' I said. 'He was going to take you to Florida, wasn't he?'

Another woman might have been hurt, but Shirley's tougher than that. 'Too right. Nothing but the best for me, and he knew it. Knows it, maybe. He could be living down the road, for all I know.'

I had a lot to think about over dinner . . . in my Mum's day, 'supper' was a cup of hot chocolate and a biscuit just before you went to bed . . . but I kept myself in conversational mode. I told Shirley about Susie's business back in Glasgow, and even mentioned casually that she'd been looking at something in our part of Spain.

'Does the name Jeffrey Chandler mean anything to you?' I asked her.

'Big grey-haired bloke,' she replied, 'in the movies like you; built like a brick outhouse, was always playing cowboys, or soldiers and sometimes Indians, because he was naturally dark-complexioned. Been dead for donkey's years.'

'This one isn't; he says he's a property developer, but he's really a con man and a thief. I wondered if he'd surfaced socially around here.'

'What does he look like?'

'He's early forties, six feet odd, dark-haired, well-spoken,' Susie told her. 'He's got a scar on his forehead. That's all I remember about him.'

'The streets are full of 'em, but I can't say that name's familiar. Ask Jo next time you see her; if he's been around here, she'll know. Did he do you wrong?'

'A couple of million wrong, and no, I'm not talking pesetas, or even euros; real money.'

'My God,' said Shirley, after a mouthful of soufflé. 'What are you going to do when you catch him?'

'Oz is going to have him killed,' she answered, with a grin. 'Aren't you, Oz? You know people who do that sort of thing.' It was a chilling thing for her to say, given recent history, but Shirl didn't know any of that, so she took it as a joke.

'Worse than that,' I retorted. 'I'm going to make him watch my new movie.'

We finished dinner, drank a couple of shots of chilled peach schnapps, then said 'thanks' and 'good night' to Shirley.

'See you at the do tomorrow?' she asked as we were leaving.

'Yeah,' I said. 'Why not? We'll give you a lift down in the new bus.'

Back at Casa Nou Camp, I checked the alarm settings and bolted the doors. When I came out of the kitchen, Susie was nowhere to be seen. I didn't have to search for her, though. I knew where she'd be. I didn't even think about telling her to go back to her own room. I was as horny as hell, and I wanted her. I undressed and slipped under the duvet. She was smiling at me again.

'You're a master of deviousness, all right,' she said. 'You're way beyond my league. The way you got all that stuff about Prim out of her, without her even knowing she was being questioned, or that any of it was news to you.'

'And was it news to you?'

'No, of course not. Prim told me the whole story a while back. I guessed she hadn't told you that much, though; if she didn't tell you the way it really was with the policeman, she was hardly going to confess to all the rest of it. What's this guy Miller like, really?'

I felt my teeth clench. 'A twerp. A real wee twerp. Shirl was right, I detest him.'

'Yeah,' Susie, whispered, laying the palm of her hand on my belly, and sliding it downwards. 'That's what she told me too. She said that every time she did it with him, all she could feel was her hatred for you. He was your penance; that's how she put it.'

What she was telling me was cutting into me like a knife. I didn't want to hear any more.

'Hey,' I said, rolling over and into her in a single smooth movement, drawing a great deep gasp from her. 'Enough about her. This one's for you, and no one else.'

24

Susie was demanding but I gave her everything she wanted, everything she asked for. We made love until we fell asleep. Then, in the morning we wakened, and we had some more.

I was lying face down, my left cheek buried in the pillow, looking at her out of my right eye alone, when she ran a nail gently down my spine. 'I'll promise you something, Oz,' she murmured. 'Even though you haven't asked me.

'After I go, that'll be it. I'm not going to hold anything over you, or threaten your marriage.'

'What if that isn't the way I want it?'

'Don't make me laugh.' She did, nevertheless. 'You're too smart for that,' she chuckled. 'You're not going to dump Dawn Grayson's sister, or your movie career will be over almost as soon as it's started. You'll work it out with Prim; at least you will for as long as it takes you to become established. And isn't this the man who told me twenty-four hours ago that he loved his wife dearly?'

'A lot of things can change in twenty-four hours. I feel like I don't know her any more.'

'So get to know her. Maybe you'll find that, inside, she's even better than the woman you thought you knew. Did you really think that she was just a little innocent who'd forsworn men for ever after you dumped her? Are you that naive? No, I don't believe that for a minute.'

'Yeah, but I chose to believe what she told me. If she'd told me the truth . . . Ah, I don't know. But come on. Answer my question. What if, just suppose, out of all this, I want you?'

'You can't have me. Simple as that. I'm going to be no one's second string. I'm going to run my business for a few more years, then either sell it or take it public and become incredibly rich in the process. Somewhere along the line I'll find a suitable husband, with a title, preferably, who'll give me a couple of nice kids then bugger off.

'I've just had one narrow escape; I nearly became Mrs Mike Dylan. No way would I get myself tied up with somebody as volatile . . . and as easy to seduce . . . as you.' She jumped out of bed and stood there, red hair tousled and tangled. 'I will do one thing for you. I'll make you breakfast. Fancy some freshly squeezed orange juice, scrambled eggs and coffee?' She took my robe from behind the door and put it on.

'Yeah, okay. You do that, I'll have a shower.' I tossed her the remote alarm control and told her to press the 'disable' button from the top of the stairs, so that she didn't set the thing off.

I was towelling myself down when I heard the front door bell ring. I had no idea who it could be. Shirley would have phoned, and I couldn't think of anyone who'd be calling on me at quarter to ten on a Saturday morning, apart from Fortunato, perhaps. Automatically I headed for my robe, then saw the empty hook on the door.

Faint sounds came from downstairs, the clop of wooden-soled sandals . . . Susie had borrowed Prim's . . . the squeak of a rusty hinge as the door opened. I strained to hear, but couldn't pick up any conversation. Then I heard footsteps trotting upstairs and drawing closer.

She appeared in the doorway and looked at me, frowning. 'Oz,' she said, severely, 'there's a prostitute at the door. Go and deal with her.'

'How do you know she's a prostitute?'

'I've lived in Glasgow for long enough to know what a prostitute looks like.'

'So can't you deal with her?'

'She doesn't seem to speak any English; nothing but Spanish. Now go on; see what she wants.'

I finished drying, and dressed quickly.

Susie had closed the front door on our caller, reasonably so, I suppose. If a mysterious prostitute presented herself at your premises, you'd hardly ask her in then go off and leave her alone, would you?

She was still there when I opened it again: a tiny girl, as bizarrely turned out for the first Saturday in January as anyone I've ever seen. Her oily black hair was piled up on top of her head and lacquered stiff, she had blusher on her cheeks and her eyelashes buckled under what must have been a whole thingy of mascara. She was wearing a yellow gypsy-styled top, trimmed with red and showing most of what little chest she had, a short, fluffed-out white skirt, white tights with gold spangles and red shoes with dangerously high heels.

It was a cold, grey morning, and a light skin of rain was falling. She stood there, a black umbrella clutched in her right hand, with goose pimples standing out on her damp shoulders. In her left hand she carried a small suitcase.

142

'*Si?*' I began.

'*Tu es el hombre?*'

'No,' I answered, in Spanish, more than a bit cagily. 'I am a man, not The Man. Step in out of the rain and tell me what it is you want.'

She did as she had been invited. 'I was told to come here,' she said.

This was something I had heard before. I took a closer look at the girl. She wasn't the same one who had called a few weeks earlier but, if I had to guess, she was of the same nationality. Beneath the pancake make-up she was brown-skinned, and her eyes said Oriental. Given that Spanish seemed to be her native language, I guessed that she was Filipina. She was also very young, sixteen at most.

'Who told you?' I asked her. As I spoke I heard, from behind me, Susie clopping downstairs, still wearing Prim's shoes and my robe. Whether that frightened the girl in any way, I wasn't sure, but her eyes went from me to the floor and she clammed up.

'Put down that case and come into the kitchen.' I said it not as an invitation, but as an order. Our visitor obeyed, without a word, following me round the stairway and through to the back of the house.

Susie had got as far as breaking half a dozen eggs into the blender, and heating oil in a saucepan. 'Make enough for three,' I told her quietly. 'This kid looks as if she's starving.'

'Freezing too. You mix more eggs and give her some coffee. I'm going to get her something warmer to wear.'

I poured her a mug from the percolator, added some milk and handed it to the strange girl. She gave me her first smile as she took it, wrapping both hands round it for warmth, taking a sip, then holding it to her chest. '*Gracias*,' she whispered.

I didn't try to question her as I broke more eggs into the mixer. She probably wouldn't have heard me, anyway; she was looking at the mug too intently. I took some focaccia from the freezer, defrosted it in the microwave for a few seconds then put it in the oven to bake. As I closed the door, Susie returned; she had her red sweater, and she motioned to the girl to put it on. I felt a pang of regret: I liked her in that jumper, and she sure filled it better than the youngster did.

She went off again, leaving me to cook. I stayed silent, letting her get used to me . . . Whoever or whatever she thought I was.

I looked across at her as I took the pot off the hob. '*Huevos?*'

'*Si, si. Por favor.*'

I tipped half of the eggs on to one plate and shared the rest out evenly. I took the warmed through focaccia, cut it into wedges on a chopping board, then set the lot out on the breakfast bar. Susie returned as I did so, in her tan trousers and another red sweater, a polo-neck that I hadn't seen before.

The girl ate so voraciously that I wondered when she had last seen food. 'What's your name?' I asked her quietly, in English, as she picked up her fourth chunk of the Italian herb bread.

'Gabrielle,' she replied, without thinking, then gave me a guilty look as she realised how easily I'd slipped through her '*No hablar Ingles*,' pretence.

'Where are you from?' I poured her some more coffee.

'Manila.'

'Have you just arrived in Spain?'

'*Si.*'

'How?'

'On a ship, a big ship from the Philippines to Barcelona.'

'Did you work on board this ship?'

'*Si*. I help in the galley and I clean the crew's cabins.'

'Nothing else?' asked Susie, fairly heavily. The kid looked at her, then back to me, with a puzzled expression on her face.

I put it another way. 'Did you have to be friendly to the crew?'

She shook her head until I thought she'd dislocate something. 'No!' she exclaimed. 'The man in Manila told me not to be friendly with the sailors. He said that if I did, you would know and I would be sent back home.'

'He would know?' Susie sounded incredulous. I waved her to indignant silence.

'Okay, Gabrielle,' I went on, gently. 'Why did you come here, to this house?'

'When the ship came to Barcelona, the captain gave me some Spanish money. Then he took me to the bus station and he put me on a bus and he told me to get off in L'Escala and to take a taxi to this house.' She lifted up the sweater, delved into the gypsy blouse and produced a folded sheet of paper from her cleavage. 'Here it is; he gave me this address.'

I took it from her and checked; sure enough, there it was, written in a big scrawl in ballpoint. Villa Bernabeu, Carrer Caterina, L'Escala, Girona.

'So,' I said. 'You were sent from Manila to Barcelona, then here to see me. What were you told will happen now?'

Gabrielle looked up at me; she was a pretty wee thing, very pretty. She didn't need any of that make-up. 'You will look at me, and you will talk to me, and you will have a doctor examine me. Then I will go to work.'

144

I knew what was coming; I could tell from Susie's expression that she did too. 'Where do you expect to be working?'

'In your club, señor; the Bluebird Club, the man in Manila told me it was called that. He tell me to dress nice, so you will like me.'

'And what do you expect to be doing there?'

'I 'spect to be a hostess; to wait on the tables, to serve the customers their food and drink, and to be nice to them.'

'How nice? You mean friendly? Like you were told not to be friendly with the sailors?'

She frowned at me as understanding began to dawn. 'The man in Manila did not say that. He only told me I would wait on tables and be nice, and I would make a lot of money and could send it home to my father and mother. My father is sick, so he cannot work. The man in Manila give him dollars; that's why he let me go to Spain.'

'You mean he sold you?' Susie exclaimed.

Gabrielle caught the anger in her voice; it scared her. 'No,' she protested. 'The man give him money to let me work for his friend. That was all.'

'So you can go back to Manila any time you like?' I asked her.

The youngster's face fell. 'No. The man said that I must stay in Spain and work at the club till you tell me I can go home. If I run away, he will hurt my father, and my mother.'

'Tell me about this man. Do you know his name?'

She nodded. 'He is an African man; Moroccan. His name is Hassani.'

'Shit,' I whispered. Susie was looking at me now; completely bewildered.

'What's my name?' I asked Gabrielle.

'Señor Capulet. You are Señor Capulet; isn't that right?'

I shoved the last piece of bread towards her, across the breakfast bar.

'No. I am not Señor Capulet, and I don't own the Bluebird Club, or any other club for that matter. Capulet has been gone from here for over a year now. I don't think the man who paid your father can have known this at the time.

'I've never heard of the Bluebird, kid, but there are plenty of places like it in Spain. Do you know what a brothel is?' She shook her head. '*En Español, un burdel?*'

'*Si.*' She nodded, and I saw her colour rise beneath the make-up.

'Did you really not know that's where you would be working?'

'No. My father said it would be all right for me to go there.' Her face fell. 'Can you find out where it is, señor? For I must go there. If I don't, the African man will do things to my father.'

'No way are you going there, kid,' said Susie. 'Do you want to go home?'

Gabrielle was silent for a few seconds, then whispered something, so quietly that I couldn't make it out, but I knew that it was 'Yes,' in one language or another.

'Then that's what will happen,' I told her.

'Susie,' I said. 'Take Gabrielle upstairs and put her in a hot bath. Then she should sleep for an hour or two. While you're doing that, I'll make a phone call.'

She nodded and squeezed my arm. 'You still have a soft side left, then,' she whispered, as she slid off her seat.

'Don't you go getting maternal on me,' I answered her, more than half seriously.

'What's your surname?' I asked the girl.

'Palacios. *Yo soy* Gabrielle Serafina Palacios.'

Left alone, I scratched my chin and thought carefully. Logically, there was only one guy I could call, but I was hesitant. There was a Catalan Society magazine lying on the bar, beside the telephone. I looked up 'Useful Numbers' and found the British Consulate in Barcelona. The telephonist told me that the only person on duty that day was the Commercial Counsellor, Ms Willis.

'Anyone will do,' I said. I introduced myself, and was wounded; the name meant nothing to her. I explained the situation, exactly as it had happened. 'Phone the police,' she advised at once. 'She's a foreign national, obviously an illegal; she's not your problem.'

'She turned up cold and hungry on my doorstep, expecting a job in my brothel!' I replied. 'Of course she's my problem.'

'What have you done with her for now?'

'My girlfriend's . . .' I paused. I had used the word without a second thought. Well, it was true for a day or two. '. . . giving her a bath.'

'That's a relief,' Ms Willis exclaimed. 'You're not alone with her; you have a female there. Otherwise she could have accused you of anything. Please, Mr Blackstone, call the Guardia at once.'

'I don't know anyone there; I do have a friend in the Mossos though.'

'Technically this has nothing to do with them, but if it'll make you feel happier, call him. Meantime, I'll get in touch with my opposite number in the Filipino Consulate. Give me all the details again.'

I repeated the girl's name, gave her my phone number, and Fortunato's, then caught him by telephone at home, just as he was about to leave for his office in Girona. He was on my doorstep within half an hour. By that time Susie had bedded Gabrielle down in one of the spare rooms. When I introduced her to the policeman she gave him one of the most unashamedly appraising looks I have ever seen, but thankfully said nothing beyond a polite, 'Hello', then went off, unasked, to make more coffee.

I told him all of Gabrielle's story, beginning with her father's sale of her in Manila to her arrival at the address to which she had been sent.

'The Bluebird Club,' Fortunato murmured, when I had finished. 'I know it all right; it is just outside Figueras, on the road to Girona. By name, it belonged to a farmer and the licence was his, too, but we knew that there were other people behind it. They had papers for all the women there, so they were allowed to do business.

'I guess now that Capulet was the other man.'

'Is there a third Hassani brother?'

The policeman nodded. 'As I recall there is. His name is Nayim, and he has a small prison record in Spain for dealing in stolen property. If you asked me to guess, he bought the girls in Manila . . . You say the first one who turned up here could have been Filipina too?'

'Yes, for sure. She was a bit older than Gabrielle, but not much.'

'That's the game then. He buys them young and fresh, finds them a cargo ship where they can work their passage, with some money to the skipper as well to ensure that the crew don't fuck them useless before they get to Spain. Once they're here, the skipper walks them off the vessel and sends them up to L'Escala, to Capulet.'

'So why are they still coming?'

'Your guess is as good as mine. Nayim can't know that Capulet has vanished. But sooner or later he will run out of money; then there will be no more girls.'

'Where did Sayeed fit in?'

'My guess would be that he delivered them to the Bluebird, once Capulet had given them the okay. The Frenchman wouldn't have been seen dead near a place like that, even if he did own it.'

'Speaking of being seen dead . . .'

'No,' said Fortunato, firmly. 'There's no sign of him.'

'How about the story I told you yesterday, about Susie's investment?'

'Hah!' He laughed. 'You know, Oz. I am not sure if I want to be a friend of yours; they are all very unlucky. However that one has taken wings; there is no longer a need for Susie to make a formal statement. I arrested Toldo, the lawyer, yesterday afternoon; for a while he tried to claim that he also had been a victim of Chandler and Hickok, but there were letters in his office which prove that he knew all about the plan.

'Once I took his statement, I phoned the Fraud people in London to tell them about it. Not long afterwards, they called me back. The British police are now looking for Señor Chandler, or Fowler, for the murder of his partner, Señor Wild Bill Hickok. So, among others, are the Guardia Civil.

'They can place him on the Costa del Sol a month ago, but there have been no sightings since then.'

'Is Susie in danger?' I asked.

'Why should she be? The story of the murder, although not of the fraud, is all over the newspapers in England, and television has shown a photograph of Fowler. He's nowhere in Europe by now, I'll bet you. But neither is the money, unfortunately.'

'I heard that last part,' came a voice from behind us. 'How much is this man Toldo worth?'

'Not enough to make it worth taking him to court,' the policeman told her. 'You will have to trace it all the way through from Barcelona to wherever it is now.'

Susie winced. 'That could be difficult. Once money goes black, it tends to move around a lot, and fast. Could we have any comeback against the Spanish bank?'

'Not unless they broke their own rules in making the transfer, and did it on one signature instead of two. I don't think that is likely, señora.'

'In that case. I'll just have to hope that the Fraud Squad is up to the job.' She gave us each a mug from the tray which she had brought from the kitchen.

'Now,' she said, fixing Fortunato with a stare, 'what are we going to do about that poor wee girl upstairs?'

'She's a good girl, you say?' he asked; a question for a question.

'She seems to be. She's lost, and scared, and thousands of miles from home, but she seems like a decent kid.'

'Then I'll look after her myself. I know she's a Guardia Civil responsibility, but if I give her to them, they will put her in a detention centre. These things can move slowly; she could be there for months, among all sorts of bad people.

'I will take her under my protection and arrange her return to Manila directly with the consulate.'

'Where will she stay?'

He gave Susie a shrug which said, *Where else?*

148

'She will stay with me tonight at least, if Veronique agrees. I will go home now and discuss it with her. I'll be back for the girl in two or three hours.'

25

Susie let Gabrielle keep the sweater. She hugged it to herself, and looked at her gratefully, as Ramon picked up her pathetic wee case. He had brought his wife with him to collect the girl, a sensible move, so that she wouldn't be frightened.

I walked them out to their car, a roomy family saloon; Alejandro was in the back, asleep and strapped into his safety seat. The girl's face lit up as she saw him. Without her make-up, her skin was a very light brown; she could have passed for his older sister.

'Are we still going, then?' Susie asked as I walked back inside.

'Where?'

'This cocktail party Shirley mentioned last night. At Fred's, or wherever.'

'Frank's. You want to go?'

'Unless you've lost your bottle, and don't fancy being talked about.'

'They're going to talk about me anyway, like Shirley said. Sure, let's go. Unless you'd rather watch rugby on Sky that is.'

'That will be right,' she snorted. 'What should I wear? Frock or trousers? Shirt or sweater?'

'Those trousers you've got on, and a shirt.' I went upstairs with her and gave the nod to her choice of a fawn shirt from the magic suitcase. I sat on the bed and watched her as she changed; I hadn't realised it before, but she was built very like Prim, an inch or two shorter, a cup size bigger in the bust, certainly, but with the same narrow waist and assertive hips. With her back to me, she could almost have been my wife in a wig.

I changed into my jeans, another white shirt, and cowboy boots. This time as we checked ourselves in the mirror by the door, me in my black leather jacket and Susie in the red one that she had bought in Torroella, I fairly towered over her.

Remembering my offer to Shirley of a lift, I called her, but she turned it down. 'I'd rather keep the option of a quick getaway, Oz. So should you, if you've any sense.'

I had been to Frank and Geraldine's house before, in my first spell on the Costa Brava. It's a nice, fairly new villa, in a part of L'Escala called Montgo and it's built on two levels, with loads of space inside and out and a small swimming pool with dark blue tiles like mine, so that it looks cool in the summer, and bloody freezing in the winter.

When we got there at about ten minutes after three, the place was already crowded. Gerrie met us at the door. 'How good to see you, Oz,' she said, enthusiastically. 'And this is your sister, that Shirl told us about, is it?'

'This is Susie,' I answered. Not a lie, and I didn't fancy any long explanations.

I gave her a couple of thousand pesetas entry money for the Catalan Society funds, and a bottle of champagne as a raffle prize, and she sold me twenty quid's worth of tickets so that I could win it back. The weather had brightened up, and it was pleasantly warm again, so most of the crowd were outside. JoJo gave us a cheery 'Good afternoon' and two glasses of some pink stuff that she said was 'punsh', and we wandered off to mingle.

I hadn't been a great player in the British Society of Catalunya during our first stay; I was given to loafing then. Still, I knew most of the faces from that time. The mingling part of it was easy; I was buttonholed straightaway by a couple from Yorkshire who admitted, in the slightly guilty way that grapple-fans of their age always have, that they watched the GWA wrestling on television, and wanted to know what it was like to be its ring announcer.

Susie saw that I was trapped for a while and slipped quietly away to talk to Shirley.

The Milligans, as the Yorkshire tag-team were called, knew every wrestler . . . they actually called them 'superstars' . . . not only by their ring names, but by their real names as well, details that normally can only be found on websites for addicts. I could tell that they were real marks, as we call punters in the wrestling business.

'Who's really the toughest?' Mrs M asked.

'Big Everett,' I told her, truthfully. 'You really wouldn't want to upset him.'

'And who are your best pals?' her husband chipped in.

'All of them,' I answered, 'but I suppose I'm closest to Everett, Liam Matthews and Big Jerry.'

'Ahh, the Behemoth,' said Mr M knowingly. 'Tell me, are these chaps really that big in real life?'

'No. They're bigger.' I thought of the first time I'd met Everett 'Daze' Davis in my flat in Glasgow, and smiled as I pictured Jan's

152

astonished expression when she came in and saw him there. I remembered Jerry Gradi lifting a Glasgow hooligan clean off his feet, without effort. But it was the fact that the thug was sat on a three-seater sofa at the time that had made it really impressive. 'You can't imagine how big they are, until you've met them.

'Would you like to go to one of the live shows?' I offered. 'I'll fix you up with a couple of tickets for an event, in the UK or in Spain. We do Barcelona quite often.'

'Oh no,' said Mrs Milligan in a millisecond. 'Thank you, but no thank you. Television is one thing, but we couldn't possibly go!'

I slipped out of their stranglehold, scrounged another couple of glasses of 'punsh' from JoJo and made my way round the pool to join Susie, Shirley and a veteran English watercolourist whom I'd met on my previous stay. His name had gone from me for that moment, but I recognised him at once, for he's blessed with the twinkliest eyes I've ever seen. Vaguely, I seemed to remember that whatever he was called, he spelled it with three 'l's.

Very often, ex-pat conversation on the Costa Brava is confined to what's happening within the community: whose family are coming out and when, whose dog just snuffed it, and who's gone back to the Elephants' Graveyard that they call 'home'.

The old artist was different though; he's been there since God retired to Augusta, and he mixes with Catalans as much as with the other Brits. It came to me at last that his name was Lionell; he kept us smiling for ten minutes with stories from way back, and he also talked me into giving him a commission for a painting of Casa Nou Camp. (I don't know what was in that 'punsh'.)

I told him, and Shirley, about our experience that morning, about Gabrielle's arrival on the doorstep, out of the blue. The twinkle left his eyes and his leathery face grew serious. 'That's the worst business under the sun, Oz. White slavery, they called it in my day, and it's bloody awful that it's still going on.'

'And Rey was into it?' asked Shirley. 'You're sure of that?'

'I'm certain of it. The kid thought that I was him.'

'Bloody shame,' Lionell muttered again, into his elegant beard.

'Sorted now, though,' I said . . . and then I felt a thump between my shoulder-blades.

At the best of times, I don't like people slapping me on the back; when it's done by someone I don't like, I really don't like it. A subtle change in Shirley's expression tipped me off a second before it happened, but too late for me to do anything about it.

'Oz, old boy! How good to see you again! And where is the lovely Primavera? Made an honest woman of her at last, I hear.'

Before I go any further, I want to say a word about car salespeople in general. I have nothing against them at all; I regard them, until shown otherwise, as honest, upright, helpful, well-trained, professional automobile consultants.

But in any walk of life, you'll always find one, won't you? Suppose he was a Samaritan by profession, Steve Miller would still be an arsehole. I had only met the guy a couple of times, and never had a civil conversation with him, yet here he was 'old boying' me like a public school chum and all over me like a cheap suit.

'My wife is very well, Steve,' I answered him, not trying to sound anything but cold. 'She's in the States right now, with her mother, who's been taken ill over there.'

I was aware that the groups nearest to us were edging very slightly away. This was not imagination on my part; they really were.

'What a pity,' Miller oozed. 'I've been looking forward to seeing her again. Talking over old times as it were.'

Right there, Susie saved him . . . or so it seemed. She stepped between us and took his arm. 'So you're Steve, are you? Oz has told me all about you. I'm Susie; a pal of Oz and Prim from Glasgow. I'll do as a substitute; you can talk to me instead. I like interesting men.'

'I say,' he said, in a voice that was pure Leslie Phillips. Yes, he did. I didn't believe that real people really say 'I say', like that, until he said it. There are those who sound camp; there are those who sound lecherous. But there are very few who can combine the two.

'And what do you do, pretty lady?' he oiled.

'I run a multimillion-pound construction group.'

'I say.' A faint look of uncertainty crossed his face.

'And what do you do, Steve?' she asked.

'I'm deputy dealer principal of a specialist automotive firm.'

'I say.' She wrinkled her nose at him, and he bought it. 'How specialist? What do you sell?'

'Imported vehicles,' he answered.

'Imported from where?' I chipped in.

'The Far East. Malaysia, actually.' He looked back at Susie, dismissing me, now that he had a quarry to pursue. 'What kind of car do you drive, my dear?'

'Just a wee runabout,' she answered.

'Ah. A Focus, Astra, something like that?'

'Porsche Boxster, actually.' She laughed lightly. I had the feeling that she was up to something, and I didn't have to wait long to find out what it was.

'So you're a friend of Prim, too,' she continued.

'Yes indeed. Very much so.'

'That's funny. I don't really remember her talking about you.'

'Oh yes, we're friends,' he insisted.

'But casual, like?'

'Oh no. We were much more than that.'

'What, you mean like . . .?'

Miller sniggered; maybe he thought he was out of my earshot, but I have very sharp ears. I tried to keep my gaze fixed on Shirley, but I wasn't looking at her at all, and she knew it. 'Well a gentleman has to be discreet,' he said, 'but yes. Like that.'

'Mmm. You do surprise me. Prim's always struck me as very reserved with men.'

'Oh no!' he exclaimed, 'not at all.' Then he chuckled. 'Maybe it's the hot climate. Why,' he bellowed, 'I remember back when she and I were in Madrid . . .'

And that was as far as he got. I turned round, grabbed him by the lapels of his navy-blue blazer and nutted him.

When a pro wrestler fake-butts another, either he stops just short of contact or the other guy gets a hand up to take the impact. There was none of that when I stuck the head on Steve Miller. I heard the crack as his nose broke, and heard a satisfying crunch of gristle. He squealed and his knees buckled, but I didn't let him fall. Instead, as the blood and snotter erupted from him and drenched his shirt front, I lifted him clear of the surrounding terrace, held him out at arm's length over the deep end of the swimming pool, and dropped him in. He went straight under, nice and clean with hardly a splash, then bobbed to the surface, spluttering and thrashing his arms about. I waited until he reached the side; when he grabbed the edging, I stood on his fingers, just for luck.

'What the 'ell's all this about?' Frank Barnett's voice boomed from the other side.

'Don't ask, Frank,' I told him.

He looked at me, then he saw who was in the pool. 'No,' he said. 'No, I won't.' Then he turned on his heel and went back indoors.

I reached down, grabbed Miller by the scruff of the neck and hauled him out. He flopped on the terrace like a beached porpoise, blood still running freely from his bent beak.

I crouched down beside him, taking care not to let the bastard bleed on me. 'If I ever hear you, or hear of you,' I warned him, 'boasting again about having my wife, I'll hold you under until the bubbles stop coming up. You better believe that, pal.'

The British abroad can be remarkable sometimes. A very nice black-haired lady, a retired doctor, someone told me, took charge of the wounded. She led him off to pack his nose with cotton wool, or string, or whatever, and a minute or so later it was as if the whole thing had never happened. The normal buzz of conversation resumed, golf matches were arranged, more 'punsh' was poured. Eventually, they drew the raffle. Lionell won my champagne, I won a bottle of Moscatel, which I donated there and then to the next raffle, Shirley won a fluffy parrot which repeats whatever anyone says to it . . . hours of fun around the pool, pity she has no grandchildren . . . and Susie won dinner for two at El Roser II, also known as Roser Dos, in which the King of Spain once ate.

Miller didn't appear again, I had a fleeting worry that he might vandalise my car on his way out, but I decided fairly quickly that not even he would be so stupid.

The party was starting to break up when Shirley took me aside. 'That was pretty vicious, you know,' she murmured. 'Steve's dad's an ex-copper. You might hear more of it.'

'I don't think so, Shirl. I don't think I'll ever hear from him again.'

She slipped an arm around my waist; she's as tall as me, so she had no trouble whispering in my ear. 'You've changed, Oz. I noticed it as soon as you came back. It's no bad thing, mind you; I think I prefer the later model. Just don't go too far in the new direction, eh.' She nodded imperceptibly towards Susie, who was just coming back from the toilet. 'And be very careful of your little friend there.

'She's absolutely deadly, that one. I reckon if she wanted something, she'd go to extremes to get hold of it: and even if you haven't realised it, it's obvious to me she wants you.'

26

I thought of Shirley's warning as we drove home; I wondered what she'd have said if I'd told her that she'd already had me. I decided not to let it fester. As soon as we were inside the house, I took Susie by the hand and turned her to face me.

'Shirl reckons you're after me.'

She looked up at me. 'She's a perceptive lady, then.'

She paused for just long enough for me to feel a frown ridge my forehead. 'But don't worry,' she swept on, 'I've told you what my game plan is, and it doesn't include breaking up you and Prim. I'm Scotland's most eligible spinster, but that's not a title I plan to keep for long.'

'So what do you want me for?'

'I want you to be my minder,' she said.

'Your minder?' I laughed, even although I could see that she was dead serious.

'Sort of. Over the last couple of days I've found out that what I've always suspected about you and me is true, right enough. We're two peas from the same pod. We're cloned from the same animal. Put it anyway you like, but what I'm really saying is that we're natural partners, you and I. If it turned out that you were my long-lost brother, like Shirley told Geraldine, it wouldn't surprise me at all.'

I smiled, and jerked my thumb in the direction of the bedroom. 'But that would make all that stuff . . .'

'So what? "The game the whole family can play", like someone said.' For a fleeting second I wondered about her and the monstrous Lord Provost, then put the thought out of my mind.

'Oz,' she continued, 'not once have I told you that I love you; because I don't. I don't love, period . . . any more than you do.

'What I have done is take shameless advantage of Prim being away to get close to you, and to make you more honest about yourself, and less naive about other people . . .'

'You mean Prim?' I interrupted.

'Okay, yes, about her; but you'd already found out some of it.'

'Aye,' I said bitterly, 'and now I've found out that when she wasn't keeping the truth from me, she was twisting it to suit herself.'

'That's as may be, but it's between you two. Just don't let it break you up.'

I frowned at her. 'Hey, you're the one who told me she hated me.'

'Past tense. She was right to, and all. I think she hated herself too, though, when she slept with that creep.'

'Speaking of Miller, don't you go thinking I don't realise you set him up this afternoon. You engineered it so that I'd fill him in. Did it give you a buzz, was that it?'

Susie looked up at me, with a delicious spark of triumph in her eyes. 'It did, as a matter of fact. But that's not why I did it. I saw the look in your eyes when he appeared, slapping you on the back like that, and I knew that sooner or later you were going to do him some damage. I reckoned to myself that if you came across him when there was no one else around, that you might have really hurt him, but that if you squared him up in a crowd, you'd be stopped before you got carried away.

'So I egged him on until he stepped over the line. Mind you, I thought you'd only punch him; I never realised you were so good at the Glasgow kiss!'

I had to laugh. 'Okay,' I conceded. 'So you kept him out of hospital and me out of jail. Thanks from us both. Now back to what you were on about before. Your minder, you said? Explain.'

Susie led me across to the big sofa, spread herself on it and pulled me down beside her. All of a sudden she looked vulnerable again, as she had when she'd arrived, two days earlier. I wondered if it was real, or if she was trying to lead me on too.

'It's like this,' she began. 'I feel closer to you, Oz, than I do to anyone else in the world. You think the way I do, you're as cunning as me, so I can't pull the wool over your eyes, and you're afraid of nothing, because the worst has happened already. On top of that, I reckon you care for me. I trust you like I can't trust anyone else, not even dear old Joe. The fact that he's my natural father doesn't make his business judgement any better.'

She put my hand to her lips and kissed it. 'I want you to look out for me, Oz. I want you to watch my back. I want to be able to come to you whenever I have a problem that I don't think I can handle on my own.'

'For example?'

'For example that Castelgolf business. I did that almost entirely off my own bat, but not quite. I went to Joe for advice; maybe he was

158

dazzled by the notion of having his own golf course, but he was taken hook line and sinker just like me.

'If I'd come to you, and asked you what you thought, what would you have done?'

'What you should have; hired Dun and Bradstreet or someone like them. Had a word with a couple of acquaintances. Sure, I'd probably have steered you away from it. But you'll learn from this experience; you won't make the same mistake again.'

'No. But there are other bigger mistakes out there waiting for me. Not just in business either. Oz, I'm a rich girlie in a greedy man's world. I might be devious, or manipulative if you like, and I might be ruthless, but I still get lonely, and in private, I still doubt myself.

'I want you to be there for me, Oz. That's all.'

I reached out and touched her face. 'That's easy. You've got it.'

'Will you come on the board of the Gantry Group, as a non-executive director?'

I laughed again. 'Fuck me, is that what all this is about? You're offering me a seat on the board. I don't know about that, Susie. I have no idea what my commitments are going to be for the next couple of years.'

'There'll be a salary involved, and shares, if you like.'

'I'll watch your back, but I won't be paid for it. You don't need to make me a director of anything.'

'It'll regularise things; it'll give me an excuse to call you whenever I need you, without pissing off Prim.'

'Okay,' I conceded. 'If that's what you want, okay. Expenses only, though; no salary. And don't worry about Prim. She doesn't have a veto over what I do.'

She moved towards me, along the sofa. 'Thanks,' she whispered. 'Now let me show you another kind of Glasgow kiss.'

Afterwards, we decided that we would cash in Susie's raffle prize that night. As I had expected, El Roser II was busy, it being the end of the Christmas festival, but they managed to squeeze another table for two into a glazed overspill pavilion on the Passeig Maritim, in front of the main restaurant.

The King of Spain went there to eat fish; if that was good enough for him, who were we to disagree?

We started with an assortment of shellfish, then majored on a stew of hake, monkfish, and sea bass with a couple of langoustines added for the sake of appearance. To drink . . . not part of the prize . . . we selected a bottle of Faustino Rioja. There are several Faustinos, each one with a number. The lower the number, the higher the price; Susie insisted on buying, so I went for number one.

When it was over, and we had scraped the last of our crêpes suzette off the plate . . . what else could we have for dessert . . . I picked up the empty bottle, and looked at the distinguished label, admiring it and wondering how I would look with a beard like that. Susie took my left hand in hers. 'You do know that we're sitting in a goldfish bowl here?' she asked.

Our table was against one of the pavilion walls. I looked out, through the glass, at the Saturday night promenaders, young couples, older couples, families with children, as they walked along the Passeig.

'Sure,' I said, 'but so what?'

'You realise that when this movie comes out in Europe, and when it's a hit, as it will be, this is how your life will be for evermore?'

'I'll make bloody sure that it isn't,' I promised. 'Anyway, you're overrating me.'

'No I'm not. You're a Brit in a Hollywood movie; you're tabloid meat from now on. Paparazzi after you and all that stuff.'

'I was cast by my brother-in-law, for God's sake!'

'Doesn't matter. You said yourself, Miles is commercial first and nothing second. You're fairly well known as it is from the wrestling stuff. Now you're going to be famous, pursued, selling exclusive rights to the first baby pics and all that stuff.'

'Rubbish. It won't be that bad.'

She gleamed at me, out from under her eyelashes, raised my hand to her lips and kissed it, lightly. 'Oh no?' she whispered. 'Then why is there a bloke photographing us right now?'

Instinctively, I snatched my hand away and looked round. Outside, on the pavement, no more than a few yards away from us, stood a man. He was wearing dark trousers and a heavy cotton jacket, with a hood pulled up over his head. The way the streetlight was hitting the glass walls of the restaurant annexe meant that I couldn't make out his face. Anyway, most of it was covered by what looked like a large digital camera, and it was pointed unmistakably at Susie and me.

The man waited long enough to take one more shot, catching, no doubt, the surprise and anger on my face, then turned and ran off. Still I had no clear view of him. I started out of my chair, but he had disappeared into the crowd, and I knew right away that it was useless. As I sat down again, I was aware of one or two people looking at me, but mostly the thing had gone unnoticed.

'How long was he there?' I asked her.

'I don't know. I was only aware of him when the people outside thinned out a bit. But it's not as if we were necking or anything. Get used to it, though, love. That's what it's going to be like from now on. "Smile please, Oz. Gie's your autograph, Oz." You'll have a fan club, you'll have a website. Soon as this movie comes out.'

'You reckon?' I growled. 'You think that was just some mark who recognised me from the telly?'

'Who else could it have been?'

I looked at her. She wasn't kidding; it hadn't dawned on her. 'I might never be able to prove it,' I told her, 'but it could have been Steve Miller.'

She gave a small gasp of surprise. 'You think so? I'd have thought he'd never come near you again after what you did to him.'

'Who else, then?'

'Another of Prim's cast-offs?'

'I only know one of them, and another by sight. It wasn't Fortunato, and it wasn't that waiter bloke.'

'Then chances are it was a punter. Anyway, you said it yourself. If it was Miller, you'll never prove it. So forget it. Let's go home.'

Susie settled what there was of the bill and we stepped out into the cold, crisp night; she wore the coat which she had bought in Barcelona, and I had on my heaviest jacket. I thought that there was a chance that the photographer might still be hanging around, so, rather than walk straight along the Passeig to the spot where the Mercedes was parked, I led her in the other direction, round the side of El Roser II. We stopped at the small headland which looks across the great bay towards Ampuriabrava and Rosas.

We stood there for a while. Susie admired the twinkling lights on the other side; I pretended to do the same, but all the time I was glancing round, to see if we had been followed. If it was Miller, and if he was still there, a broken nose would be only the start.

But there was no one lurking, either with a camera or without. Eventually we walked on; past L'Olla and El Pescadors, two cheek-by-jowl restaurants which are open all year round, then back to the car.

Although I knew that there was no longer any threat to Susie, I bolted the doors automatically once we were home. 'Nightcap?' I asked.

'Not that sort,' Susie replied.

I felt accustomed to her being there with me, even though it had been less than three days. I knew that it was short term, an encounter, an adventure; but in its course my life, or at least my outlook on it, had changed dramatically. Old delusions had been swept aside and new truths had taken their place. I knew myself now, for sure, and I had my wee Glasgow provocateuse to thank, or blame, for it. I felt as if I would be ready to live in the real world again . . . in a couple of days.

'Come on then,' I said. She was wearing the dress that she had worn to Shirley's the night before. She undid a single catch at the one covered shoulder; it slid gently to her feet and she was naked. I lifted her clean out of her shoes and carried her upstairs, once again.

Our first night, or morning, had been sudden and violent, our second had been filled with my anger. Our third was different, it was gentle, warm, and assured. Maybe it was because we knew that it had to end, but we were terrific together. We knew what each other wanted, what to do, where to go. And, into the bargain, we fitted together, piston and cylinder precision-matched like a formula one engine.

If we had been trying to tire each other out, which we weren't, then the outcome was a draw. We slipped into sleep together. I dreamed. I saw the two of us, on a sailing boat, knowing that we were due in harbour but without a wind to blow us home.

When I woke next morning, she was standing at the side of the bed, looking down at me, and she was dressed. 'I'm going home, Oz,' she said. 'I've just phoned the airport, and they can get me on to a flight this afternoon.'

I wasn't surprised; I had known that the third night was it. Still I asked her. 'Wait another day?'

She shook her head. 'No. If I did that, it could fuck up my game-plan big-time. I might start to want you in that way after all.' She smiled. 'Not love you, you understand. Susie doesn't love. Just want you.'

'Okay.' I stepped out of bed, right side as always. I'm superstitious that way; I never get out of bed on the wrong side. 'You put the coffee on. I'll shower and dress, then I'll drive you down.'

'No, I'll get a taxi.'

'You've got one: no arguments.'

We ate a quick cereal breakfast then I loaded Susie's case into the Voyager, and we took to the road. We spoke very little on the way down, not at all, in fact, just listening to CDs, until we were past the hilltop prison. 'What would have happened over the last couple of days, d'you think,' I asked, 'if you hadn't gone down those stairs?'

'I don't know,' she admitted, with a smile. 'I caught you off-guard, and it was wicked of me, but I needed you awful bad.

'Probably we'd just have had a nice chaste weekend, but . . . You weren't exactly in the best frame of mind yourself, were you?'

I had to agree with her. In truth, I still wasn't, but that was something to be confronted later, even though a wee, lurking, bit of me wanted to say 'Fuck it', and get on that plane with Susie.

'I'm glad you came,' I told her. 'I don't regret what happened, and I'm not going to feel guilty about it. You were right about many things, one of them being that I like women. I enjoyed you, Susie; I loved having you, one might say. I hope you enjoyed me too.'

She smiled again at my sudden declaration. 'You were all right,' she conceded. 'Yes, okay, it was great; never better.

'But that's the least of what you did for me. Three days ago, when I walked up your drive, I was hurting, I was insecure and, for all that my business is doing well, inside I had the self-esteem of a gnat. Now I feel like me again, I know where I'm going and I have the self-belief to get there.

'I was glad when I found that Prim was in the States. I was glad to have you to myself. I never meant to blurt out the truth about her and Fortunato, but I don't regret that either. You don't deserve to be allowed to live a lie; even if I do understand why she kept those things from you.'

'Do you think it would have made any difference to how I felt about her,' I asked her, 'if she'd told me the whole story from the start? Every fucking detail?'

'No.'

But it does now, I thought to myself. *It means that she's not the person I thought I married.*

'I just wish she had, though,' I said.

'Maybe, but now you're even. You've got a secret to keep from her.'

'What if I don't want to?'

'Hey, I thought you'd stopped kidding yourself. You won't because it's in your interests not to. Sure you'll say that it would only hurt her, but in terms of this great new career of yours, it could hurt you more. You'll stay with her.'

'But what if I didn't? What about you and me?'

She gave me a look that bored into me even though I had my eyes on the road ahead. 'I thought we'd agreed how you and I are going to be in the future. You're going to be the strong man behind the Gantry throne.'

'Yeah but what if . . .?'

'No what ifs,' she exclaimed, suddenly, sharply.

'We're too alike, Oz. We're hard, clever, ruthless, ambitious, rich and however many other adjectives we've got in common. The thought of you and I together full-time scares the hell out of me, as it should you. You get on with your life, I'll get on with mine, and we'll be there for each other as need be. That's all I can handle. Susie doesn't love; Susie can't love.

'Deal?'

'Sure, it's a deal. Oz doesn't love either, not any more. Just as well, eh?'

It was Sunday, so the airport was relatively quiet. I parked and we walked together to the check-in, me wheeling that bloody great case behind me.

The departure gate was at the top of a big escalator. Having ditched the luggage, we rode up it arm in arm, Susie, clutching her passport and boarding card. At the top she turned towards me.

'One last confession,' she said.

I looked at her, intrigued; I'd thought that everything lay bare between us. 'When I came out here, I wasn't just concerned about the Castelgolf thing: I knew it was a con. The other investors and I finally twigged a few weeks ago that something was up. We put detectives on Chandler and Hickok, and we heard about the suicide, supposed, when it happened.

'We didn't call in the police at that stage for one reason only. One of the other investors is chief executive of a major public company, and he crapped himself about what the City might make of the news that he'd been the victim of a professional scam. When I heard that you and Prim were here, so close to the action, I volunteered to come out, and go to see the banker and the lawyer, Toldo, to find out whether the money was safe.

'We didn't have much hope of that, though. The day after Hickok's death, the detective we put on Chandler reported back that he'd flown to the Costa del Sol, then out again to Rio, using another of his names.'

'You know what that means, don't you?' I murmured. I had been keeping pace with her.

'Yes indeed. Whoever it was that chucked me down your stairs . . . and I agree that someone did . . . there's precious little chance that it was him.'

'So who did?'

'Exactly. And, just as intriguing . . . why? It wasn't Chandler, and if it was linked to my business in Glasgow, then it would just have happened there. I would understand if someone had seen me and had to have my fabulous body, but why would anyone want to break into your house, just to attack me?

'Christ, I'd been in town for less than a day. Who would even know I was there?' .

164

I didn't have an answer for her, but I didn't have time to dwell on it either, not then at any rate. Susie slipped her passport and boarding card into her shoulder-bag, put her arms around my neck, and pressed herself to me; we kissed, a mix of Glasgow and Fife style, a long and slow goodbye. If either of us had been wearing shades they'd have steamed up.

Finally, we came up for air. 'I'll write to you when I get back,' she said. 'Formally inviting you to join the board. You'll let me know when you leave here, won't you?'

'Sure. I have the Glasgow premiere of *Snatch* coming up in a couple of weeks. I'll be back for that, certainly: we'll be back, I should say. You're on the invitation list, by the way. It'll probably be there when you get home.'

'You make sure it is "we",' she cautioned me. 'But don't look for me there; not just yet.'

'Fair enough,' I acknowledged. 'Hey. Just you remember, when you go looking for your titled consort, don't go selling yourself short.'

She looked at me as if I was daft, her brown eyes flashing, the light glinting on her hair. 'Selling doesn't come into it, honey. I'll be buying.'

I laughed at her frankness, but doubted if she'd have to get her chequebook out.

She kissed me again. 'Hey,' she whispered. 'If Susie did love . . .'

'Yeah,' I answered. 'Oz too . . .'

She turned and walked towards the gate, passport produced and offered for the cursory inspection, then she was through, beyond the metal detector and gone. She didn't look back; to my complete surprise, I experienced a sudden surge of loneliness. It was nothing new to me, yet it signalled the truth of what she had said. My life had changed.

27

All the way back up the *autopista* I could think only of Susie, and what she'd told me at the airport. I had accepted Chandler né Fowler as her attacker not just because it was convenient but because it was the only logical explanation.

But if it wasn't him . . . and it wasn't . . . then who on Earth, and, yes, just as important why on Earth?

If Susie didn't have an enemy, that just left me. I ran through the field.

Fortunato? Never in a hundred; I was the answer to the guy's prayers. When Prim turned up in L'Escala again he must have been the most relieved man in town to see that she had brought a new husband with her, after the way he had ditched her. The grief she could still have given him over that must have weighed heavily on him, especially with things patched up with Vero and her believing, as naively as I had, that he knew nothing about Prim's aborted kid.

Steve Miller? He was an even less likely candidate. His remodelled hooter gave him something against me, but until then he hadn't taken me seriously. I knew quite well that he'd seen me as no more a sap over whom he held a supposed edge, by virtue of having shafted Prim once upon a time. Anyway, no way was he capable of picking a lock expertly, nor could I see him manhandling Susie either.

Reynard Capulet? Even if he was still in the vicinity, which I doubted in a big way, what could he possibly have against me? I was the guy who had bought his house, and given him a big slab of money for it into the bargain. Okay, I had found the stiff in the pool, but someone had to, eventually, especially if they'd been meant to.

Someone from my recent, fairly exciting, past? Again, no, for one good reason; those who might have had an axe to grind against my skull are all dead. Okay there's one who isn't, but if he had been going to have a pop at me he'd have done it long ago, and somewhere else.

No one came to mind; no one at all. By the time I hit L'Escala I was back to thinking of Susie again, about our incredible three days together, and of the many truths she had told me and shown me, about herself, about Prim and about me.

No, Oz doesn't love any more, not anyone alive, at least, but he can be attracted if the magnet is strong enough. I hadn't thought of her in that way before. Back then, she was with Mike Dylan and he was my pal, and the old Oz didn't do things like coveting a pal's lady, far less covering her. Now, I thought of her, of our last kiss at the airport, of her retreating back, and I felt that pang again.

I swung the Voyager into the driveway, through the gate which I had left open, and drove it into the garage, beside the Merc. I took the shorter route to the back door, unlocked it, and stepped inside, my hand going up quickly to disable the alarm. But the active light was out. I frowned and walked along the short corridor, into the kitchen.

She was leaning over the dishwasher, with her back to me. I looked at her, and felt even more disorientated than I had on the previous Thursday, when Susie's voice had sounded behind me. I had had more than enough surprises for a while; and I sure wasn't ready for this one. I had wanted time, time to think about her, and of what I was going to say to her.

My foot squeaked on the tiled floor and she jumped. She turned quickly, gasped with relief and smiled.

'I know that "Welcome home" is in order,' I said, 'but I have to ask. How the hell did you get here?'

'It's a short story, really,' she answered. She came to me and hugged me. 'After we spoke on Friday, I went out for lunch with Miles and Dawn. We met an actor friend of his, Nicky Johnson. You've heard of him, I'm sure. Miles mentioned that I was there from Spain, and he said that he was about to fly to Madrid, in his private jet. He offered me a lift, said he would drop me off in Barcelona.

'I thought it was too good a chance to miss, so here I am. I beat you home by five minutes; my taxi's just gone.' I had passed a Barcelona Airport taxi as I crossed the town boundary; its green light on top had caught my eye.

'So where's Susie?' she asked.

'She's gone home. She felt awkward,' I lied glibly, 'with just the two of us being here, so she brought her flight forward. I'm just back from the airport myself.'

'It's a wonder I didn't see you there, with our luck.'

Too right, I thought. Then something important came to me. 'Put on the coffee,' I said. 'I won't be a minute.' I strode out of the kitchen and up the stairs. Quickly, I stripped the sheets and pillowcases from our bed and shoved them into the laundry basket in our bathroom; then I crossed the hall and did the same in the bedroom which Susie had used, if only briefly.

Prim was in the living room when I came downstairs; a mug of instant lay, waiting for me, on the coffee table. 'So,' I began, 'tell me all about Elanore.'

'She's recovering well from the surgery,' she replied. 'They decided to hold off on the chemo for now: they're going to give her time to regain a bit more strength. I had a long talk with the surgeon who operated; he's as optimistic as he could be under the circumstances.

'He thinks he got it all, and he thinks that the follow-up treatment will minimise the risk of spread, but he can't say for certain.'

'Worst case, what could happen?'

'She could develop another tumour, maybe in the liver or colon, and that in time would be that. I prefer to think of best case, that she has full remission from the thing and dies of old age.'

She sipped her coffee as I settled on to the sofa beside her. 'What about you, now? What did you and Susie get up to?'

I looked at her, poker-faced. 'What do you think?' I replied. 'We shagged each other senseless.'

Prim laughed. 'I'd know if you had,' she said. 'You'd have bags under your eyes and you'd be tripping over yourself with guilt.'

'You can see though me in a second, can't you?' I murmured.

'You better believe it. No, really, what did you do?'

'Saw the sights, ate well; that was it. I told you about going to Barcelona on Friday. We did Pals as well and some of the other sightseeing places.

'One very odd thing did happen, though.' I told her from start to finish of Gabrielle's arrival on the previous morning, and of the strange story she had to tell. As it unwound, I watched her expression become more and more indignant.

'Do you mean to tell me that the girl's father sold her to a pimp, as if she was livestock?'

'Exactly so; and she turned up here looking for Capulet, so that he could give her the once over, make sure the sailors hadn't given her the clap, or anything like that, on the way across, then put her to work. The poor wee lass is completely innocent. She really did think she was going to be a cocktail waitress.'

'Can we find her father, Oz? Can we trace him and report him to the Filipino police?'

'We won't have to; your old boyfriend's taken her under his wing.

169

He's going to arrange her repatriation through the Philippines consulate. When they hear the story, I'm sure that Papa Palacios will get what's coming to him.'

'Let's hope so.' Prim frowned and chewed her lip; that mannerism always means that she's about to come out with something. It didn't take long.

'Darling,' she murmured. 'Have you considered that if the girl was sold out of poverty, it might not be the kindest thing in the world to send her back to it?'

'The thought did flutter across my mind, my jewel, to be followed by another. What the fuck's it got to do with us? I'm not, we're not, sending her anywhere. We just happen to have bought a house that seems to have been used as a dropping-off point for prostitutes on their way to long-term horizontal employment.

'I'm as angry as you are about what happened to the kid. But I'm chuffed that we've saved her from a life of shame, as the *Daily Star* would put it. What more can we do?'

She turned on the full persuasive power of her baby blues; until that time, that would have been enough. 'Couldn't we give her a job?' she suggested.

'Don't be daft. Give her a job as what?'

'I don't know. A live-in maid, something like that.'

'But we don't need a live-in maid! We're not going to live here full time. What would she do while we're away?'

'Look after the place for us?'

'God! Prim, you've never even met Gabrielle. She's a nice kid, sure, but she's a kid nonetheless. She's too young to be given a responsibility like that.'

'Did you tell Shirley about her? Maybe she'd take her on.'

'Sure, and I'll bet Lionell would give her a job as well, cleaning his brushes. Prim, the best is being done for her; Fortunato has her and he'll make sure that she's sent home under better conditions than she came here. The Philippines is a modern, developing country; she's not simply going to be given back to her father so he can sell her again.'

'Mmm,' she muttered, 'maybe you're right. Still, I think I'll phone Ramon just to make sure she's still all right.'

'Why?' I asked her. 'Don't you trust him with the kid?'

She flushed. 'Of course. I just thought that maybe he and Veronique could use a nanny. That wee Alejandro's a handful.'

'Too much of a handful to give to a sixteen-year-old . . . If she is sixteen, that is. No. Take my word on this and leave things as they are.'

170

She looked reluctant to do that, but I knew that in the end she would. 'We'll see,' she said grudgingly. 'Do you have any other strange stories to tell me? Anything else I'm going to find out about?'

I hadn't planned to raise the subject, but I knew that there was a better than even chance that someone else would, the bulk of the ex-pat community having been witnesses at Frank and Geraldine's cocktail party.

'Well there is one thing,' I began. 'Someone bust Steve Miller's nose at a drinks do yesterday afternoon. He was boasting too loud about one of his conquests, and a guy took violent exception. Guess who the guy was? Guess who the conquest was?'

'Why didn't you tell me you fucked him after I left?' I looked her in the eye as I asked her.

It took her a while to answer me. When she did, her voice was small, not hers at all, someone else's, that of someone uncertain and insecure. 'Didn't think it was any of your business.'

'You're right. It wasn't.'

'Who told you?'

'He did, in effect. He told everyone else too, round the Barnetts' pool, when he started talking about you getting horny in Madrid. But most of them knew about it anyway, I suppose.' She stared at the coffee table. 'You couldn't stand the guy, Prim, any more than I could. Did you hate me that much, that you let him . . . into you?'

Her face flushed again; I thought I could feel her shaking, beside me on the couch. 'Yes,' she yelled, silence-shattering.

'At the time I did. You were such a calm, cruel bastard when you told me you were leaving me for Jan; cunning too, the way that you seized on my friendship with Davidoff as a counterweight for your conscience . . . if you had one at all.'

'A bit more than friendship, I remember. You told me so yourself, in some detail; about the two of you. "He was my lover", I recall you saying, only a few days ago.'

'No, it wasn't!' she snapped at me. 'It couldn't have been any more than it was.'

'If he could have, you would have.'

'No! Oz, he was very special, to you too. And he was very sad, and very old. It was nowhere near the same as you and Jan. You just chucked me to one side and you went back to her. Not out of the blue either. I knew that you'd got together again in Edinburgh before that, when you went back on business.'

She paused. 'You were pretty late admitting that too. And you didn't

171

have to anyway; I knew for sure at the time, as I told you.

'I found a credit card slip, from Laing the Jeweller. A gold necklet, as I remember.' She laughed, short and shrill. 'I actually thought you were going to surprise me with it. Oh you surprised me all right. Too fucking right I hated you! Too fucking right I had Steve Miller!

'Good old Steve. "I say," ' she mimicked. ' "One size fits all." '

'What?'

'That's what he used to say; when we were in Madrid. "One size fits all!" It was a sort of a war-cry with him, as he was struggling into his condoms . . . Not that he was talking about them. God, he's so crass, and God how you deserved it.'

'Fine,' I said. 'But did he?'

'What do you mean? I'll bet I'm the best lay he ever had.'

'I wonder if he'd think you were worth it now?'

She frowned at me, her anger turned to fear. 'Why? What have you done?'

'Less than I might have at another time. I might have done a hell of a lot more than just spread his nose all over his face. I told you, he was mouthing off at the Society do yesterday. Of course I let him have it.'

'Stupid bastard!'

'Who? Him, or me?'

'Both of you!'

'No. All three of us, you included. If you had told me, Prim, I'd have understood. I might have said that you'd dropped your knickers to spite your face, so to speak, but I'd have understood. Yet you didn't, even though you had going on two years to bring it up. At first you even made a point of telling me you hadn't been with anyone after me. Then you sort of let it slip that there had been one casual thing. Fine; that didn't bother me.

'Then we get married, come back here on honeymoon, and I find out that it was more than casual. You will agree that living together and making a baby is more than casual, will you? Still, I understood; I felt as guilty as sin, in fact.

'But now, I find out about Steve Miller, not from you at all, but from the local grapevine and from him. Too right I filled him in, and you can blame yourself for that just as much as me. You set him up for it by not telling me, just as much as he did himself.'

'So much for your understanding then,' she murmured, bitterly. 'You found out and you battered him.'

'But that's my whole point!' I yelled at her, shoving myself up from the couch. 'I didn't find out from you! You even let us get married without telling me.'

'And if I had?'

'It would have made no difference. I might even have admired you, in a strange way.'

'Now?'

'Now, nothing. It's none of my business, just as it never was. Yes, I was mad when I found out, but I took that out on Miller's nose. End of story.'

I looked down at her. 'It is the end of the story, isn't it?' I asked, quietly. 'There's nothing else I might hear around the pool at someone else's party?'

She shook her head and said, 'No.'

If she'd come out with everything then, I think I'd have told her about Susie, to clear all the decks. But she didn't, so I didn't, and I let it go at that, for that time. Life can be a bit of a poker game, you know. It might be against the rules, but it's always comforting to know that you have an ace up your sleeve.

She stood up, and came to me. She took my hands in hers and laid her forehead on my chest. 'I'm sorry,' she whispered. 'I'm also very tired. I didn't sleep at all on that flight; Nicky Johnson talked non-stop all the way across the US, and all the way across the bloody Atlantic. Can I go to bed?'

'Sure you can,' I said, 'once I make it up. I took the sheets off to be washed. Have yourself a drink, while I go and do that.'

She nodded and headed off towards the kitchen. I trotted upstairs and found a fresh fitted sheet from the linen cupboard; to be on the safe side, I changed the duvet cover as well. The room smelled fresh enough, but I raised the shutter and opened the window slightly, just to be on the even safer side.

When I went downstairs, Prim was on the couch once more. She was asleep, and the gin and tonic which she held was about to slip from her fingers. I took it from her, put it on the table and picked her up. As I carried her to bed it occurred to me that I had hefted enough weight up those stairs over the last few days for it to be classed as part of my work-out programme.

I turned back the duvet on Prim's side of the bed, laid her down and undressed her. As I tossed her knickers on to the pile of clothing on the floor, she came half awake. 'Get in?' she murmured, half request, half question. I realised that I was tired too.

I hadn't been sure of the time we'd gone to sleep, but when I came

173

back to the surface, it was just after five in the evening. The fresh air from the open window was overcoming the heating, and the room felt chilly. I got up to close it, then wakened Prim, not wanting her to sleep so long that she'd be awake all night.

She smiled at me, and I felt sorry about our confrontation. I couldn't have handled it worse, and I knew it. 'Hi,' she whispered. 'How are things?'

'My thing's fine. How's your thing?'

She laughed and opened her arms to me. 'Missing your thing. Come here.'

I had been half afraid that it would have been different; it wasn't. Well it was, different from Susie, that is, but I forced myself to look on her as a closed chapter in my life. With Prim it was as good as ever, with maybe, even, an added touch of wickedness. 'One size fits all, indeed,' I whispered in her ear as I thrust into her. 'Poor bastard, that's all he knows.'

We showered together and dressed, then realised how hungry we were. I made a sandwich to keep us going, we watched some television, then at around eight we drove into L'Escala for a pizza in La Dolce Vita, up there in a window seat watching the traffic. We had just been presented with two pizza sorpresas when Prim glanced outside, then did a double take. I followed her eyes and saw that she was looking at a Lotus Elise with British plates, its top open even in January. The driver was jammed behind the wheel, wearing a heavy jacket, and distinguishable by a white plaster over his nose. I didn't know whether he had seen us or not, but, sure as hell, I didn't wave.

'Just think,' I said, with a certain amount of acid in my tone, but not enough to spoil the taste of the pizzas, 'if you had played your cards right, all that could have been yours.'

'I'll stick to the Mercedes, thanks,' my wife replied, with a smile which made me decide that whatever I knew about her, I would do my best to forget it.

'It's a pity about Susie,' she murmured, a little later, after we had found and dealt with the surprises in our pizzas. 'I'd have liked to have seen her. Just why did she go home, Oz?'

I was sure that the question was completely straight; that no suspicion lay behind it.

'I told you, she felt awkward. After the thing with Miller yesterday, she got scared that people might start to gossip about us.'

'You took her to the party?'

'Of course. We had dinner at Shirley's on Friday; she suggested it.'

'I'm not surprised she went, then, after what you did to poor Steve.'

I frowned at her, not in jest at all, even if she thought it was. 'You call him poor Steve again and you and I will have another row. I was protecting your tattered reputation, remember.'

She made a face at me; just like the old times. 'Thank you, sir. But what did Susie say?'

'Nothing. She was a bit surprised that good old Oz could have done such a thing, and that I was so good with the head; but then, I've been coached by professionals.

'Actually, there was another reason why she went home. It has to do with a piece of business out here that's gone sour on her.' I filled her in on the Castelgolf fiasco, and on its resolution. Naturally, I said nothing about her other misadventure.

'That's terrible,' Prim exclaimed. 'Two million down the toilet!'

'Probably so. They might trace the money, but it's touch and go. The man Fowler will be under deep cover by now; they've more chance of finding Lord Lucan than him.'

'I'm really surprised,' she said. 'I wouldn't have thought that Susie'd have fallen for a scam like that.'

'Both her partners were heavy hitters, apparently. I think that helped to persuade her. Anyway, it was an investment; some pay off, others crash. As for the amount, it would be a disaster to you and me, but not to her. She's still rolling in it.'

'That's good, at least.' She paused. 'How is she, though, Oz? Is she still broken up about Mike?'

'She's better now,' I told her, truthfully. 'She's got herself a new goal in life. She's made it in business, now she's after a titled husband to help her climb the social ladder.'

Prim looked at me, incredulous. 'Susie said that?'

'Yup.'

'That'll be the day. Susie Gantry's a Glasgow girl through and through, and proud of it. The idea of her in the drawing rooms of Mayfair . . . No, she had to be kidding you.'

'I don't think so. Susie's out for herself now; she's through with sharing. She wants a husband only as a necessary part of having a couple of kids. When she goes shopping for one it'll be in Harrods, not M&S, and there are plenty of ex-hereditaries around with an eye to the main chance, now that they can't hang around the House of Lords, drawing money for the privilege of being privileged.'

'I'll believe that when I see it.' She paused as a waiter brought two cappuccinos. It was a different bloke from the guy who had served us until then. I recognised him; I hadn't seen him in La Dolce Vita before, but he had come up in conversation at Shirley's a couple of nights before. He gave Prim what was meant to be a knowing smile. She frosted him out, completely.

'Change of subject,' she said briskly, as if he had never been there. 'My brother-in-law said I should ask you how you're getting on with that script. Next month is drawing nearer, my darling, when you learn to become a real actor.'

What the hell does she think I am now? I wondered.

28

Prim was up and about before me next morning. Her half of the bed was empty, not even warm, when I awoke. I rose and stumbled downstairs a few minutes later, showered but unshaven . . . I had decided that if I was an actor, then I might as well look like one.

As I shambled into the kitchen, in search of cornflakes and coffee, I heard the phone being replaced.

'Who was that?' I asked Prim.

She gave me a slightly guilty look. 'I phoned Veronique,' she admitted. 'I wanted to know how your girl was.'

'You didn't suggest that she give her a job did you?'

'No I did not. If you must know, I thought I'd quite like to meet her. I'm too late though. You'll be pleased to hear that Ramon's taking her down to Barcelona this morning. The Filipinos have arranged her return home.'

I was mildly surprised. 'That was quick,' I said as Prim vanished through to the living area. 'I thought it would have taken a week at least, not forty-eight hours.'

I filled the percolator, put it on the hob and filled a couple of bowls with cereal. Then, as soon as the coffee was ready, I poured two mugs, put the lot on a tray, with a large jug of milk and carried it through.

Prim was sitting on the smaller of the two sofas, with her back to me as I came into the big room. I put the tray on the coffee table, 'Dig in,' I said, glancing at her. She looked back at me with narrowed eyes. Her mouth was a slit. I had never seen her face like that before, never in my life. Then I saw the envelope on the floor; A4 brown manila, with 'Prim', printed on the outside in big, bold letters.

She was leaning forward slightly, obscuring the papers on her lap. Then she seized them and thrust them at me, furiously. I took them from her.

They were photographs; of me, and of Susie Gantry. The first had a matt finish, and I guessed it had been taken by a digital camera then run off from a computer through a colour printer. It showed the two of us, in Roser Dos; Susie was holding my left hand to her lips, kissing it lightly. The second had been processed conventionally. It had been taken with a telephoto lens at Barcelona Airport, a perfect candid shot of our last goodbye kiss.

'You weren't kidding, were you?' Prim hissed. 'I asked you what you and she had done, and you told me you'd shagged each other senseless. You weren't kidding, were you, you fucking horrible bastard?'

I thought, as I stood there looking at the prints, of many things; of Susie and me, of Prim and me in the good times, of the sneaky bastard who had taken the things and was going to pay for them in broken bones, and, most urgently, of how I could cool the situation.

'Come on, they're not what they seem. They're just innocent gestures between good friends,' was certainly an option. But all that it would have bought me was whatever time it took for Prim to confront Susie.

So I confessed. 'No, I wasn't. Things happened.'

I told her how it had all come about, after Susie's near-calamity on the stairs. 'She was frightened,' I said. 'She thought she'd been sleepwalking. So did I at that point; it was only afterwards that I realised what had really happened, that someone had broken in and thrown her down there.

'So I stayed with her, till she settled down. I fell asleep and . . . Like I said, things happened.'

'Rubbish,' Prim snarled. 'Even if that far-fetched crap is true, which I doubt, it's quite obvious to me what happened; the conniving little bitch thought you'd chuck her out if she just came on to you, so she staged a sham at the foot of the stairs.'

'No!' I protested. 'When she went to bed she was too drunk to come on to anyone. I just dumped her on the bed and left her there. She didn't stage anything. She had bruising on her arms where she'd been picked up and carried; not by me either, I promise you.'

'Your promises are worth shit. These things that happened . . . just the once, was it?'

'No. It might have been, but things changed.'

'Sure, things changed. You found that she was a good fuck, that's what changed. Or did good old Oz feel sorry for her, and think that good old Prim wouldn't mind her borrowing your services for the weekend?'

It was time to reach up my sleeve and produce my card. 'There is no good old Oz,' I shot back at her. 'There never was, any more than there's a good old Prim. We're just a couple of yuppies with false glossy fronts.

'You've lied to me since we've been here, Primavera. You gave me your version of your affair with Fortunato, but it wasn't bloody true, was it?'

I saw the blood rush to her cheeks. 'Who told you that? Susie?'

'Susie thought that you'd told me. She went out of her way not to shop you, my dear. It doesn't matter how I found out, you told me the opposite of the truth, didn't you? You wanted to have the copper's kid; it was Fortunato who wouldn't hear of it. He did a runner back to his wife and set the abortion up without even asking you. What do you suppose he'd have done if you'd refused to go through with it?'

'How could I,' she exclaimed, 'in those circumstances?'

'The same way that many other women do. It would have been called a love child, I guess, and you'd have been called a single parent. Look around, you'll see plenty of them.

'But sure, your body, your decision, your right. So why did you lie to me? Know what I think? I reckon that when I turned up, just after it had happened, and when I found myself suddenly single again, you saw me as an easy option. But you were afraid that if I knew the truth, any part of it, I might have walked away.'

She started to yell something back at me, but I stopped her.

'Does that sound conceited? Sorry, but tell me that I've got it wrong.'

She answered me with silence.

'As it happens, I found out about it by accident, on Friday night. You must have been mad to think that I wouldn't, eventually. Then I got a bit shifty, and I found out about Steve bloody Miller. You know what that led to; you've seen the damage.'

'And that excuses you, does it?' she shouted. She was on her feet now, in my face.

'I'm not making excuses. I was angry, Susie was here and at the time I fancied her as much as she fancied me. That's it.

'But you know what? I'm still fucking angry, not about what you did then, but the fact that you can't even be honest with me now. You lied to me last night, even, when I asked you if Miller was the end of it. How do you think I felt in that bloody restaurant when a waiter came to our table, and I had to look at him knowing that he'd fucked my wife?'

Prim gasped.

'Don't say anything,' I said. 'If I'd doubted it, the way he smirked at you and the way you chilled him out was enough to confirm it.

'And how many more, eh? What about the lad from St Albans, and the racing driver from Sussex?'

'Who's been . . .? Shirley.'

179

'I let her think you'd told me. She assumed that you would have, and she said that it served me right. At the time, I'm sure it did, but the lies that have followed since we've been here, I didn't deserve those, honey. When we married, I thought you were a princess, Cinder-bloody-ella, no less. I don't mind you not being perfect, but I do mind you conning me into thinking that you were.'

I stopped and took a deep breath. 'Right. Now you let me have it.'

She shook her head. 'No. You really don't want me to do that.'

'Sure I do,' I said bitterly, 'go on.'

'If you insist. When you left me and went back to marry your ac/dc childhood sweetheart I thought you were the lowest of the low. I felt defiled, especially when I found out that you'd been with her and then come back and been with me. So I reacted by behaving like the slut you'd made me feel. I had Miller, I had Fredo, the waiter, I had those other two and a few more that Shirley never knew about.

'Then Ramon came along, and for a while he was different. I fell in love with him and he moved in with me. Yes, I did think I was Cinderella. When I became pregnant by him, I'd never been happier. Yes, it was a real fairy tale, sure enough.

'He was so delighted that he left me, just like that. When he told me I was having an abortion and that he'd fixed it, I felt like topping myself.

'I didn't though; I got rid of it, as he demanded.

'Afterwards, I might have gone back to being a slag, but I was too bruised even for that. Not long afterwards, I saw an ad on telly for some silly wrestling circus; and there you were, right in the middle of it. All of a sudden it came to me that I didn't hate you after all. I had been very, very angry, and very, very hurt, but somehow, Ramon had put that into perspective. So I bought a ticket and I went to your show in Barcelona, and like you just said . . . things happened.

'Yes, I kept my mouth shut about my life in between times. And yes, if it gives you any satisfaction, you nailed the reason, right on the head.'

Prim grabbed the prints back from me and crushed them in her hand, waving them in the air. 'But now, you bastard, you've done it again. You've been with her and you've come back to me and I feel defiled all over again. Did you even bother to wash it this time?'

She hit me, punched me in the chest, once, twice, three times, over and over again, not hurtful blows, more gestures of frustration and anger. 'Why couldn't you have been good old Oz, after all?' she moaned. 'Not the horrible shit you are.'

I shrugged. 'Because, as I told you before, I never was. I was just another crafty little bastard on the make, a horrible shit, if you like. Susie showed me that much.' I held her arms and pinned them by her side, my temper cooled by the tears running down her cheeks.

'So you know my secrets and I know yours. I slept with Susie, and before that with Jan, before I went back to her, even. And you were indeed the village bike, as you put it recently, and then you came back to me on the rebound from the nice police captain. Tell me, then: what do we do, now that we know we're not Mr and Mrs Perfect?'

'Are you going to leave me for Susie?' she asked.

'Of course not, you're my wife. Are you going to leave me for Ramon?'

She shook her head, briefly and violently. 'No,' she muttered.

'Even if that was possible?'

'No. Not even if.'

I chanced a smile. 'How about "One size fits all"? Him maybe?'

She gave a spluttering, laugh, snorted, then sniffed. 'I'd rather drill holes in my feet,' she said.

'Look, I am sorry,' I told her, 'but I'm not going to throw myself on the ground before you and beg forgiveness. I can't do that. I didn't set out to even scores, but that's how it stands. Call me a heartless bastard if you like.'

'You're a heartless bastard.'

'Okay. I admit it. Do you want to go on?'

'Do you?'

'Sure, for better or worse. That's what I said.'

Her mouth took on that tight look again. 'From where I'm standing it's still me who's come off worse. Oz, I'm not saying I'm going to leave you, but I need some space to think about all this. I'm going to go down to Barcelona for a few days ... On my own,' she said. 'Fair enough?'

'Eminently.'

'What will you do while I'm away? Call Susie?'

'No, I won't do that. I'll think about us as well, I'll get on with learning that script and, in the spare time I have left, I'll see if I can figure out who might have chucked Susie down those stairs.'

'If you find him,' she said, 'tell him from me he did a rotten job.'

'Hey!'

'Don't "hey" me, Oz. I promise you this. Whatever happens with us, Ms Gantry will be a poor little rich girl when I catch up with her.'

29

I booked Prim a suite for the next five days in the Husa Princesa in Barcelona, and loaded her cases into the Mercedes. She didn't kiss me goodbye, and I didn't wave her off either.

As soon as she had left, I changed into a tee-shirt and shorts and went into my makeshift gym, where I spent half an hour pressing weights and another twenty minutes knocking ten bells out of the heavy punchbag. When I was finished, I went upstairs to take my second shower of the morning. None of it did me any good. As I stood there in the shower turning the mixer colder and colder to stem the sweat that was pouring out of me, it came to me that I was alone, not like I had felt after the family had gone, but really alone, for the first time since just after Jan died.

I dressed again, but I gave no thought to getting down to the script or anything else. Before I did that there was something else I had to do; and for that there was something else I needed. I looked through my copy of the Catalan Society magazine, but that did me no good. I thought about phoning Shirley, but decided against that, because I didn't want to get into a discussion with her just then.

In the end, I phoned Lionell. He gave me the information I was after and, to my relief, he didn't ask any questions.

I found Steve Miller's parents' villa easily enough, in a narrow street in Riells de D'Alt, where most of the houses are holiday homes. The little Lotus was parked in the driveway, with its rag-top up.

There was no preamble, no discussion. I rang the bell, he opened the door and I hit him; in the middle of the forehead, not directly on his broken nose, but close enough to make him scream in agony as he fell to the floor.

I took the crumpled photos from my jacket pocket and tossed them down beside them. 'Did you really think that you could get away with sending those to Prim?' I barked at him.

He was dazed and his eyes were unfocused, but eventually his head began to clear and he picked up the prints. He gazed at them, blankly.

'Don't know anything about them,' he protested, his voice thick.

'Sure you do, Steve. You spotted Susie and me in that restaurant and you photographed us. I clocked you then, but I couldn't catch you. Then you had the idea of hanging around the house to see if you could get some really incriminating stuff. We left for Barcelona, you followed us, and you took that other one at the airport.

'Great, thinks you. I'll slip copies of these to Prim and that bastard Blackstone will be really in it. Congratulations, mate, I am, but so are you. Oh, how deeply you are in the shit!'

Miller looked up at me. 'I didn't take these,' he squealed. 'They've got nothing to do with me.'

'Of course they have. Prim only got back yesterday morning, but she was a couple of days early; nobody knew about it. But you saw us last night, sitting in the window of La Dolce Vita. You knew she was home.'

'Oz, I swear on my mother's grave . . .'

'Your mother isn't bloody dead!'

'All right, I swear to you on the grave of somebody who is. My grandmother, I'll swear on her grave, I didn't take those photographs.' I reckoned he had a deal more swearing to do, though, before I started to believe him.

'When were they taken?' he asked.

'You know damn well.'

'Tell me.'

'The Roser Dos shot was taken on Saturday night, the other one, yesterday morning.'

A huge smile of relief crossed his broken face. 'Then I couldn't have done it. I was on the golf course yesterday, with Frank, Gerrie and Maggie. We played a foursome at the Torremirona Country Club, up past Figueras. Ask them; they'll tell you I couldn't have been in Barcelona.'

Still I didn't buy it; I suppose I wanted him to be the one, I wanted to punish someone and he was the easiest to fit in the frame.

'So someone else took the second shot. So what? You got a pal to tail us and take it.'

He stared up at me. There was a lump the size of a pigeon's egg above his left eye. 'Oz,' he said, in a sad voice that I just couldn't doubt, 'I don't have any pals.'

I helped him up, the poor hopeless sod, sat him on his parents' couch, stepped into the open-plan kitchen and made us two mugs of coffee. It turned out to be a foul own brand instant, but I didn't care. Steve didn't either; he was still slightly stunned, from my big righthander.

'I'm sorry I shot my mouth off on Saturday, Oz,' he mumbled. 'Not very gentlemanly, was it? Not very clever either. My father's told me often enough that I'd get myself really done over some day.'

I was relieved to find that the new model Oz Blackstone still had a conscience, of sorts. 'It's you who's due the apology, mate,' I told him. 'Not just from me either. Prim owes you one as well; she worked you over worse than I did.'

He looked at me. 'Mmm,' he murmured. 'Truth is, I guessed that when she agreed to come to Madrid with me, your leaving had a lot to do with it. Still, I hope you won't thump me again if I say that one doesn't look a gift horse, and all that. Good for any chap's morale, when he lands a lovely like her, whatever the story.'

I tried to think back to a time when I had morale; it was difficult. Success doesn't mean anything unless you feel it inside yourself. There was I, my name on billboards all over the States, and soon to be all over Europe too, and inside I felt like shit.

'I'll push my luck a bit further, shall I?' Steve went on. He must have guessed that I was no longer dangerous by that time. 'What possessed you to take a chance like that? I mean, old boy, be sure your sins will find you out, and all that.'

'They sure will,' I agreed. 'As to what possessed me . . . apart from the obvious . . . that I have to figure out. There's only ever really been one woman for me, Steve, and I even messed her about too. Now she's dead, and I can't tell her I'm sorry.

'As for Prim, she and I got back together and got married because each of us thought that the other was a safe port in a storm. For different reasons, both of us were wrong.'

'I take it that she's gone, because of those photos, and that's why you came knocking my door down.'

'Yeah, she's gone, and I don't know whether she's coming back.'

I've never been one for self-pity; I'm like my dad in that respect. I don't wallow in it, I turn it into anger.

'I do know one thing, though,' I said, sincerely. 'I am going to find the bastard who took those pictures, and when I do . . .

'Sure, it's my own fault, I've been caught at the naughties. But I don't care about that; when I find whoever it was shopped me, I'll fucking well kill him . . . Or at least, by the time I'm finished he'll wish I had.'

'Will that make you feel better?' Steve asked me.

'No,' I answered, 'but it'll make him feel worse than I do, and that's important to me.'

185

I left him there, the poor, battered Proton salesman, and headed back home. I stopped for petrol on the way, and was just leaving the *gasolinera* when my mobile phone sounded. I pulled into the car park of the furniture store across the road and answered the call. I found myself hoping that it was Prim, telling me that she had turned the Mercedes around and was coming back, but it wasn't. It was my Other Woman.

'Hi,' said Susie cheerily. 'I'm in the office, and I've just dictated a letter to you, inviting you to become a director of the Gantry Group. Today's a no-lunch day, so I thought I'd give you a call and see how you're doing on your own.'

'Not very well,' I answered. 'Not very fucking well at all.' I told her about Prim's early return and about what had happened that morning. When I was finished, she was silent for what seemed like quite a while.

'Oh dear,' she sighed at last. 'I must have been crazy to assume that she'd never find out. She'll be after my blood, I suppose.'

'Several pints of it. The least you can expect is a fairly ferocious phone call,' I admitted. 'I guess I should have called you, to warn you, but the red mist came down. As a result, I'm just on my way back from making a fool of myself yet again.'

'How?'

'Miller. I assumed it was him and I went to his place to give him another doing. It wasn't.'

'So who did take the photos?'

'I haven't a bloody clue, Susie; not yet, at any rate.'

'Don't go overboard when you find him, Oz. Promise me that.'

'I'm promising nothing any more. Promises just get you into bother.'

'What about the one you made to me? About looking out for me?'

I had actually thought about that. 'That still stands, whether Prim comes back or not. I gave you my word.'

'Listen,' she said. 'I really am sorry. I never meant to mess things up between you two.'

'What would you do differently in the same circumstances?' I fired at her.

'Nothing.'

'Me neither.'

'Do you want to come over here?' she asked.

'No. We've been over that, and you were right.'

'What about the new movie? What happens if Prim doesn't come back, and tells Dawn and Miles why?'

'Right now, I don't give one damn. But we're contracted, Miles and I, for one more picture at least, and he has an option on me for the one after that.'

'Will she come back?'

'I don't know.'

'Do you want her to?'

I had been thinking about that, on and off, from the moment her car turned out of the driveway. 'Susie,' I replied, 'you made it pretty clear that I've been misusing women all my adult life. I've got to start being honest with someone.'

'Be honest with me, then. If Prim did leave, and I turned up again, would you throw me out?'

'I . . . Oh shit, I don't know. I'll tell you one thing, though; I wouldn't have any bloody illusions about you.'

Susie gave the short, brittle laugh that was one of her trademarks. 'Now there's a fine basis for a relationship. Oz, don't be an idiot any longer than you have to; get your arse down the road to Barcelona and ask her to come back home. Even if a wee bit of begging's called for as well. What's the name of her hotel?'

'The Husa Princesa. Why?'

'Because I'm going to phone her, take my punishment like a big girl, and apologise for my part in messing up your nice, yuppie, beautiful people future.'

'She probably won't speak to you,' I warned.

'Oh she will. She'll speak to me all right. It'll take me a while to get a word in, but when I do I'll tell her the truth, that when a couple of self-indulgent schemers like you and me are left alone under the same roof, by accident or design, then sparks are bound to fly.'

A recollection came to me. 'And she did tell me not to put you in a hotel, I recall.'

'That's better!' Susie exclaimed. 'You're sounding like your real self again; conniving, crafty and quick on your feet.'

'Just like you?'

'Absolutely. By the time we're finished, the pair of us, she'll be apologising to you because her mother got cancer.' She giggled.

'If I thought you really meant all that,' I murmured into the phone, 'you would terrify me. Happily, I know that most of it's just front.'

I heard her take a deep breath. 'I'm glad you said that; I really am. I can take anyone else thinking I'm nothing but a brassy wee cow, but not you.

'Oz, Prim's a good woman who had a hard time and didn't deserve

187

another. Yet I've given her one, and as a lady who's been hurt herself, and knows what it's like, the truth is that I'm just a tiny bit ashamed of myself. And so, when you've run out of ways to justify yourself, will you be.'

Deep in my heart of hearts, I wished that I could agree with her . . . but I didn't tell her that. 'Go on then,' I said. 'If you're serious about calling her, do it. Just don't take all the blame on yourself.'

'Oz Blackstone,' she gasped. 'You are some piece of work. As if I would!'

I could feel her hair against my face as she spoke, catch her fragrance, taste her lips. 'That's good,' I laughed, 'because neither will I.'

It would be wrong to say that I was preoccupied as I drove home. I knew that Susie was right and that there was a case for contrition, but I hesitated. I knew that I was a degree-level, out of the closet, male chauvinist pig, and I had my doubts about whether I could pull it off. I once heard a famous comedian say that when you can fake sincerity, you've cracked it. He got a laugh, but I knew that he was serious. Budding actor or not, I doubted whether I was in his class.

The garage looked enormous as I drove into it. Even with the Voyager in it, there was still a big aching void where the Mercedes had stood. I had grown to love that car.

I went in through the back door for the second time that day, disabling the alarm, and wandered through to the living room. The envelope in which those damned photographs had been delivered still lay on the floor where Prim had dropped it. I picked it up and looked at it, in a vain attempt, I suppose to find something familiar in the way the letters P. R. I. M. were printed. Nothing did. A name scrawled in ballpoint, that was all I saw. I wandered back to the kitchen, to get myself a beer and to think about fixing myself something to eat.

The tray lay on the work-surface; the one which I had used to carry our breakfast through to the lounge, before our world blew up, and on which I had carried it back afterwards. The cereal was still in its bowls, the milk was curdling in its jug, the coffee was cold in the pot, and the two mugs stood empty waiting for it to be poured.

I sighed and then I frowned. The mugs didn't match. I picked them up, one in each hand and looked at them closely. They didn't match.

We all have our characteristics, every one of us; mannerisms, habits, phrases we use to flag up and emphasise meaningful statements. 'To be honest with you . . .' is one of my stepmother's, and it's meaningless, because she always is.

One of my peculiarities is symmetry; I like things to match whenever

188

possible, to the point that I'm obsessive about it. I've been known to spend half an hour with a pile of black socks from the tumble dryer sorting them into absolutely identical pairs . . . As if one black sock is any different from another as far as your feet are concerned.

So, when I had loaded the breakfast tray that morning, naturally I had picked out, from the crockery and cutlery which we had inherited with the house, two identical bowls, yellow, to go with the milk jug, two matching spoons carefully picked out from among the odds and sods in the drawer, and two blue mugs with raised square markings.

The mugs which I held in my hand were both blue, but the ridges on one were round, rather than square. I put them back on the tray, then opened the wall cabinet and looked inside. When we had done a kitchen inventory we had found eight blue china mugs, made in Italy, four with square and four with circular contoured patterns. Only five remained in the cupboard, two square, and three round. I never had a moment's doubt that I had done my usual matching trick that morning, whatever else had been on my mind, but I checked in the dishwasher just in case. It was empty. I had hand-washed the breakfast dishes that Susie and I had used the day before, and everything since. I pulled out the slide-away rubbish bin and looked in that. It contained a couple of blackened banana skins, and nothing else.

I looked again, and I was certain. While I had been out on my abortive mission of revenge against the innocent Steve Miller, someone had been in the house. I dropped to my knees and peered at the kitchen floor. It was tiled, a deep terra-cotta shade which made it difficult to spot crumbs and other fragments, but I started to go over every inch, until I found what I was looking for; a sliver of broken china, bone white with a blue glaze.

I knew I hadn't broken anything. I knew that Prim hadn't. I knew beyond any self-doubt that when I had opened that cabinet in the morning there had been eight mugs inside. Someone had been in the house, someone in enough of a rush to have knocked a mug off the work-surface to smash on the floor. The damage done, that person had replaced it with another from the cabinet, cleaned up the fragments, or as many of them as he could see against that dark-coloured floor, and taken them away with him to cover his tracks. Tough on him that he was dealing with an obsessive in the midst of a very bad day.

He? I thought. It had to be; had to be the same person who had broken in and attacked Susie, and no woman had done that. The size of the hands that had left those marks on her arms had told me that for sure.

'How?' I asked myself, aloud. That was an easy one; he had to have come in by the back door, through which I had left when I had gone off in my rage in search of Miller. The windows were all secure and the front door was bolted. 'Did I lock it?' Yes, I had, and I had set the alarm. So the intruder had picked the lock again and had switched off the alarm again, at the panel by the door. This time, undisturbed, he had had time to set the alarm on the way out, and to lock the door behind him.

'Can you do that?' I asked myself again. 'Can you unpick a lock?' I didn't know the answer to that, but if it was 'No,' it led to only one conclusion, and a very disturbing one at that: my visitor had a key.

I went out to the back door once again, knelt down and looked at the lock on the outside, searching for scrapes, scores, scratches in its bright brass facing. It was unmarked. 'Change this son of a bitch right away,' I muttered as I walked back into the house.

'Now just hold on, Oz, hold on. Think this through.' I was talking to myself, but I'm my favourite audience; that's because I'm never heckled, as sometimes I have been at GWA shows. I remembered why I'd come into the kitchen in the first place, so I took a beer from the fridge, uncapped it and strolled back through to the living room. As I settled on to the couch, the phone rang, but I let it go unanswered. I didn't want to speak to anyone just then.

'What's happened here?' I asked myself.

One, someone took a shot at me in Capulet's Lada.

Two, someone broke into the house, grabbed Susie from her bed and threw her down the stairs.

Three, someone sent Prim compromising photos of Susie and me. Not Steve Miller; who?

Four, someone broke into the house as soon as I went out; maybe someone with a key.

'Why Oz, why?' I said, aloud once more.

What if Susie had been killed by that fall? I'd have been arrested, sure as God made wee green apples.

What if I'm wrong about an enemy of Capulet shooting at the car, thinking that it was him. Maybe he knew it was me all along and thought he could scare me out of town.

Why would anyone want to break Prim and me up? Maybe, he didn't, or didn't care one way or the other. Maybe what he really wanted was just to get us out of the house.

Who might have a key to this place? The Frenchman, that's who. But why would he sell us the bloody house then try to get us out of it so that

*he could break in? Answer me that one, smartarse. No, you can't can
you?*

'No, I bloody can't,' I admitted to myself. 'The answer's in here, I'm
sure of it. There's something about this house. But as to how it all fits
together, and how, or even if, the body in the pool relates to it, there I
don't have a bloody clue.'

There was only one logical thing to be done at that point. I searched
the place, from top to bottom, looking for signs of the intruder, looking
to see if anything else was missing other than that one giveaway mug.
It took me three hours, and it was dark outside when I was finished.
While I was working, the phone rang three more times and my mobile
sounded twice. I ignored them all.

There wasn't a thing out of place. My passport was still there; my
chequebooks and the passbooks for our Spanish bank accounts in the
Caixa de Girona were still in the bedside drawer where I'd left them.
The bed itself was rumpled, just as we had left it that morning.

I looked in every cupboard, every wardrobe, and every drawer. I
checked the wall safe behind the mirror in our bedroom; it had come
with the house too. We had found it open and empty, and I had
programmed in my own combination. I kept some cash in there in
pesetas and sterling, some receipts given to us by the notary and by
Sergi when we had completed our purchase of the house, and a few
valuable jewellery items, like my white gold Piaget watch and Prim's
necklace; gifts which we had bought for each other when we were
married. They were still there, every item.

Nothing in the house was out of place as far as I could see; yet I
knew that he'd been there. I could sense it.

I walked out of our bedroom, wondering what he could have been
after, and whether he had finished searching for it. I was halfway
down the stairs when another question jumped up in my mind and bit
me.

*How did the guy know when he broke in that Susie wouldn't wake up
and scream the place down?*

'Because he'd seen her, son, that's why and possibly because he
knew she wasn't drunk, but drugged. Those two guys in JoJo's; the two
playing pool in the back room. Who the hell were they, and could one
of them have spiked her drink while I was in the bog?'

I tried to remember what had happened that night, and who they
were. Then I recalled that I had only seen one of them, a veteran
L'Escala anchovy fisherman called Miguel. When I'd gone into Jo's
unisex toilet, one of the two cubicles had been occupied. When I had

come out of the other one, it had been empty and the pool players had both been gone.

Suddenly, right at the top of my list of priorities was another visit to Bar JoJo.

I was thinking about that and about going out for something to eat when the phone rang once more. This time, I picked it up.

'Hi. You're back at last. I was beginning to think you were headed for Glasgow.' Prim sounded quiet and subdued, far from her normal breezy businesslike self.

'No. I'm still here; I just didn't feel like talking to anyone for a while, that's all.'

'You spoke to Susie, though. You told her where I was.'

'That was earlier, when I was out in the car. She called me to tell me she got home safe. I told her she didn't.'

'You told her right.'

'What did you say to her?'

'Nothing you'd want to hear.'

'And what did she say to you?'

'That it was all her fault, that it began by her taking shameless advantage of you, and that it all got out of hand after that.'

'That's not true. It wasn't all her fault.'

'I know that, for God's sake,' she snapped.

'Listen to me,' I said. 'I am truly sorry that I've hurt you, and so is Susie. But there's someone else to blame, to an extent.'

'You mean me?'

'No, I do not. I mean the person who took those photos and sent them to you. If it hadn't been for him, you'd never have been any the wiser, Susie and I would have had our little secret and that would have been that.'

She gasped. 'Oz, you incredible bastard! I don't blame him at all. I blame you and Susie Gantry; end of story. If you've made someone mad enough at you to do that, then it's down to you. Who do you think it was anyway?'

'I thought it was Miller, but I don't any more.'

She let out a small sound; it could have been a yelp. 'Oz, you didn't . . .'

'No, at least not much. He convinced me that he didn't do it.'

'So who do you think did?'

'I don't know, Prim,' I told her. 'But I'm certain it has something to do with this house. You maybe don't believe that someone broke in and chucked Susie downstairs, but it happened. Then today, after you'd gone and while I was off questioning Mr Miller, he broke in again: this time he searched the place.'

'Are you serious? Or is this some story you've cooked up to make me feel sorry for you.'

'I don't give a shit whether you feel sorry for me or not, my love. It's the truth. There is something in or about this house, and someone wants it.'

There was silence between us for a while. I could sense that she was working herself up to say, or ask something. It turned out to be both. 'Oz,' she exclaimed, finally, 'I don't think that me sitting down here brooding for a week is going to do either of us any good. Do you want me to come back?'

'Frankly,' I told her, 'I'd rather you stayed in Barcelona. Until I've got to the bottom of what's happening here, I'm not sure this place is safe. Give me a few days to sort it out.'

'Is that the real reason you want me to stay away?'

'Sure it is.' Actually I wasn't sure at all, but it was certainly a reason.

'Okay then; a few days. I'll stay for the five I've booked. If it gets too scary up there, you can always come down and join me.'

'Honey, the mood I'm in, it's me that's scary. I'm going to catch this bastard.'

'Why don't you tell Ramon? Ask for his help.'

I had to laugh at that one. 'First, unless it was in my interests, I wouldn't ask him for the time if he had an armful of Rolexes. Second, I'm not entirely certain that he isn't the guy I'm after.'

'Ramon?'

'Think about it. This guy has to have kept me under pretty close observation for the past few days. Who's more capable of that than a policeman?'

'No,' she protested, 'he wouldn't have attacked Susie. I don't believe it.'

'Why not? He fucked you over badly enough, and that's for sure. Or are you still in love with him just a bit?'

'No.' Her answer wasn't quite quick enough for my liking. 'But Oz, I know him too well to believe that of him.'

'Are you kidding me?' I asked her. 'If there's one thing we've both learned over the past few days it's that we never know anyone as well as we think; sometimes, not even ourselves. Your ex might not be at the top of my list, but believe me, he's on it.'

We called it quits at that, before we got angry with each other again.

30

It took a few minutes, but after Prim had hung up, I started to feel lonely. I gave some thought to what Susie had told me to do, and for a while I thought about getting into the car and driving down to Barcelona after all, leaving the bloody house to my mystery visitor.

I got over that urge by reminding myself that there was someone out there who had tried to kill Susie, and frame me for it. That got me sufficiently mad once more for me to forget everything else.

No way, I decided, was I going to be held a prisoner in my own home. Equally, if the bugger did come back, he was going to be warned off.

I had precious few leads, only one in fact, so I set out to run it down. But before I went out I took a couple of simple steps, just in case. First, I took the brown manila envelope and turned it over, found a marker pen on the drawer, and wrote on it, 'I am not a mug, but you do owe me one.' Then I went upstairs to our en suite bathroom and picked up a tin of talcum powder that Prim had left behind.

I left the note in the kitchen, on a work-surface, then headed for the back door. I didn't bother to set the alarm, instead I uncapped the powder and sprinkled it liberally on to the floor of the short entry corridor, backing towards the exit as I did so, to avoid marking my trap with my own footprints. When I was finished, I put the lid back on the tin and chucked it back inside.

That done, I locked up and headed into L'Escala to kill time by grabbing something to eat before JoJo opened her glass door at around ten thirty. I found a table in La Taverna de la Sal, just up from the town beach. It wasn't difficult; there was no one else in the place.

I had a Catalan salad and a steak, glancing up, as I ate, at a television above the bar. The Spanish football season was back in full swing after its holiday break, and one of the local channels was showing a review of all the weekend's matches. The presenter and the pundits were all speaking Catalan, but football is a universal language, so I understood what was going on.

Just about the only thing I miss about Edinburgh, apart from my loft, and the fun times I had there during my days as a swinging single bent on building up a track record, is the weekly kickabout which I had with a bunch of like-minded pals, including the unforgettable Ali the Grocer, who has to be the most foul-mouthed shopkeeper in Scotland.

My meal and the programme finished virtually simultaneously. There were a few minutes left until Jo's standard opening time but, rather than have another coffee, I paid my bill and strolled out on to the small beach-front. The night air was as sharp as you would expect in the second week in January, but there was no wind and the skies were as clear as they had been forty-eight hours earlier when I had stood not far from there with Susie.

The place was deserted; the Café del Mar was doing a little business, but its neighbour, La Caravel, seemed to be closed for winter refurbishment. I sat on the wall, looking out to sea and wondering what the fuck I was doing there, and how I had got myself into this mess. My cell phone sounded and I answered it, a touch impatiently.

It was Susie. 'Hello again. You don't mind me phoning, do you? If you can't talk just disconnect.'

'Oh, I can talk all right,' I assured her. 'Don't you worry about that.'

'Prim's still in Barcelona then?'

'Yes, and I'm sitting on the beach in L'Escala, staying angry with the bastard who's been setting me up for all this grief.' I told her about the missing mug, and the second break-in.

'Hey,' I asked her, as soon as the thought occurred to me, 'tell me something, if you can. Think back to last Thursday night when we were in the bar.'

'Okay.'

'Now tell me, can you remember anything about the drinks you had? How many, for openers?'

'Two brandies; big ones.'

'Did they both taste all right?'

She thought for a moment. 'Now you mention it . . .' she murmured, slowly. 'The first one was fine, very smooth in fact, like very good Cognac even though it was Spanish. But the second, when I sipped it, tasted just a wee bit sharp; which was odd, since the lady poured it from the same bottle as the first.

'That's it, though. My next memory, apart from you taking my boots off, is lying at the foot of the stairs in the buff, looking up at your baby blues.'

'After Jo poured it, did you drink it straightaway, or did you let it lie on the bar?' I felt as if I was back at my old job, interviewing witnesses for lawyer clients.

'No, it lay there for a bit. I know, because . . . That's right, one of the pool players, the younger one, came in to pay JoJo for his drinks. He got out his wallet and all his cards and stuff fell on the floor. I helped him pick them up.'

'Aye, and while you were doing that, he slipped something into your drink.'

'You think so?' Susie exclaimed.

'I'm bloody certain. Either he or the other guy did. Given the amount you'd had to drink, a simple sleeping powder would have done you in.'

'Well, it couldn't have been the older bloke. He was just coming through from the back room when the other fellow dropped his stuff. I remember seeing his feet when I was picking it up.'

'This first guy. What did he look like?'

'Let me think; tall, but then most men look tall to me, clean-shaven, wore glasses, dark hair, around thirty maybe.'

'Nationality?'

'I don't know. JoJo spoke Spanish to him, but he never said a word; not even thanks to me, just a wee nod when I handed him his stuff. Then he put a note on the bar and left without waiting for his change, as if he was in a hurry.'

'I guess he was.' Maybe because he didn't want me to see him.

'Wait a minute, Oz. If this guy spiked my drink, then broke in and tried to do me, and it was all planned and everything, how did he know we'd be at JoJo's in the first place?'

'Who says he did? He might just have seen his chance and taken it. But no; I think he must have spotted us together earlier on and followed us there. I think his real aim was to get rid of me, not you.'

'How?'

'By having me huckled off by the police for doing you in, or at least for trying to.'

The breath she took was so deep I heard it clearly down the phone.

'Oz. Get out of there now, please. You're starting to worry me. Go and patch it up with Prim in Barcelona; come to me, even, if that's what you want, but do something.'

'You think I'm cracking up?' I laughed.

'No, of course not, but you have had a hell of a time. I don't like the thought of you being there on your own.'

'It's the way I want it, and don't worry about me. Now, how are you?'

'I'm all right. I phoned Prim and she tore me to ribbons, but when we were finished, I sort of had the impression that she would go back home in a couple of days, once you've had time to stew in it.'

'That's okay by me. I don't want her here right now. Not till I get this sorted out.'

'You sure about that?'

'Yes, no. What the fuck.'

'Och, Oz honey, I'm sorry. I wish I'd stayed in Glasgow.'

'Do you really?'

'No. But now I've traded one care for another, and I don't know what's worse. Last week, I was worried about myself and tripping over my lack of self-esteem. You cured that, and no mistake, but there's been a trade. Now I'm worried about you. Take care of yourself, pretty boy. You've got too much going for you to chuck it all away. G'night now.'

'You too.'

Sometimes it's a hard life just being yourself, you know. After Susie's call, I sat there on the beach wall, still looking out to sea. Offshore, the lights from the small anchovy boats shone like fireflies as they bobbed on the surface of the untroubled Mediterranean.

Lucky bloody Mediterranean. My troubles were pressing down on me like the world on the shoulders of Atlas and, without knowing it, my weekend lover had just added another. I didn't know if I wanted Susie worrying about me, because that meant caring too and no way did I want that; I might feel obliged to care back, or to be really honest, and admit that I did already.

The ludicrous thing about the whole situation was that she was dead right about one thing she had said. Not many guys on the planet had more going for them than me right at that moment. Millionaire, movie actor, plenty of places still to go and the ruthlessness to make sure that I got to each and every one of them.

So why the hell was I getting myself involved in a dangerous situation into which I had stumbled by accident, and away from which I could walk without fear of retribution?

'So why am I, Jan?' I asked, out loud, my breath cloudy in the sharpness of the evening.

'Good question, Oz,' she answered. 'And you don't have an answer to it, my daft darlin' do you?'

'Not a good one, other than . . . It's a bit like sleeping with Susie; if

198

I hadn't, I know I'd have spent my life wondering, and probably regretting it.'

'But what if it has consequences that could follow you, looking over your shoulder for the rest of your life . . . just like sleeping with Susie?'

'What consequences could that have?'

'Time will tell. But what if . . .?'

'They can join the queue of Oz's secrets. The man in Geneva, Davidoff's tomb, Mike Dylan's death, the real Noosh Turkel story; it's getting crowded back there. I'd ask you to say hello to them, love, but I know they'll all be somewhere else.'

'Thank you for that, darlin'.'

'Do you think I'm going to wind up where you are, then?'

'Count on it. You'll always be where I am. I'll always be where you are.'

'But how can that be if I'm the heartless bastard that Susie showed me I am?'

'You're not. You're angry and hurt about what happened to me. You tried to hide from it by making Prim a substitute for me, just like she tried to make you a substitute for Ramon, and for another man in Perthshire, before she ever met you, before she went to Africa. Someone she never told you about . . . the reason she went to Africa, in fact.

'But you can only cure that sort of hurt one way: it's beyond all other forms of repair. I know, because I feel it too.'

'So what am I?'

'You're what you've been made into. When you were a boy you were artless and innocent, like Jonny. Then you became a self-indulgent young man, fulfilling your own desires, first and foremost. Then you found yourself again, and me.'

'How could you love someone like that?'

'Because I was someone like that. That's what Susie doesn't know. Artless like you as a child, then just as self-indulgent as a young adult. Until I rediscovered you, and myself. Then it was all cut short.'

'So what do I do?' I asked her, aloud again.

'You know what to do. Just don't hurt anyone . . . unless they deserve it.'

'And what if it's dangerous?'

'Then you might be with me sooner rather than later.' I'll swear I could hear her laugh, but it was bitter, unlike any I'd ever heard from her in life. *'What do you want me to say? "Live long and prosper, darlin'?"'*

'Just look out for Jonathan, that's all. Colin's like his mum, but look out for Jonny . . .'

And then the spell was broken and she was gone, into the night. I blinked and sat bolt upright on the wall, wakened from my dream. Yes, dream for sure, except . . .

I had to do it, there and then. I called the Husa Princesa in Barcelona. When they dialled her room, Prim answered on the fourth ring.

'Oz, what is it?' she murmured, huskily, as if she had been asleep. 'Are you all right?'

'I have no idea, love. I just want you to promise me something, that's all. Next time I see you, I want you to tell me about the man in Perthshire, before you went to work in Africa.'

There was a long silence, so long that I began to wonder whether she had hung up on me.

'You bastard,' she hissed. 'You've been interrogating my father. He and my mum are the only people you've ever met who know about him. Not even Dawn . . .'

'No!' I told her, trying to cut short her anger. 'I promise you I haven't spoken to Dave, or Elanore either. I can't tell you how I knew, not over the phone at least. I just did, that's all. But it's okay, Prim; no more blame, no more recrimination, I promise. Come home tomorrow, okay?'

'What?' Her voice could have engraved the word in granite. 'You've forgiven me for marrying you under false pretences, have you?'

'Put it this way. If you did, so did I. Let's just see what we can make of it, eh?'

'I'll see,' she whispered.

'Shit, check out of there right now and come home tonight.'

'No, we agreed earlier I'd stay here. I'll call you tomorrow, sometime or other. But now, just let me go back to sleep.'

She hung up and I stood up, my backside chilled by my stone wall seat. I remembered why I was still in L'Escala and headed for Bar JoJo.

It was open, of course; during my interlude everything else had shut down, but its light still burned like a campfire torch at the furthest oasis in the Sahara.

The Queen of the Night was at her station as always. Lionell was seated in a corner watching Sky News on the small television set. The only other customer, apart from a large black former tomcat, was perched on a stool at the bar, his broad shoulders hunched. I had recognised him even before he turned to eye me up and down and I saw the thick, grey-flecked beard.

'*Noches*,' Miguel grunted. I asked for a beer and, as JoJo was pouring it, sat on one of the available stools, near the heater.

'And a good evening to you,' I replied, in Castellano.

'What brings you here on this fine night?' Jo asked, as she topped off the head of my drink to a perfect depth. 'And on your own too. I don't ever remember seeing you without a lady.'

I gave her my best, gauche, John Hannah grin. 'I'm fresh out,' I said. 'My wife's in Barcelona.

'Actually, I'm trying to find someone,' I told her. 'Remember when I was in last Thursday night, with Susie? There was a guy here, and when he was at the bar he dropped all the cards and money out of his wallet. She helped him pick them up, but after he had gone, she found a ten thousand peseta note sticking to her shoe. We reckoned that it must have been his.

'D'you remember who he was?'

She shook her elegant head, slowly. 'No. I remember who you mean, but I don't know him. Never been in here before . . . and I'd know if 'e had.' She turned to Miguel. 'You were playing pool with him. You musht know who he was.'

The gentleman of the sea looked at her. 'Why should I?' he growled in Spanish. 'I was at the table alone and he came in and picked up a cue. He didn't even ask if I wanted to play, he just joined in. Then, after a while, he went into the lavatory, came out again and went away.'

'Yes,' said Jo, 'and he gave me a five thousand note for one beer and didn't wait for his change, just took his stuff from your Susie and shot out the door!'

'Do you know anything about him?' I asked Miguel.

He looked at me, sideways. 'Only that he was English, like you.'

'I'm Scottish, mate, not English.'

He treated me to his full frontal glare. 'Is all the same!' he barked.

201

31

For at least an hour after I woke next morning, I regretted becoming involved in a discussion of sub-national identities. It took a litre of Evian and a session on the weights before I felt anything like normal, and I don't think I'd even won the argument that Jocks are in just the same constitutional position as Catalans.

Still, I had been sober enough when I got home to remember to check my talcum powder burglar trap. It hadn't been sprung and my note was still there, untouched.

It was quarter to ten before I settled down to my script, sitting close to the phone in the living room, to be handy for Prim's call, whenever it came.

When I was at secondary school, I studied French and Spanish. For the first couple of years I found them difficult; but I stuck at it. (I didn't have any choice: my mother and my sister saw to that in their different ways.) Then about halfway through my third year, when I was fourteen, it just clicked. I looked at a piece of Spanish text one day, the words meant something and it all just fitted together. I never looked back after that. I scored 'A's in my Grade Highers, and for a brief period I thought about becoming a modern languages teacher, until the thought of a lifetime in the classroom chilled me to the bone.

I had a similar experience that morning. I sat down with the screenplay, closed my eyes and went through it from memory, scene by scene. I was almost at the end when the realisation came to me. I could do this thing: it wasn't beyond me. Indeed, even on my own in Spain I knew that I was making a passable job of delivering my lines. With coaching, and firm direction from Miles, I would be pretty good. For the very first time, I looked forward to getting back on to a sound stage, and to giving it my best shot. Apart from anything else, it would be a blessed relief from everything that had happened.

I had to tell someone. I realised that I hadn't spoken to my dad for a while, so I called him. I had lost track of the days, and almost forgotten that he still filled teeth for a living. I was lucky, though; I caught him between patients.

'Guess what,' I began, 'I think I'm an actor.'

'I could have told you that when you were four and I caught you dressing up in your sister's clothes and putting on your mother's make-up.'

I felt myself blush through my tan at the memory. 'Well, please, please don't tell anyone else.'

'That'll depend on how much the tabloids offer me. How's it going with you anyway? What's the news on Elanore Phillips? I've been meaning to call to ask you.'

'I'm in seclusion with my script, and that's going pretty well. As for Elanore, everyone's fingers are crossed, but the signs are still good. They think she might be all right.'

Mac the Dentist heaved a great sigh. 'Thank the Lord for that. My blood went cold when I heard about her; it brought your mother back, all of that awful time.' He paused. 'Is that what's been eating you?'

'What do you mean?'

'There's still something up with you, I can tell that. Is Prim still in America, is that it?'

'No, she came back on Sunday. Hitched a ride with a mate of Miles.'

'Let me speak to her then.'

'I can't; she's in Barcelona for a couple of days.'

I could almost see his eyes narrowing. 'Have you two had a fight?'

For a moment, I almost blurted out the whole story, but I kept myself in check. I didn't want him going back into the surgery and drilling a hole in some poor bastard's gum. 'Slightly,' I admitted. 'Let's just say I found out some stuff about her and she found out some stuff about me that puts neither of us in a good light in the eyes of the other.

'Dad,' I asked him suddenly, 'since I'm your son, and Mum's, how can I be a cruel, ruthless, self-centred bastard?'

'Who said that about you?'

'I did.'

'Hmphh. If it was anyone else, I'd batter the crap out of him. But since it's you . . . You're not cruel, Oz, or not knowingly so, at any rate. And you're not a bastard, I promise you. As for the rest, you can't help it. In truth, I envy you in a way. In the last few years you've gone from a state of sloth into one of restlessness; you've always got to be moving forward, doing something new.

'I think you're running away, son.'

'From what?'

'From the hurt, and from the loss. From what happened to Jan, and to your baby. But I tell you this from experience; you can run as fast and as far as you like and it'll keep pace with you. It'll be with you until you die.'

'That's a coincidence,' I said to him. 'Jan told me exactly the same.'

'When?'

'Last night.'

'Did she now?' I could tell from his voice that he didn't doubt me, or think me crazy, not one bit. 'And did she tell you how to cope with it?'

'She told me to do my best . . . Oh aye, and she told me to look after Jonny.'

'I'm with her on both counts,' he murmured.

'About you and Prim; you probably expect me to tell you to forgive and forget, but I'm more of a realist than that. Just concentrate on forgiving each other. Forgetting's beyond most of us, but as long as we keep on forgiving, it's usually all right.'

He paused. 'And speaking of you two,' he went on. 'I'm going to a seminar at Glasgow Dental Hospital tomorrow; I'll look in on your flat while I'm there.'

'Thanks, Dad.'

'I might even look in on your wee pal Susie, if I've time. She was like a wee wounded bird at your wedding, and when she called me the other week, she still didn't sound like her usual self.'

I didn't like to tell him that she did now, so I let it go. We left it at that, and he went off to his eleven fifteen patient.

I went back to the script, and I was feeling mildly exultant again when Prim called, bang on twelve. 'Hi,' I said, breezily.

'Hmmph,' I heard her sniff. 'You sound full of yourself. What's up? Is Susie back?'

'Chuck it. I've had a good morning's work, that's all. I needed it, too. It helped bring me back to a degree of sanity.'

'You mean you've stopped thinking that someone's out to get you, and accepted that Susie staged that wee stunt on the stairs just to get her leg over you?'

'You can cut that out as well,' I told her, firmly. 'No one's out to get me as such . . . other than you, maybe . . . but someone is trying to get us both out of this house. I think they're looking for something, something connected with Capulet.'

'If you're right, can't it be Capulet himself?'

'No, otherwise he'd know where it was, wouldn't he? Anyway, enough of that. Are you coming back home?'

'Maybe tomorrow,' she said. 'I'm going to stay another day. Twenty-four hours in the sin-bin isn't punishment enough. Apart from that, what you asked me last night really threw me. It stirred up a lot more stuff I'd hoped was buried, and I need to think about it before I talk to you.'

'You really didn't get it from Dad?' she asked.

'I promise I didn't.'

'Then you've either had a call from Fergal . . . his name was Fergal Keenan . . . or you're a bloody psychic.'

'Maybe there's more to life than we can see and touch,' I said.

'What do you mean by that?'

'I'll tell you when I see you. Go on, make it today.'

'No! Tell you what, the day after tomorrow, for sure. I'll be back for lunch; book somewhere expensive.'

She hung up. Again, I thought about Susie's advice to drive down to Barcelona. I might have done it too, if the doorbell hadn't rung.

I hadn't a clue who it might be as I walked to answer its call; Lionell, maybe come to start his painting of the house, or Shirley, come to investigate Prim's renewed absence. The last person I expected to find was Veronique Sanchez i Leclerc.

It was a cold, grey day outside and she was wrapped up in a heavy coat, with a silk scarf round her head. She still looked beautiful, though; nervous, agitated, but beautiful.

'Vero,' I exclaimed, surprised, but secretly pleased to see her. 'Come on in. Where's Alejandro? You haven't left him in the car, have you?'

'No,' she replied, in Spanish. 'He is with my mother.'

'Sit down,' I told her. 'Or come with me if you like, while I make us some coffee.' I remembered that my script was spread all over the coffee table, and began to worry about the draught from the door. 'Go on through to the kitchen while I tidy up these papers.' She nodded and walked through without a word, past the staircase. I was sure that on the night of the party she had never left the living room, other than to put Alejandro to bed upstairs.

When I rejoined her, she had laid her coat and scarf on a kitchen stool and was cleaning out the percolator, flushing the used grounds from the receptacle into the waste disposal in one of the twin sinks. I took the Bonka from the cupboard and handed it to her, together with the measuring tool. 'Here,' I said. 'You do it. I never seem to get the strength right in that thing.'

She smiled at me faintly, then measured out three and a half scoops, filled the water container up to the valve, and put it on one of the fast rings on the hob. I felt as if I was watching her in her own kitchen.

'This is a pleasant surprise,' I began, breaking the silence once more.

'Prim is not here?' she asked.

'No. She's in Barcelona . . . shopping,' I added. 'Why? Was it her you came to see?'

'No, I came to see you rather than her. I am worried about the girl.'

'What girl?' Then it dawned. 'You mean Gabrielle? But I thought that Ramon was taking her to the Filipino Consulate yesterday, for her flight home.'

She nodded, vigorously. 'Yes, he did, late yesterday afternoon. But on the way south he called into his office in Girona, to pick something up. He left her in the car while he went inside, and when he came out, she was gone. He doesn't know whether she just ran off or whether someone took her.

'He has had all his men looking for her ever since; last night he stayed in Girona and went round all of the clubs in the area, just in case he might find her in one of them. He called me this morning to say that she is still missing.'

Given that he had been reluctant to investigate the stiff in my pool, I was surprised that Fortunato had pulled out all the stops for one runaway Filipina, but I guessed that he felt himself to blame for losing her, and wanted to find her before he had to answer some awkward questions.

'So what brings you here, Vero?'

She looked at me with her big amber eyes. 'I thought that if she has run away, she would know very few places to go. In fact this would almost be the only place she would know. So I came to ask whether she had returned here, and to warn you, in case she does.'

'Is your telephone out of order?' I asked her, as I switched off the hob and filled two mugs with coffee, handing one to her. 'I know mine isn't, because I've had a couple of calls already this morning. You could have phoned to tell me all that, but you didn't. You parked the baby with your mother and you came here.'

I smiled at her, wanting to put her at her ease as much as I could, while finding out why she had really come. 'Did you hope to see Prim, on her own, maybe? So you could thank her for kicking Ramon out of her life and sending him back to you?'

She returned my grin, contriving to look awkward and embarrassed. 'Something like that, perhaps. Yes, I used Gabrielle as an excuse.'

'Then it's probably as well she isn't here, because she couldn't have gone along with it, not any more. Ramon knew about the kid and

Ramon made her abort it. She didn't kick Ramon out, he walked out, and damn near broke her in the process.

'But you're not stupid. None of that is news to you, is it?'

She shot me a narrow-eyed look that scored up one to me.

'So come on, what's this visit really about? I know I'm a damned attractive guy, and I'm in the movies and on the telly and all that stuff, but you're no groupie. Not that I'd say no if the offer was made, you understand . . . I have absolutely no moral fibre, as my wife will tell you.

'Let me take a guess. You're here because you wanted to be in this house again, just one more time, back in his house, Rey Capulet's house. Or one of his houses. What was the Paris place like? As big as this?'

She tried to speak but I wasn't ready to let her. 'Why did you want to be here, then, Vero? Are you looking for something? Are you and Ramon looking for something, maybe?'

'Did Capulet give you a key for this villa at one time? Do you still have it, perhaps?'

She looked me up and down for a while, then she put down her mug and moved towards me, without a word. She threw her arms around my neck, and kissed me, pressing her body against me. It was some body.

Of course, I had meant what I said about not turning down any genuine offers. I carried her up that great big staircase . . . God, but it was getting to be a habit . . . and into the master bedroom.

I wish I could say that it was great, sensational, Earth-shattering and all that other stuff, but it wasn't. She was grim, tense and determined; I was just along for the ride, so to speak. 'Who was that for?' I asked her, when we were finished. 'Ramon? Capulet? It wasn't for my sake, that's for sure.'

'It was for both of them, and yes, maybe it was for you too. You're bastards, all three of you, and I despise you all.'

'Hey!'

'Don't protest to me,' she retorted, getting out of bed and walking, naked into the bathroom. The door was closed, and it could have led to a cupboard, but she walked straight to it, knowing exactly where she was going. I heard water splashing; not the shower or the basin, but the bidet as she tried to wash me off her, and out of her.

'You're no better than they are,' she said, as she slipped back into bed. 'Remember how you left Prim here.

'Ramon? He had countless affairs before I met him, and just as many afterwards. Finally, I left him for Capulet after I saw him coming out of a sex club near Figueras . . . And no, he was not on duty.

'Rey? He turned out to be the worst of the three of you. I didn't know the business he was in when I went with him; his business with those poor girls, those poor slaves. As soon as I found out I left him and came back to Albons.

'Now, to answer your questions. No, I do not have a key for this house. I had a key for the apartment in Paris, but not for here, although of course I have been here often enough before. No, I am not looking for anything here, and neither, as far as I know, is Ramon. I came here because at your party, I found that I could still sense Rey in the place, and I felt that maybe if I confronted him here again, I could get rid of the dirty feeling I have had ever since I found out about him.'

'And have you confronted him?'

'No,' she whispered. 'Only you. As for the dirty feeling, after this, time will tell. But I owe Ramon nothing now.'

A look in her eye troubled me. 'What do you mean?'

'How long has Prim been in Barcelona?' she asked.

'Since yesterday afternoon.'

'And when is she coming back?'

'The day after tomorrow.'

'And you believe she is alone?'

I felt a hot surge of rage inside me. It was a while before I could answer her. 'I booked the hotel for her,' was all I could say.

'So? Listen, Oz, I have never known Ramon to spend a night in his office. It's an old cover story of his, but I've checked and I've never known him actually to do it. Today he tells me that he will be there for another night, and maybe until they find Gabrielle. Which they won't, of course; I'm sure she's on her way back to the Philippines already.

'I don't know why, but I didn't expect to find Prim here when I arrived. I saw the way he looked at her at your New Year party. And, yes, I know how she really felt about him. So? Will we go down there ourselves and find them?'

My anger had gone. Also, I didn't truly believe her. I thought that she was adding one and one and making six hundred and sixty-six. 'No,' I answered. 'I don't exactly have good moral grounds for doing that.' I looked down at her long tanned body. 'And neither, I have to point out, do you.'

I lay there for a while and thought about things; about everything in fact, and about people hurting, and being hurt. Then I thought, *What the hell? 'Unless they deserve it,' you said, my angel. I guess we all deserve each other.*

'There's just one other thing I'd like to ask you, Vero,' I said.

She raised herself on an elbow and looked down at me. 'What's that?' she whispered, in English.

'That back there? Was that the best you can do?'

Her smile told me that she was no better or worse than the three guys she despised. The light was blotted out as her hair fell down around me. 'Oh no,' she said. 'That was far, far from it.'

32

'When does you mother expect you back?' I asked her, as we ate a mid-afternoon lunch in the kitchen.

'This evening,' she answered. 'I told her I was going to Girona.'

The truth is dead, I thought. *We are all Satan's children, right enough.*

'Why are you smiling like that?' she said.

I hadn't realised that I was. 'It's nothing,' I assured her. 'Other than that I was thinking that you were right . . . you could do a lot better.'

'Why is it always men who say that kind of thing?' she mused.

'Because that's the way our sad, selfish minds work.'

It was Veronique's turn to smile. 'What unexpected honesty. Here's some in return; some good news and some bad news you might say. The good: you're much better in bed than Ramon. The bad: neither of you are in the same class as Rey Capulet. He is an artist, whatever else he might be.

'Most men think of a woman's body as no more than a piece of exercise equipment. He sees it as an instrument to be played with skill . . . And believe me, he is a maestro.'

'I'll bear that in mind,' I grunted, giving her a sour look.

'What are you going to do about Primavera?' she asked me suddenly.

I didn't have a considered answer for that one, at that moment; so instead I told her that our future wasn't at my disposal alone, and that Prim and I would have to talk it through together. 'Maybe it's what she wants to do about me that will decide things,' I added.

'What are you going to do about Ramon?'

'Drop him,' she answered vehemently. 'For good this time. Whenever the moment is right, he's out.'

'Are you going to tell him about this morning?'

'I might. Does that scare you?'

'No.'

'He's a policeman, remember. He has a gun.'

'I've seen guns before. Carrying one is one thing; having the balls to pull the trigger is another. I'm not sure Ramon has. Anyway,' I laughed, 'you're forgetting, I'm a public figure; I'm in the movies. I don't have a lot of influence myself, not yet, but I know people who do. If your old man tried to make trouble for me or for Prim . . . especially for her . . . I'd have him squashed like a fly.'

She gave me an appraising look. 'You have it all thought out, Oz, don't you?'

I shook my head. 'No, only some of it. I'm working on the rest.'

'And what is the rest?'

'Having the sort of power for myself that I've seen in others; in people like my brother-in-law, Miles Grayson, and my friend Everett Davis. The power to reach out and influence things.'

'How do you do that?'

I considered her question carefully. I was voicing thoughts that had been idle, fanciful ambitions until then. All of a sudden they were falling into place, as the last of the old Oz façade crumbled away.

'My first step is completing this next movie, and making it a personal success. That will cut me free of Miles, and break the only sort of hold that Prim has over me. After that, I'll stay in movies for a while, until I'm seriously rich, instead of fairly so.'

'And somewhere along the line you'll ditch Prim.' It was a prophesy, not a question.

'Not necessarily. Prim's had some bad things happen in her life, all of them male, including me, including Ramon. As far as I'm concerned, when she gets back, maybe we can start on a new chapter, one where it's all good for a change.

'Down there in Barcelona right now, with your old man, she's playing a part. She's being tough and vengeful, she thinks, doing what she has to do, just as you've been. But that's not the real her . . . any more than it's the real you.

'There's no way I can change what I am, but maybe I'd like to help her get back to the person she was before all the crap happened.'

'But do you love her?'

'Oz doesn't love. I can't; not any more.'

'Then shouldn't you let her try to find someone who does?'

I drank the last of my mineral water. 'I prefer it when you ask easy questions. But, of course, if she wants to, I can't stop her.'

'You'll try to keep her for a while, though; if only for the sake of your career.'

'You're the second person to tell me that. I wish I could tell you that I wouldn't, that I was above that; but the fact is . . .

'So what are you going to do after Ramon?' I asked her, changing the flow of the discussion.

'I don't know. I'll teach again, and bring up my son, but beyond that . . . maybe nothing.'

'You won't go off in pursuit of Capulet, the maestro?'

'No way. Ramon isn't a bad man: Rey is. I wouldn't let Alejandro anywhere near him.'

'Speaking of Alejandro, are you sure you'll be able to keep him?'

'I'll take him to France if I have to. But Ramon won't want him, I don't think. I will be surprised if he even tries for custody; it would cramp his style.'

I thought of Fortunato's style for a moment, and that flame of hypocritical anger flared again for a moment. I began to believe Vero's notion of the two of them in Barcelona, and I realised that if it was true, it couldn't have been planned in advance. Ramon couldn't have known she'd be going down there, for she hadn't known herself until half an hour before she hit the road.

'Has your husband changed his cell phone recently?' I asked.

'No. He's had the same number for years, since he was in the Guardia Civil.'

Prim has a remarkable memory for numbers; once they're lodged in her brain she can recall most of them, and certainly the most important, within seconds. If Vero was right, she'd called him and he'd come running . . . IF she was right.

'You know what?' I told her. 'You should go to France. You should get your son away from here and bring him up somewhere new. If you raise him here there's a fair chance that he'll never leave. This place is fine for retired Europeans and for Catalans who are born to the lifestyle, but there really is more than that.'

She frowned. 'I don't know, I'm half Catalan too, remember.'

'I do know; I'm all Fifer, and that's worse.'

'So why are you here?'

'Because I like the place, yet I have the ambition and the will to go away from it when I need to. In a couple of weeks, I'll be gone from here, back to Scotland. A few weeks after that and I'll be in Los Angeles.'

'Lucky you. And here was I thinking that Rey Capulet's palace had hold of you for ever, with its sunshine, its luxury, its fine wine cellar. Did all of that come with the house as well?'

I shrugged; maybe I was starting to turn into a Catalan myself. 'The wine? There was some in racks in the house, and in the storage area at the back. It was good stuff but I wouldn't describe it as a cellar.'

'No, no. I mean the cellar itself. Rey had some very valuable wines there, laid down long-term. I suppose he must have had them taken away when he left.'

I was more than a bit puzzled. 'Vero,' I assured her, 'this house doesn't have a cellar.'

She looked at me, blankly. 'Of course it does, down below; a big one where Rey kept his wines, and some of his files.'

'You're kidding.' Then I remembered another cellar I'd been in once. 'Does it have a secret entrance?'

'Don't be silly. There's a door under the staircase.'

'There isn't.'

'There is.'

'Listen, this is my house now, and I'm telling you there's no door there.'

'Come on,' she insisted. 'I'll show you.'

She led me out of the kitchen and round to the far side of the big staircase, into the passage which led to our small office. 'There . . .' she exclaimed, pointing. Then she stopped and looked, blankly.

There was no door of course. Like the other, the side of the stairway from the steps down to the floor was finished in fine wood panelling. English oak, I'd been assured by Sergi, although I was fairly sure it was really good quality Spanish pine, well treated and finished.

'This is new.' She turned to look at me. 'Oz, I swear, this is new. It wasn't here when I knew this house before, and there is a door behind it.'

'Okay,' I said, 'I'll take your word for it.' But once I had, a big question came to me. Why would anyone block up a doorway in a house they were selling?

'Do you know any good carpenters around here?' I asked Veronique.

'One or two. Why?'

'Because I'm going to need one shortly.'

I went out behind the house, into the workshop and selected the biggest chisel I could find and a black-handled steel claw hammer.

She looked at me with a degree of awe as I set to work on the panelling. 'You're going to tear it down?'

'Of course. I can't have all that wine going to waste.' I worked as carefully as I could, trying to remove the wood, rather than just rip it out. The panelling job had been done by a real expert; the joins were there, but you couldn't see them, and the nails which secured the timber to the framework behind had been filled over and varnished to make them undetectable.

In the end, it came off easily. I worked until all the sections were loosened, then removed them together.

Yes, there was a door; but it hadn't just been covered over, it had been bricked up. Whoever had done the job had been much better at carpentry than at building walls.

Veronique was looking frightened now; I guess I was looking pretty serious myself.

'Listen, kid,' I told her. 'I think you should leave.'

'No.'

'Humour me in this, okay. This was done for a reason, and I'd rather that you were long gone from here when I find out what it was. Go back to your baby; better still, nip down to Girona and buy something to prove to your mother that you really did go there.'

'Why?'

'Common sense. Keep all your options open, for now at least; so that this morning never happened, if that's the way you decide you want it.'

'And you?'

'I'm going to knock this wall down. This morning? As far as I'm concerned, it certainly didn't happen.'

I recovered her coat and scarf from the kitchen, kissed her quickly, and rushed her to the door before she had a chance to protest.

I watched her from the window, and listened to the sound of her engine, until I was sure she had driven off. Then I went back out to the workshop and found a bigger hammer . . . a much bigger hammer.

As it turned out I could probably have nutted my way through the badly built wall. The bricks were soft, and I guessed that they hadn't been properly soaked before being put in place. Three good whacks, middle, top and bottom, and there was a hole big enough for me to step through.

As the last chunk fell, the smell seemed to come out in a 'Whoosh!' Staleness, mustiness, and something that could have been the notorious surge from the L'Escala town sewers, but wasn't. I waited until it had subsided, then opened all the doors and windows in the living room to let it escape outside, before I contemplated going down to trace its source.

I brought my wide-beam torch through from the kitchen, but as it turned out I didn't need it. There was a switch at the top of the stairway, I flicked it, and lo, there was light, from three neon tubes suspended from the ceiling of the big, pillared chamber.

Capulet's wine . . . mine now, legally . . . was still there, racked high; row upon row of it, dozen upon dozen. I picked one up as I reached the foot of the stairs. I didn't recognise the label, but it was 1968 vintage, whatever it was. I hoped I would enjoy it.

I moved on past the racks, towards what I knew must be the front of the house. Facing me I saw a big double-fronted, metal filing cabinet. It was open and yellowed papers were strewn all over the tiled floor.

I came to the last rack and looked round, shivering from the chill as I did . . . At least I think it was the chill.

This time, as I looked at the body lying face-down . . . a technical description; it didn't have a face any more . . . I was one hundred per cent certain that I'd found Reynard Capulet, the maestro. I didn't have to prod him to find out whether he was dead or not, and I didn't have to be an ace pathologist to know what had killed him either. The big kitchen cleaver that had done the job was still lodged in the back of his skull.

'Don't you move, now,' I warned him. 'Not till the ambulance gets here.'

Then I went back upstairs and found Captain Fortunato's card, the one with his mobile number on it, the number that Prim must have known a couple of years before.

I almost dialled it until I thought to myself, *Fuck it; might as well know one way or another*.

So instead I called the Husa Princesa and asked for Prim's room.

'Did you decide to stay in this afternoon?' I asked her, unnecessarily, as she picked up.

'Yes,' she replied. This time she sounded hesitant, not drowsy.

'Fine. Listen, if you're alone, I apologise. If you're not, put him on.'

There was a silence, broken eventually by Fortunato's voice. 'Yes?' He sounded a hell of a lot more hesitant than had Prim.

'Tea-break's over, Ramon,' I told him. 'Time you went back to work. I want to see you here, at the house, inside an hour and a half. You're a copper; you can go lights and sirens if you have to.'

'What's this about, Oz?' he asked.

I had to laugh at him. 'If you don't mind my saying so, that might be regarded as a fucking stupid question in the circumstances. But as it happens, it isn't about you. You'll see when you get here. Now just do what I tell you.

'Oh yes, and come alone. But from what I hear, you always do anyway.'

33

I regretted that last, thoughtless, crack as soon as I had said it, but I was fairly sure that Ramon would link it to Prim, not Vero . . . if his English was that good.

He certainly didn't mention it when he arrived, an hour and twenty-three minutes later. Allowing him four or five minutes to get dressed, he had made pretty good time.

As he walked up the drive, in his crisp uniform, everything about the policeman's body language suggested that he expected me to take a swing at him as soon as he came within range. I had spent most of the time since we had spoken in my gym, pressing weights, and punching the bag, so I probably looked ready for it, too.

Instead, I clapped him on the back, almost sympathetically: from the way he flinched I could tell that it had thrown him.

'Come on in, lover boy,' I said. 'I hope you haven't eaten recently.'

He gave me a bewildered look. 'Oz,' he exclaimed. 'I don't know what to say.'

'Fuck all would just about cover it. I'm sure that Prim's told you everything that happened between us, so the best that you and I can do is put a lid on it. If you insist on talking about it, I'd probably start behaving unreasonably, like a stupid jealous husband, and we don't want that.'

'So what is all this about?' he asked. We were still standing in the doorway, so he couldn't see the mess at the side of the stairs.

'Are you any good at carpentry?' I asked.

He gave me a stare that hovered between paranoia and idiocy. 'What?' he croaked.

'You heard.'

'*Hombre*, I can't even hang a picture straight.'

'How about bricklaying? Are you any good at that?'

'I've never laid a brick in my life.'

I studied his eyes as he answered me; they're a better guide than any truth drug. He didn't know what I was talking about.

'You've laid just about everything else, though,' I said, with a light laugh which made him wince.

'Come on. Let me show you what I'm talking about,' I led him into the house.

'I got the deed for this place back from the notary a couple of days ago. I didn't look at it closely when we completed the purchase, so I decided that I might as well read it. When I did, I found a reference to a cellar, accessed by a door in the side of the stairs.

'But there was no door, only wood panelling.' I pointed to the pine sections, which leant against the wall. 'It had been bricked up, then covered over. For a bloody good reason too, as you'll see when we go down there.'

His face had gone pale. He started for the revealed doorway, but I put a hand on his sleeve to stop him; just to make certain. 'Listen, before you do anything that might have consequences, I want to tell you something. I know about Veronique, and the Frenchman.

'If you want me to block that door up again, and to replace that panelling, I'll do it, and it'll stay there for good. I worked on building sites when I was a student, so I'll make a passable job of it.'

He frowned at me. 'I honestly do not understand what you are saying to me, Oz,' he murmured.

'Okay,' I told him, 'if you don't, that's good enough for me. Go on down.'

I followed him down into the cellar. I was right behind him when he saw the body, and I put a hand on his shoulder to stop him as he jumped back, involuntarily.

'Mother of Christ!' he gasped, in Spanish.

'I shouldn't think so for a minute. Reynard Capulet, I'd say; beyond a shadow of a doubt this time.' I pointed to the left wrist, and the heavy gold, diamond-set watch which hung loosely round it. 'That's a pimp's Rolex if ever I saw one.'

Fortunato had recovered his composure, enough to let him lean over the body. 'We should be able to trace its ownership, certainly; with a bit of luck we'll still be able to lift some prints too. It's very dry down here.'

He turned. 'Come on, let's get upstairs before we contaminate the scene any further.'

I led the way this time; we went round the stairway and into the kitchen, from where the policeman phoned his office to call out detectives and technicians, while I took a couple of beers from the fridge.

220

He looked me in the eye, as he took his first slug. 'Sayeed in the pool, now Capulet in the cellar. What do you think, Oz? You're a sharp guy. Any ideas?'

'Bloody obvious, isn't it? The Moroccan was killed and planted in the pool to make it look as if Capulet had shot him after a quarrel, then run off. At first I thought that the Frenchman might have killed him to fake his own death . . . until I found that thing downstairs.'

Fortunato nodded. 'I agree with that. I guess we'd better contact Interpol, and round up his known associates.'

'I guess you'd better,' I agreed, 'only that can't be the whole story.'

'What do you mean?'

'Clearly, the sister has to have been in on it; Lucille, the one who's gone missing. With her brother dead, she took the decision to sell all his property, the three places in Paris, Florida and here, that were owned technically by the company she controlled.

'Maybe one of his Mafia pals was involved in it, but she had to be too.'

He scratched his chin. He must have shaved very quickly, for blood began to run from a fresh nick just above his jaw, on the left side.

'I suppose so,' he conceded. 'I don't imagine Interpol have been looking for her . . . not too hard at any rate. They'd better start now.'

'So should you,' I said. 'I don't think she's gone far away.'

His look wasn't just a question. It was a whole cross-examination in itself.

I answered it by telling him all the stuff he didn't know about Susie's visit, about her dangerous fall down the stairs in the middle of the night, and about my certainty that her drink had been drugged earlier in the evening, by the same guy who had sent her flying, to try and incriminate me and get me out of the house.

I told him about the envelope which Prim had received, the one which had put me in deep shit and him back in her bed, and I told him about the missing mug. Finally, I told him about the trap I had laid for the intruder, the one which hadn't been sprung.

'He may have found what he was after, or he may have felt that he'd pushed his luck far enough: I don't know. I do know that whatever it was, or is, must be extremely valuable, for he and Lucille have had all that time since Capulet was killed to find it, and they're still looking. More than that, they're taking big risks to do it.'

'Yes,' Fortunato agreed. 'But why? If this is something in the house, and Lucille is involved, why did she sell it to you in the first place? Why not refuse your offer and keep looking?'

'I don't have an answer to that one,' I told him. 'But I know a man who does. Why don't we go and find him, once your people get here, and once you've contacted Interpol and asked them to find a photograph of Lucille Capulet and fax it to you.'

34

He wasn't hard to find. He wasn't in his office, but his secretary sent us to a bar at the far end of Riells beach; he was there, sitting at the bar, drinking café solo and talking to the attractive owner.

'Hello Sergi,' I hailed him in Castellano as we walked in. 'Just the man I want to see. How about buying my friend and me a beer out of your commission on the sale of Casa Nou Camp?'

'*Que?*' he blurted out, then laughed. 'Ah, you mean Villa Bernabeu.'

'Not any more. I'm a Barça fan.'

'Whatever. Sure I will buy you a beer, and your pal.'

'You know him, do you? If not, let me introduce you to Captain Fortunato, of the Mossos in Girona.'

Sergi's lantern jaw seemed to tense, but his expression stayed amiable as he shook the policeman's hand.

'You were just passing by?' he asked, as the young man behind the bar poured two beers.

'Not exactly,' I admitted. 'We were looking for you.'

'Ah,' the estate agent said slowly. 'This is about the unfortunate business with the body in the swimming pool. I told the other policemen that I had no idea it was there, and they believed me.'

'So do we.'

'Ah, then maybe you want to talk about a discount on the price. I am sorry, but . . .'

'No,' Ramon interjected. 'Señor Blackstone does not need the money. I want to ask you something, actually: some new questions.'

'Okay.'

'During the time when the villa was for sale, did you have other offers?'

Sergi nodded. 'Yes, several. I had four, in fact. One was even for the full price.'

'What did you do when each offer was received?'

'I called the lawyer in Geneva who acts for the company which owned the villa. They said that they would consult Señora Capulet, but

223

each time, they came back and said that she didn't want to accept.'

'So why did she accept our offer?' Fortunato shot me a glance; he was annoyed at my joining in the questioning, but I didn't give one. This was my line of enquiry we were following.

Sergi hesitated; I guess he was considering whether it was safe to tell the truth to the Mossos. Eventually he decided that it would have been risky not to.

'The fact is,' he admitted, 'that she didn't. I did.' The policeman's eyebrows rose, threateningly, but he went on, quickly.

'I was annoyed with her. I am not in business for fun; I had been doing my best to sell her house, and four times before I could have done so. So when you offered, I said to myself, "Man, enough is enough", and so I used the power of attorney which the company had given me at the beginning to complete the transaction.'

He glanced at Fortunato. 'It was all quite legal, you understand. Ethical? In the circumstances I'd do it again. Silly woman; her brother Rey would not have messed me about like that if he hadn't gone away.'

'Sergi,' I asked, 'when the house was put up for sale, were all the valuables taken away?'

'Sure. Lucille sent a man to take them to her.'

'What was his name?'

'He called himself Martin Guerre. His French accent was odd, so I guessed he was Swiss.'

'Have you seen him since?'

'I think I may have seen him about L'Escala once or twice, but I'm not sure.'

'How about Lucille Capulet? Have you seen her?'

'I wouldn't know. I've never met her in my life.'

The captain would have left it at that, but I tried him with one more. 'When the valuables were cleared away, what happened to the wine in the cellar?'

Sergi is not a guy who would recognise a trick question, even after he'd tripped over it. 'What wine?' he asked. 'What cellar?' As if to confirm his innocence, he gave me the biggest shrug I have ever seen. Even Fortunato was convinced by that.

We drank our beers, I bought two more, and a Campari and soda for our friend, and then we went back to the villa to see what progress the technicians were making.

35

As it happened they were only just starting, but while they were away something of greater interest to me had finished, for the time being at least . . . my marriage.

After Fortunato had driven me back to Casa Nou Camp, instructed his men to report any significant finds to him at once, and headed home to God Knew What from Vero, I went wearily upstairs, stripped off my clothes and stepped straight into the shower.

I had finished towelling myself off, when I saw the note, in an envelope bearing the Husa Princesa crest, on the dressing table. Before I even picked it up, I went to Prim's wardrobe and threw it open. Most of her clothes were gone.

I almost crumpled the letter and threw it away unread, but, once I had finished dressing, a mix of guilt and curiosity made me tear it open. It was more or less what I had expected.

Oz

We really have made hash of it, haven't we? You more so than me, from where I stand, but you'd expect me to say that wouldn't you.

I'm sorry that I kept so many things from you; things like Fergal going off and dumping me, how it really was here after you did the same thing, and what really happened between me and Ramon. I don't know how you guessed that he was with me in Barcelona, unless you called Veronique looking for him, and she told you that he was away. I should reproach you for not thinking better of me, only you were right. I am no better than you. You took your revenge with Susie, and I took mine with him.

From your tone when you called earlier, I suspect that if I stayed and said that we should call it evens and try to start again, you'd agree. I can't do that, though, and I think you'll understand why.

The thing is, I don't know you any more; I know you'd say the same to me, if you were honest. If I did come back, we'd be strangers to a large extent. We might say the right things and do the right things, but it would be for the sake of it and there would be raw resentment burning just under the surface in both of us. Sooner or later one of us would explode, and that really would be the end of it.

I'm not going back to Ramon, that I can promise you, even after Veronique kicks him out, as I expect she will after you tell her what's happened. You're too vengeful not to. I've seen too much of his weakness, just as I've seen too much of your ruthlessness. It wasn't just me who kept things secret, you know. You were worse in a way; you kept your secrets from yourself.

What I am doing is going back to Los Angeles, back to Mum, and back to help Dawn after she has the baby. I'll say nothing to them about what's happened, I promise you. I won't screw things up between you and Miles. No, you go back to Glasgow for the premiere, and for your acting coaching. Maybe you'll go back to Susie, I don't know. Nothing I can do about that. If you don't, when you come out to Los Angeles to start rehearsals and filming, maybe we can see each other again and see what the prospects are for a salvage operation.

I don't know what's going on under the stairs. The police wouldn't tell me, and I don't think I want to know, anyway. I've put the Merc in the garage and taken a taxi to Perpignan. I'll fly to Paris from there, then on.

Love

Prim

PS I really would like to know how you found out about Fergal. That's the one thing that nearly made me stay.

'Yeah,' I said. 'But not nearly enough.'

I tried to call her, on her mobile, until I heard it ring, and I realised that she'd left it by the side of the bed. I thought about racing after her in the Voyager, thought about it seriously, until I knew for sure that I didn't want to. She was right; if there was any chance for us, we had to put time and distance between us and all that shit. We had to do that even to find out whether either of us wanted there to be a chance.

I had to call someone; my sister drew the short straw. I told her that Prim and I had split up and why. I had expected Ellie to give me the bollocking of all time, just as if I was a lad again, but she didn't.

'You poor loves,' she said. 'I could tell at Christmas that there was something wrong between you. I blame that place, Oz.'

'What? The house?'

'No, the whole bloody town. You had nothing but trouble when you were there before, so whatever made you go back?'

'There are dark forces which guide our destiny,' I told her grimly. Until that moment it would have been one of my poorer jests, but that was the point at which I became convinced that it was entirely true.

'Maybe so, but if they come around my house I'll give them a good leathering. Do you want to come and stay with me for a bit?'

Never once in my life, not even when she was slapping me around as a kid, had my sister ever made me cry . . . until then. I felt my eyes moisten and a tear ran down my cheek. More than anything else, it came from the knowledge that there was still someone alive, as well as my dad, who really loved me.

'Thanks Ellie,' I said wiping it and that flash of self-pity away, 'but I've got some stuff to finish up here. I'll come and see you when I get back to Glasgow. I'll tell you what: you can chum me to the premiere. You up for that?'

'Haud me back!' she exclaimed. 'You're on, boyo.'

I left her laughing, then went out to eat. The techs were still at work when I got back, and when I went to bed. They were still at work next morning, when I got up, although I have no idea what they were doing by then . . . having a wine tasting, maybe.

They had only just gone at three thirty, when the phone rang. I picked it up, half-hoping that it would be Prim. But it wasn't. It was the Other Woman.

'Oz,' Susie burst out, as I answered.

'Just saying my name gets you that excited, does it?'

'Could do, boy, you never know. Don't repeat this to anyone who might know me, but I've been missing you.

'Prim back yet?'

'And gone.' I filled her in on what had happened . . . with the notable exception of my horizontal encounter with Veronique Sanchez.

'*Que sera, sera,*' she said.

'When did you join the Tartan Army?'

'I helped to found it. Now shut up and listen. I've just had a visit from your old man. I think he came along to see that I was all right . . . bless his wee heart, or did you put him up to it?'

'No,' I told her, truthfully. 'It was his idea.'

'Glad to hear it. Anyhow . . . he brought along some holiday snaps to show me. They were of your place, so I thought I'd better act as if I'd never seen it before.

'Then he showed me one that was taken at your New Year party.' She paused: she was winding up for something big, I could tell.

'He was in one of them, Oz. The guy in JoJo's that night, the one you reckon spiked my drink. I recognised him.'

I gasped, struck dumb for a moment. 'Who was it, then?'

'If I knew that I'd have told you in L'Escala, idiot.'

'I suppose so. I'll just have to wait until my old man can send me it.'

'No. I guessed you'd want to see it, so I asked him to leave it with me. I'll post it to you tonight.'

I thought about this for a bit. 'Better than that,' I said. 'Have you got a scanner in the office?'

'Yes.' She paused. 'I'm with you. I'll turn it into a file and send it to you by e-mail. Gimme half an hour.'

'I'll hold my breath,' I told her. 'Susie, if I did, right now I'd tell you I love you.'

'Aye, but don't, until you do.'

I heard the phone go down. I didn't quite hold my breath, but I didn't wait for half an hour. I logged on after fifteen minutes and, sure enough, Joanna Lumley told me that I had post.

Susie had named the file, 'Villain'. It took just under a minute to download.

I felt my fingers tremble as I opened it and watched it scroll down the screen. I adjusted the magnification to one hundred and fifty per cent; any more and I'd have lost clarity.

There were quite a few people in my dad's wide-angled snapshot. Prim and me for two, kissing, Mary, Ellie, Jonny and Frank Barnett. I didn't have any trouble working out who Susie had meant, though. She had printed a great big 'X' right above the smiling face of John Gash.

36

I sat for an hour after I'd printed out the picture, staring at it, caressing a couple of beers until they'd evaporated, and thinking. I knew I should call Fortunato right away and tell him what I'd found out, but I wanted to get a handle on the complete picture before that.

Almost from the moment I discovered that Gash was the guy trying to get Prim and me out of the way, I developed what I used to call Quasimodo Syndrome. I had a very large hunch.

We were agreed, the captain and I, that Lucille Capulet had to be involved in her brother's murder. Someone had to be instructing the company lawyer and it could only be her. We were agreed too that there was a man involved in it, because of what had happened to Susie.

Therefore, there was only one conclusion as far as I was concerned. The lovely Virginie, the new girlfriend John had sprung on Shirley, was Lucille Capulet. How they had met didn't interest me; maybe John had been alarmed by the Frenchman's courting of his mother, and had sought out his sister to see what she might be able to do about it. Maybe, but it didn't matter.

Lucille had never been to L'Escala as far as anyone knew; not even Sergi, her estate agent, had ever seen her. She was Virginie, simple as that; I knew it and I didn't need any faxed photos from Lyon to confirm it.

So what were she and John after so badly? Towards the end of my contemplation, something came back to me, something that had struck me as slightly off at the time. After all his determination to get his hands on Capulet's old Lada, even to the extent, I was now sure, of taking a shot at me to scare me into selling it, he had buggered off and left the thing in his mother's garage.

I left my beer and the photo on the kitchen work-surface and walked along to Shirley's house. She was in, and met me with a great big smile, which made me feel all the worse about what I was going to do to her life.

'Shirl,' I began, 'that car I flogged to your lad: I think I may have left a pair of sunglasses in it. Can I have a look?'

'Sure,' she said, handing me a remote control device which had been lying on her hall table. 'That'll open the garage.'

I pressed the button and the door raised. It was starting to get dark, but there was still enough light for me to see that John had given the car a real going over. The seats had been taken out and were upside down on the floor. The roof lining had been cut out completely, and all the door panels stripped off. HM Customs could not have done it more thoroughly: this was not how a car was broken into spares for export.

I closed the door quickly and gave Shirley her zapper, plus a 'No luck', story. Then I hurried back to Casa Nou Camp.

Whatever they were after, he and his girlfriend, was a big mystery, but there was also a 'why' to be considered. I could have asked Shirley a couple of questions, but she was too smart not to ask me a couple in return. So instead, I called someone I'd met the last time we were in L'Escala.

One reason why I remembered her . . . far from the only one, she's a very memorable lady indeed . . . was that she's the Clerk to one of the City livery companies, the one which covers makers of fine furniture.

I didn't know the name of Shirley's family firm, but I'd a fair idea that it wasn't called Gash Furniture. She did know it though, as soon as I mentioned John's name.

'Oh yes,' she said. 'I know them.'

'A profitable business is what I hear,' I ventured.

'Believe that if you will,' said my friend, a remark which told me nothing, but everything. I thanked her, looked forward to seeing her in L'Escala, and said so long.

Still, I kept Fortunato on the back burner, instead, I phoned his wife. She wasn't exactly delighted to hear from me. 'This isn't going to become a habit, is it?' she blurted out.

'Vero,' I promised her, 'I've got enough on my plate without you. But I need to see you now, here at the house.'

'Are Ramon's people still there?'

'Of course not.'

'And is . . .?'

'That's an even dafter question. They took him away last night.'

'I meant your wife, you idiot.'

I felt like one; that notion had never occurred to me. 'No. She's been and gone; off to see her sister and mother in the US. What about Ramon?'

'He's at work,' she replied. 'I haven't kicked him out yet, if that's what you mean. I'm biding my time. Look, is this important?'

'Yes.'

'Okay, I'll take the baby to my mother and come over.'

She made it in twenty minutes; I had coffee ready and waiting for her, in the sitting room. She surprised me by kissing me as soon as I closed the door.

'I thought you didn't want this to be a habit.' I murmured.

'I don't. I'm just indulging myself, that's all. I still feel very strange.' She walked over to the big couch and sat down.

'Why?' I asked.

'Why do you think? The thought that yesterday, while we . . . That Rey was lying beneath us all that time.'

'Hey! I've been living with the bastard for a month, and he's brought me nothing but grief.'

She shuddered, then smiled. 'Poor you. You want me to feel sorry?'

'A little consolation wouldn't go amiss right now,' I admitted.

'We'll see about that when you tell me why you had to see me . . . Or was that the reason? It didn't sound that way.'

'No. How much has Ramon told you about what happened last night, and about what we found out?'

'Nothing, other than that you had found Rey Capulet's body, for real this time.'

'Okay.' I filled her in on the story from the beginning, then brought her right up to date. 'I know who killed him.'

'Who?' she gasped.

'John Gash; Shirley's son. You met him at our New Year party. Remember the girl with him? Virginie?' She nodded. 'I'm betting she's really Lucille, Rey's sister.'

Vero gave a wee cry. 'Ahh, yes!' she exclaimed. 'That's it. I remember her, and I remember thinking that she reminded me of someone I'd seen. Rey had her photograph, here and in Paris. But she was different in that; she wore spectacles and her hair was much darker.'

'Good. I win the money, then. So, the score is that those two killed Rey and walled his body up downstairs. They also killed Sayeed, and left him as a sort of time-bomb in the pool, either to be identified as Capulet or as the reason for his disappearance.

'But they didn't just do it for the value of his three properties. They were after something else, something which they couldn't find, after they killed him. They've looked for months, and they kept on looking even after Sergi sold me the house . . . which he wasn't supposed to do.

'You were here, Vero, with Capulet, in this house. Do you have any

231

ideas about what, or where, this thing might be?'

She stood up. 'Take me to bed,' she demanded.

'Vero, I'm serious.'

'So am I. Take me to bed and then I'll tell you what I think.'

She made it up the staircase under her own power this time. I was quite pleased about that. She's a bigger girl than either Susie or Prim.

I did my absolute best for Scotland, as they say, and she did hers for Catalunya. After a while we lost track of time, but eventually, when all the heavy breathing, sweating, shoving and shouting was over, I noticed that we'd been at it for a good forty minutes. I found myself wondering when Ramon usually got home for his tea.

'Okay,' I said to her, summoning up a threatening tone that I'd been practising for my next movie role. 'You gonna spill the beans now, or do I have to do all that again?'

She laughed out loud and pulled herself up until she was sitting with her back against the shiny frame of the big brass bed. Then she reached up and over her shoulder with her right hand, grabbed the big knob which topped the post, and twisted it, clockwise, as hard as she could.

It began to unscrew, slowly and stiffly.

I watched her, fascinated, then jumped over her and out of bed, taking over from her. The big brass dome was screwed into the post, not just slid in there, but the normal thread pattern was reversed. Even if they had thought to look there, John and Lucille would have tried to unscrew it in the normal way, anticlockwise, and the thing wouldn't have budged.

It took a while, but eventually the heavy knob came loose and I lifted it out. There was a chain attached to it, and on the end a cylindrical metal container, like the kind they used to have in some big department stores in the days before credit cards when all the cash transactions were completed and change given in a central counting house, connected by tubes to all the sales points. I've never seen that system, but my dad described it to me in detail, one day in Edinburgh. That's what I thought of when I saw Reynard Capulet's secret treasure.

The lid of the box unscrewed too, but in the normal way. I opened it and shook out on to the bed, eight long keys on a ring, and a single sheet of paper.

'They're for safe-deposit boxes,' said Veronique quietly. 'Rey turned all his real wealth into bonds and diamonds and kept it in locations all over Europe. Each box has two keys. Rey had one, his sister held the other. But only Rey knew where they all are, and that piece of paper there is the only record of the addresses of the banks where they are kept and the names in which the boxes are held.

'I know this because I walked in on him once, while he was putting a new key into the box and adding its details to the paper. I thought he would be angry at first, but he just said, "Now you know where the Capulet riches are hidden. Of course, if you tell anyone, I will have to kill you, and them." He smiled when he said it, but I knew that he meant it.'

'Jesus,' I whistled. 'This is dangerous stuff.'

Vero's right hand flew to her breast. 'What if they are still watching this house?'

I looked at her. 'I wish. I want to meet young Mr Gash again; I've got some real pain in store for him. But if they are, they'll know we've found Rey's body, and that they'll be rumbled.'

I picked up the bedside telephone. 'It's time I called in your old man again. Better get your kit on and beat it home, unless you want to be here when he arrives.'

'Maybe I do. And why not? He's never going to believe that you found this hiding place all on your own, in a day, when other people have been looking for it for a year.'

'Okay, but meet me halfway on this. Get dressed and be downstairs before he gets here.'

37

In deference to Veronique . . . not that she was too bothered . . . I changed the sheets and aired the bedroom for a good ten minutes after I called her husband.

He didn't say anything when I let him in and he saw her there. He didn't have to; his eyes did it for him. For an instant I thought we were going to have to do the macho thing right enough, but his wife crushed him with a few words.

'I have often wondered how good a policeman you really are,' she said to him, speaking in Spanish rather than Catalan, to make certain that I understood too. 'Now I know. Señor Blackstone . . .' Nice touch, I thought, to sweep away any thought of familiarity between us. '. . . is a civilian, and yet he had an idea all on his own, one which the entire Mossos d'Esquadra overlooked.'

Fortunato looked at me, as if he was glad of an excuse to escape his wife's withering gaze. 'What does she mean?'

I tossed him Capulet's key-ring. 'That's what they've been after. His set of keys to his treasure house; his sister has the others, but she doesn't know where the boxes are.

'I was told that your wife and the Frenchman had a relationship once, so it occurred to me that she could have an idea about where they might be hidden. She did.'

He nodded. 'Very good, my dear. Very good, Oz. But I don't suppose she could tell you who "They" are . . . or "Him", at least.'

'She didn't have to.' I picked up my dad's Hogmanay snapshot and handed it to him.

He stared at it, pop-eyed, taking in the face below the 'X'. 'The son of Señora Gash? What makes you say that?'

'My father showed that picture to Susie Gantry. She identified him as the man in JoJo's; the guy who spiked her drink. I sold him Capulet's old car; to be broken into parts, I thought, and shipped to Russia. He tore it apart looking for those keys, and the paper that goes with them, pointing the way to all his safe-deposit hoard.'

I paused. 'Have you had that photo from Interpol yet?' I asked him.
'Of Lucille Capulet? Yes.'

'Right. So take a look at John's girlfriend and picture her with glasses and darker hair.'

His pop-eyes went narrow. '*Puta,*' he whispered.

'Shirley thinks they went home last week, only they didn't. They hung around, trying everything they could to clear me out of this house.' I laughed. 'They should just have killed me . . . No fucking way you'd have caught them, if you'd even tried.'

He ignored the crack. 'Are you saying they are still here?'

'I don't know, chum. They may have cut and run after I found Capulet's body; but they may be hanging around for one last shot at the goodies, after I go back to Scotland.'

'But where could they hide? L'Escala in the winter is a small place, in terms of people at least.'

'Exactly. There are thousands of empty properties here; they could have broken into any one of them, and be using it as a hide-out.'

The captain shook his head. 'That could be risky. They would need to know for sure that the owner didn't employ a caretaker.'

He had a point there. And then a light flashed on and off, off and on, in my head, directing me to the obvious hiding place for John Gash. 'Shirley's old house,' I exclaimed. 'What's the betting that it's empty right now? She sold it to an Aussie; it's their summer and they're playing a test match at the moment.'

'I know where it is,' he said. 'But it has an alarm system. Again, too risky.'

'Don't you believe it, mate. There's a summerhouse there, with everything they'd need in a hide-out. And last time I saw it, it wasn't alarmed.'

'It's worth a look. I'll go up there now. Thank you, Oz. Vero, you can go home now.'

'Hold on a minute,' I told him. 'I'm coming too.'

'You can't,' he exclaimed, as he picked up Capulet's list, folded it and put it in his pocket. 'This is a police matter. I'll go alone; if I have to break into the property and there's no one there, I don't want any of my men to see.'

I looked at him even harder than his wife had. 'It is also a personal matter, Ramon. This lad could have killed my wee pal Susie. He probably took a shot at my car when I had my nephews in it. I want at least one good pop at him before you cart him off to the nick.'

'On top of that, he's killed a couple of people so far. No way will I let you go up there on your own.'

He gave in more easily than I'd expected. I guessed that my last point had hit the mark.

I realised that Veronique was staring at us, from one to the other. 'You have your gun, Ramon?' she asked. He flicked aside his jacket to show her a revolver in a hip holster. It looked like a Colt 38. I'd used one as a prop in my first movie. I hoped that Ramon's wasn't loaded with blanks.

'Be careful, still,' she said; but she was looking at me when she spoke.

She left as we did, driving off in her Ford Ka, and we climbed into the policeman's Seat Cordoba.

Shirley's old house was on the other side of town, in a place called Puig Sec by the locals, and Millionaires' Row by the ex-pats. It took us ten minutes to get there. I knew the lay-out better than Fortunato; he would have parked at the main entrance, but I directed him round to a street at the back. The night was clear and moonlit; I looked at the silhouette of the villa and realised that the Aussie had knocked it around a bit. A structure not unlike the look-out tower of a prison had been added to the upper floor.

I tried the back gate; it was unlocked. We slipped inside, relieved that the hinges didn't squeak. A silver Ford Cougar sat on a paved area inside; I recognised it. It had British plates, and the last time I'd seen it, it had been parked in Shirley's drive.

I nodded to Fortunato and led him down the sloping path, towards the garden. All the windows of the summerhouse look out on to the villa's big swimming pool, so I knew there was no chance of us being seen; not at that point, anyway.

The summerhouse was actually meant by the architect to be a glorified barbecue, but somewhere along the way a couple of bedrooms were added and it was turned into a guest bungalow. But the main living area was open to the elements, enclosed by two big wooden doors. As we drew close, I could see that at least one of them was open. A little light spilled out, although it was almost overwhelmed by the moonlight reflected by the pool.

I held up a hand. The captain took the signal and stopped beside me. We stood stock-still and listened. We couldn't make out the words, but we heard voices, one male, one female; the fragments of conversation which did drift out to us were in English.

Fortunato drew his gun and pointed; I followed him as he stepped round the door.

John Gash and Lucille Capulet were sitting on plastic seats on either side of a black butane gas heater. They gasped in harmony as they saw us, then John jumped to his feet. He was close enough so I hit him, a lot harder than I had hit Steve Miller, bang on the temple, right on the spot you should aim for if you really want to lay someone as broad as they're long.

He dropped like a stone, spark out for at least as long as it would have taken a referee to count to ten, even in a wrestling ring. *Liam would have been proud of that one*, I thought.

Lucille didn't say a word; she just gave us a cold killer stare, and I knew right then who had shot Sayeed and put a cleaver through her brother's head.

John started to come round, but his eyes were still glazed as the policeman waved him to his feet with the Colt. He struggled upright on shaky legs.

'Go on,' Fortunato barked, pointing to an open door which led to one of the bedrooms. 'In there.'

They did as they were ordered, the two of us following, Ramon closing the door behind us all. The room had a double bed and a small dressing table . . . on which lay eight long keys.

'You know what those are, Oz, don't you?' he said.

I smiled, and nodded. And then he shot them, both of them; Lucille first, John second. No messing, right in the head. Bang! Bang! One shot each, no more needed. I'd been wrong. He did have the *cojones* to pull the trigger, after all.

The sound in that small room almost deafened me, but the nearest neighbours were a long way off. I looked down at the two of them, stunned. Lucille was still, with her right eye gone. John had a hole in the middle of his forehead; he twitched for a second or two, then stopped.

'What the f—' I gasped at last. 'That was a bit peremptory, wasn't it? I thought you guys didn't do that any more.'

'They don't,' he said, cheerfully. 'I do . . .' He picked up Lucille's eight keys and put them in his pocket with their twins. '. . . when the stakes are high enough.' Then he pointed the gun at me. I thought that I was about to keep my date with Jan, right then, but he nodded towards the door.

'Go on,' he grunted. 'Back the way we came.'

'Why?'

'You're going to have an accident. You're going to fall off a cliff, into the sea. No one's going to report you missing for a few days; by that time the fish may have finished with you.'

'And what about them?' Pointless question, since the answer was so obvious.

'Killed resisting arrest. I have another gun that I'll plant on them, unless they have one already. After they give me my medal, I'll empty Capulet's boxes, one by one.'

'Very good. But there is someone who'll report me missing.'

He frowned at me, and then it dawned on him. 'Ahh, my wife. I thought so. Fair enough, it doesn't matter now.

'She might report your disappearance, Oz, but she'll report it to me. I'll tell her that you opted out at the last minute and ran off into the night like a chicken.'

'She won't believe you.'

'Then I'll kill her too; probably stage it as a robbery gone bad. After that, I'll have Prim. There's a fine last thought for you.' He gestured with the gun again. 'Go on. Out to the car.'

I did as he told me. 'This is definitely the last time I will ever trust a policeman,' I murmured, seeing Mike Dylan grin in the dark.

When we got to the Cordoba, Ramon tossed me its keys. 'You drive. I'll tell you where.'

It wasn't far. We drove over the hill and down towards Montgo, then took a side road which was signposted 'L'Estartit'. I knew where we were headed.

The track was tarmaced at first, but when we crossed the L'Escala town limit that ran out and became rough and rutted . . . they must be tight buggers in L'Estartit.

'Turn left,' Ramon grunted as we came to a gap in the hedge alongside. I did as I was told, driving through woodland until we came to a clearing. 'Stop.'

I could see the cliff path in the headlights; I had walked it, a couple of years before. I knew how far down it was to the rocks and the water. I knew also that once I got out of that car I was dead.

Happily, Ramon had made two big mistakes; one, he had underestimated me, and two, he hadn't made me wear the seatbelt.

When you're holding a gun on someone, you don't expect him to throw an elbow into your throat. But equally, it's bloody difficult to do it accurately in the dark. That's where luck came into it.

My forearm whacked up under his chin, then my hand chopped down on to his wrist, numbing it and knocking the Colt to the floor of the Seat. I reached across, opened the door and shoved him out of the car, scrambling across after him, leaving the weapon where it was.

He rolled away from me, choking and coughing as he scrambled to his feet. 'Right pal,' I yelled at him cheerfully, 'what was that you were saying about Prim?

'You guessed it right back there. While you were having my wife, I was having yours and just like with the two of you, it was her idea. You're a fucking loser, Ramon. You didn't need to kill me. For all you knew, you just needed to split Capulet's dough with me; there's well enough for two.'

He held his hands out before him. 'Okay! Okay! Okay!' he squealed. 'I'll do that now.'

'Too late. Anyway, I'd have shopped you: I'm many things but I'm not a thief.'

A gleam came into his eye. 'I'll say you killed them,' he shouted. 'That you grabbed my gun and did it.'

'Don't be daft. You shot them; so the traces are on your hand, not mine. And anyway, how are you going to say it?'

He looked at me, terrified, edging back and away from me.

And then his foot caught the root of a tree which grew no more than a couple of metres away from the crumbling face of the cliff. He fell backwards, and seemed to bounce, realising too late where he was.

He went over, his hands scrabbling at the edge of eternity. I threw my left arm around the tree-trunk, bracing myself, and grabbed him by the right wrist, at the very last second. I was strong from all that lifting; I took his weight easily.

He hung there, looking up at me, begging with his eyes. 'Oz,' he croaked.

'Sure, Ramon, but just one thing first. The girl, Gabrielle. What did you really do with her? Vero thinks you took her to the airport and put her on a plane, but I know different.

'Did you kill her, or did you sell her?'

'I sold her,' he screamed. 'To Madame Midnight's, a club near Girona.'

'That's fine,' I said. 'I'll get her out of there before she's hurt too badly.'

'Okay,' he called out, mishearing me. 'I'll do that; now pull me up.'

I looked down at him, and thought about what my dad had said about forgiving and forgetting, and decided that I couldn't come close to doing either. I thought about my ghostly Jan's words, 'Unless they deserve it'.

If she'd meant anyone, she'd meant him.

So I let him go. I started to haul him up, so that just for a second, I could see the light of relief in his eyes, then I simply let him go. What the hell? Vero was going to drop him anyway. I just saved her the trouble, that's all.

He screamed for half the way down. Then, as I watched him in the moonlight, he hit a rocky outcrop, and I heard the crack of his breaking neck even above the sound of the sea. I'm certain he was dead before he hit the bottom.

38

They arrested me, believe it or not. I called the Guardia Civil . . . not the Mossos; no way did I want Ramon's people dealing with this . . . on my mobile phone. I waited for them, told them an acceptable version of the story, and took them back to the summerhouse.

Their response was to stick me in a van and drive me to Figueras.

I wasn't there for long, though. I called the nice lady in the Consulate and she had me released inside fifteen minutes. There was never a problem, really. Fortunato's body didn't go into the sea; it was recovered, and they were able to determine that he had shot John and Lucille, just like I said.

They also found the safe-deposit keys and the note on his body; that clinched it. The whole thing was hushed up, of course, as always. The official story was that the three of them had died in a fire-fight when he had gone to arrest them for Capulet's murder. My part in it was never mentioned; my name didn't even make the Spanish papers, far less the British tabloids.

I went to see Vero, of course; they had fed her the official version too, but I could tell she didn't believe it. So I told her what had really happened, including the bit about Gabrielle. By that time the Guardia had rescued her from the brothel, and handed her over directly to the Filipino consul, in person.

The only thing I left out was what happened at the end, but from the way she thanked me, I suspect that she guessed that too.

I couldn't stand to see Shirley, though, not then anyway; I couldn't have lied to her. Thankfully, she had gone back to the YUK to make arrangements to bury her son, and begin what would turn out to be the recovery of the family business.

Once I'd done more or less right by Vero . . . which took me a couple of days . . . tidied up the mess in the house, and sampled a couple of the better wines in my new cellar, there was nothing to do but lock the place up, hire Sergi as a caretaker, and bugger off back home, a couple of days early for the premiere.

Ellie loved it, of course. I was the star attraction, and so was she, done up to the nines in the new dress I'd bought her, and with a professional hair and make-up job. She even picked up a bloke at the party afterwards; big Darius Hencke, one of the wrestling crowd for whom I'd fixed guest invitations.

The nephews would love that, I reckoned.

I had another surprise at the reception too; Susie turned up after all. In Glasgow, she can go anywhere she wants.

Once Ellie's limo had taken her and Darius off to God knew where, she and I went back to my place; for a board meeting, she said.

In the morning, after I'd told her all . . . and I do mean all . . . about what had happened in Spain after she'd left, she told me what she'd been doing.

'I'm late, Oz,' she said.

'What do you mean? It's Saturday; you're not working today are you?'

'No, you fucking idiot. I'm late; as in ten days late. I've done a test and I got the black dot.'

'You mean . . .'

'I mean there's going to be an heir to the Gantry empire, my dear.'

'Fucking hell!' I'm never at my most articulate on a Saturday morning.

'What are you going to do?' I asked, when I could.

'I'm going to have a baby.'

'Just like that?'

'Yup.'

'Our baby?'

'Absolutely.'

'Whatcha gonna call it?'

'Something appropriate, given its parentage. Damien, maybe, if it's a boy. Or Lucrezia, if it's a wee girl.'

'Should I ask you to marry me?'

'What a lovely proposal!' She let out a peal of laughter. 'Don't be daft. Susie doesn't love, remember?'

'That'll change in eight months or so.'

'True. But not that much. Like I said back in Spain, think of the couple we'd make. Doesn't it scare you?'

'No.'

'Well it bloody should. Anyway, it's academic; I hate to remind you, my boy, but you're married already.'

'I'm not so sure about that.'

244

'The Crown Office would be certain, if you tried marrying me. Listen, the only things I'm going to think about till next October are my baby and my business. You go and make your movie, and sort yourself out.' She looked at me, and her eyes went all soft.

'But if you want and you can make it, I'd like you with me when he or she arrives. You're my minder, remember.'

'It's a deal.'

She left an hour later . . . just before Ellie came in like a trollop, still in her new dress . . . and that's the last time I saw her. I phoned her every couple of days though, all through my intensive acting class.

That was worthwhile; it took the confidence I'd built up in Spain, broke it down and then built it up again, even stronger.

So, Hollywood, here I come. My plane gets into LAX in twenty minutes. Prim won't be there to meet me, but I'll see her when I get to Miles and Dawn's place.

And what am I going to do about that situation?

Quite frankly, the Devil alone knows.